BEAT THE BAND

BEAT THE BAND

DON CALAME

This is a work of fiction. Names, characters, places,
and incidents are either products of the author's
imagination or, if real, are used fictitiously.

First paperback edition 2011

The Library of Congress has cataloged the hardcover edition as follows:

Calame, Don.
Beat the band / Don Calame. —1st U.S. ed.
p. cm.
Sequel to: Swim the fly.
Summary: Paired with the infamous "Hot Dog" Helen for a
health class presentation on safe sex, tenth-grader Coop tries
to regain his "cool" by entering his musically challenged
rock group in the "Battle of the Bands" competition.
ISBN 978-0-7636-4633-2 (hardcover)
[1. Popularity—Fiction. 2. Rock groups—Fiction.
3. High schools—Fiction. 4. Schools—Fiction.
5. Humorous stories.] I. Title.
PZ7.C1241Be 2010
[Fic] — dc22 2010006607

ISBN 978-0-7636-5663-8 (paperback)

11 12 13 14 15 16 BVG 10 9 8 7 6 5 4 3 2 1

Printed in Berryville, VA, U.S.A.

This book was typeset in Melior.

Candlewick Press
99 Dover Street
Somerville, Massachusetts 02144

visit us at www.candlewick.com

To my wife, who reminded
me to just have fun

CHAPTER ONE

BORN TO RUN

THIS IS IT, DAWGS," I say. "From boys to men. Tenth grade is the year we tag all the bases. First, second, third, and then we *slide* into home."

"I'd just be happy to step into the batter's box again," Sean says.

I shoot him a gimme-a-break look. "Don't be so mopey, dude. Tianna was just a practice swing. Now you're primed to aim for the fences."

Me, Matt, and Sean shortcut across Dreyfus Park, our bikes kicking up the dust that settled over the summer as we head toward the beige brick building of Lower Rockville High that looms like a penitentiary. A penitentiary chock with hotties, to be sure, but a lockup for most of the daylight hours, nonetheless.

"I don't know," Sean says. "I don't think I'm over her yet."

"Of course you aren't," Matt consoles. "It's only been a week since you split up."

I laugh. "Are you kidding me? They were only going out for a month. A week is more than enough time to get over it. It's standard formula: One day of angst for every week you were dating. Four weeks, four days. Over and out. Any more time is just a wank."

Matt looks at me in disbelief. "Where do you get these things?"

"It's common knowledge, dude. Google it."

"What do I do if I see her in the hall?" Sean asks.

"What do you mean, *if*?" I say, pumping the pedals on my creaky mountain bike, feeling the strain in my legs as we split the goalposts and ride over the football field. "You *are* going to see her in the hall. She might even be in a bunch of your classes. Who gives a crap?"

"Just say hi," Matt offers.

"No." I glare at Matt. "Wrong. Do not take advice from the Whipped One." I turn to Sean. "You say nothing. She dumped you, so she no longer exists. Simple as that."

"Ignore her?" Sean says. "I don't know if I can do that."

I sigh, exasperated. "Look, Sean. You're a changed man. We all are. This past summer was epic. Look at all we accomplished. Our first party, yours and Matt's first girlfriends, Matt kicking ass in the butterfly, seeing our first naked babe—"

Sean cringes. "*Please.* Do *not* bring that up ever again.

I'm still having nightmares about Ms. Luntz threatening to suffocate me with her gargantuan gazongas unless I swim a thousand laps."

"What I'm trying to say is, you're no longer wet behind the ears. Tianna breaking up with you is the best thing that could have happened. I mean, seriously, why would you want to waste the best years of your life tied to just one babe? No offense, Matt."

"Why would I be offended?" Matt says. "It's not like me and Valerie are getting married."

"No," I say. "You're just having her baby."

Matt scowls. "You're so full of it, Coop."

"Sean-o? A little backup here. Matthew is, in fact, carrying Valerie's baby, is he not?"

"Leave me out of it," Sean says, the wind whipping his hair.

I raise my eyebrows at Matt, like "Need I say more?"

"Jealous much?" Matt says.

"Oh, yeah, without a doubt. Green as hell. Aren't we, Sean? We'd love to have to ask permission anytime we want to do something. And be dragged to every chick flick that comes out. And have to drop everything whenever our 'honeykins' calls."

Matt shakes his head. "Everything you just said is total bullshit. And you know it."

I smirk. "Then why is your face getting red?"

"Because it isn't."

I glance at Sean. "Sean-o?"

Sean looks off in the distance. "I said, leave me out of it."

Matt rolls his eyes. "Yeah, you guys have really matured this summer. It's staggering."

We hop the curb into the student parking lot and pedal toward the bike racks. The lot is already full. I don't have my driver's license yet—another thing I need to get started on this year—but everyone knows that if you want to nab a parking space you have to get to school at least twenty minutes early. We pass my sister Angela's car, recognizable by the fact that it's the only one in the lot with a car cover. It's her sickness. One of many.

"Look, Matt," I say. "You're acting like we think it's a *bad* thing. So, Valerie's got a tight grip on your Mr. BoDangles. At least you're getting some. Some of *what,* I'm not sure. But you seem comfortable with the trade-off. Personally, *I* wouldn't be. And I'd be lying if I said Sean and I don't miss you sometimes. But we get by. Don't we, Sean?"

Sean says nothing. Jesus, I hope he's not going to use this Tianna thing as an excuse to be such a soggy turd all year long.

The three of us coast up to the bike racks and leap off our bikes.

"All I'm saying is, we have an opportunity here." I pull a key from the pocket of my jeans, unlock my bike lock, and unravel the chain from around the seat post. "Our summer goal was a success. We saw a live naked—"

"Hey!" Sean shouts, waving a yellow coil lock at me like a weapon. "Did I not just ask you never to bring that up again?"

I laugh. "Sorry. But remember what I told you at the beginning of the summer? About the natural order of things? Internet porn, live naked girl, and then the dirty deed? Well, we're ready to take that next step."

"Would you stop it with that stupid theory of yours?" Matt says. "You wouldn't know the natural order of things if it crapped on your head."

Sean snickers. I ignore him and give Matt a you-can't-be-serious look. "Correct me if I'm wrong here, Matt. Maybe I shouldn't be including you with me and Sean. Maybe you've already rounded all the bases. If you have, just say so."

"If I did, I wouldn't tell you," Matt says, snapping his lock shut for emphasis.

"So, *no*. That's cool. Maybe they're more conservative up in Canada. Valerie probably wants to wait until you tie the knot or something. Tell me you've at least gotten to second, though?"

We start our trek past the soon-to-be-smelling-like-hell dumpsters toward the back doors of the school.

"You know what?" Matt sighs. "The only people who talk about sex as much as you are the ones who haven't even gotten up to bat yet."

I slap my forehead. "Oh, my God. Not even second

base? Jesus. What's the point of letting Val cinch the choke chain so tight then, Mattie?"

"Valerie and I are doing just fine, thank you very much."

"Well then?" I ask.

"It's private."

"It's private," I mimic. "Dude, you don't think she's gabbing about it to all her galpals? That's all babes do. They talk and talk and talk about *everything*."

"Whatever," Matt says. "Anyway, even if I was going to tell you—which I'm not—I have no idea what *your* definitions of the bases are. I'm sure they're probably incredibly sick and twisted."

I place my hand on my chest. "Hey, when it comes to the bases I happen to be a purist. First is Frenching. Second is fondling the floppers. Third is rummaging in the basement. Home run is all the way."

"I thought third was oral," Sean says.

"No, that's choking up on the bat," I say. "And then of course there's the conference on the mound. The knuckleball. A doubleheader. Extra innings. A grand slam. And, of course, the triple play." I waggle my eyebrows at my friends. "Which also happens to be in my plans for this year."

"In your dreams." Matt grabs the door and holds it open.

"All great things begin with a dream, Mattie," I say as we enter the building, ready to start what promises to be an epic first semester.

CHAPTER TWO

COME TOGETHER

"AND HERE WE GO," Mrs. Turris says, reaching her soft, pork bun hand into the blue shoebox that sits on her desk. I feel like I swallowed a still-buzzing bee as she pulls two slips of paper from the box.

I can't believe we're already being subjected to the humiliation lottery and it's only third period on the first day back to school. Mrs. Turris says that this will be a "glorious and enriching opportunity" for us to work with one of our classmates for an *entire semester*. Each couple will get to research a specialized health topic, after which we will—as a pair of studied-up experts—present our findings to the class by "teaching" everyone what we've learned.

Not a ten-minute presentation. Not a twenty-minute demonstration. A *full class period* lesson with handouts, visual aids, questions and answers, and who the hell knows what else, the whole of which will make up 85 percent of our grade in Health.

It's a big old diaper load if you ask me. Sounds like a way for our Health teacher to get out of doing her job. Make the helpless slaves do the dirty work.

When I brought this up to Mrs. Turris—in not so many words—she just laughed and said, "Cooper Redmond, you rascal, you've found me out." Like it was all a big joke or something.

But she's going forward with it anyway.

If this were one of those work-with-a-partner-for-one-week deals there'd be a lot less at stake. But we're talking about being shackled to a person for *three solid months*—in and out of class. Depending on who you get, it could either be genius or a world of pain. If I'm lucky, I'll get Matt or Sean. If I'm super lucky, I'll be partnered up with one of the Phenomenal Four—Prudence Nash, Kelly West, Bronte Hastings, or Gina Lagotta. It's rare you get four of the school's hottest girls in one class, which I take as a solid omen for the year. Working that close with any one of them will give me ample opportunity to play some serious *babes*ball.

The papers make a rustling sound as Mrs. Turris unfolds them. "Andrew Bennett and Nicholas Hickey," she reads.

All the kids in the classroom snicker.

Andy winces.

Nicky's head drops.

Class assbag meet Cabbage Boy. Sometimes there *is* justice in the world.

I can breathe again. The first pairing has been decided, and already two of the biggest booby prizes have been awarded. And to each other. Which is classic.

The only thing you have to know about Andy Bennett—besides the fact that he's been desperately trying to grow a mustache for the last two years—is that he likes to spit Jell-O cubes at all the babes and can't understand why this move doesn't make them lie down naked at his feet.

And Nicky Hickey? Smells. Bad. Real bad. Like brussels sprouts rolled in fish food. He might not even be such a terrible guy, but you just can't hang with him long enough to find out.

Me, Matt, and Sean share a thank-holy-Jesus look.

Mrs. Turris brushes a curly blonde lock from her forehead. "The topic you will be researching and teaching a lesson on will be . . ." She grabs the nearby yellow shoebox and blindly plucks an index card from it. Drum roll please. "Alcohol."

"I did a few pints of research on that very subject this past weekend," Andy quips, running his hand down the baby beard he's sprouting on his chin.

One person sniggers in the back corner, but really, nobody wants to encourage him.

Mrs. Turris ignores Andy's comment and continues reading the card. "Its effects on the body. Consequences of driving under the influence. Alcohol addiction. Et cetera."

Personally, I don't give two turds what subject I get. But I *have* to get a cool partner. Everything else is dealable.

Mrs. Turris dips her paw back into the blue shoebox and draws two more names.

"Sean Hance and Matthew Gratton."

Matt and Sean fist bump. The bastards.

They both turn to me and make apologetic faces. I give them a shit-happens shrug, 'cause what else am I supposed to do? Threaten to ignore the food pyramid and eat a crap diet until Mrs. Turris pairs me up with one of them? As if I've ever eaten "heart healthy" in my life.

It would have been stagg to work with Matt. We would have had a ton of laughs and maybe even gotten a decent grade, 'cause Matt's actually pretty smart.

I wouldn't even have minded Sean. I mean, sure, we'd have barely passed, but at least we're friends and neither of us smells like anus.

Mrs. Turris scratches hard at her pad, trying to get the ink running in her pen so she can write down their names.

I take a breath. No need to panic. Everything's chill here. I'd rather get one of the lovely ladies anyway.

I lean over to Prudence Nash—her soft brown hair framing her Victoria's-Secret-model face—and shoot her my irresistible, whadda-ya-say grin. "Looks like our odds just got a little better, huh?" I whisper.

"For what?" Prudence says, staring straight ahead. "A reason to commit suicide?"

"For you and me, babe. That is, if your luck holds." I give her a sly head tilt as Mrs. Turris rummages in her drawer for a new writing implement. "Who knows? Maybe we'll be assigned the *Kama Sutra*. We can demonstrate the seventy-two most pleasurable lovemaking positions. What do you think about that?"

Prudence flips me the middle finger. Still not looking in my direction.

"Mee-ouch. You do know that's how the deaf talk dirty to each other."

Prudence whips around and gives me the slow burn.

"And your topic is," Mrs. Turris says, finally ready to reveal Matt's and Sean's fate. "Sexually transmitted diseases. STDs. Contraction, prevention, and treatment."

Matt's and Sean's life-is-great expressions suddenly sour. Pube lice and penile scabbing. Not exactly a car for Christmas, is it, fellas?

My cheeks start to tug a smile, but I wrest control.

Mrs. Turris scribbles the topic down, then grabs two more names.

"Gina Lagotta and Kelly West," she calls out.

Jesus Christ. Two more of my prospects paired up with each other. I don't like how this is shaking out.

Okay, just stay positive. There's still Bodacious Bronte and Primo Prudence.

I smile at Prudence to let her know she's still my number one. Waggle the eyebrows. "The plot thickens."

Prudence's hand rockets into the air. "Mrs. Turris?"

"Yes, Prudence," Mrs. Turris says, her sausage-fingers hovering over the yellow shoebox.

"I'm not feeling well. May I go to the nurse?"

"What seems to be the problem?"

"I just got *really* nauseous."

"How about you wait until we see who your partner is, so you two can schedule a time to meet. Then you can go to the nurse."

Prudence huffs and crosses her arms.

"Kelly and Gina, the subject of your lesson will be . . ." Mrs. Turris pulls an index card. She's having way too much fun with this. "Nutrition. What constitutes a healthy diet? Effects of an unhealthy one. How to read a nutrition label. And the like."

I scan the room to assess the situation. Beyond the two choice babes left, all the other potentials are bottom-feeders at best. I suppose I could deal with most of them if I absolutely *had* to. Anyone except Justin "Stoned Senseless" Sneep. I'd end up having to do all the work, which would be a giant sack of blowage.

Come to think of it, if I wind up working with Prudence or Bronte, I'll probably have to do the whole project myself as well. Although, if they'd be willing to work out an appropriate barter system, it might not be so bad.

Still, I think I should have a plan B. So I'm not completely devastated if I lose out on my first tier of partners. Preferably someone who's so concerned about being paired with me and my slothful ways that they'll take up the lion's share. Someone who's too nice to get mad at me. Someone like . . .

"Sam Shattenkirk," Mrs. Turris reads, fumbling with the folded second slip.

Yes! Smart, clean, friendly, non-threatening Sam. He's my backup man. My backup plan. A lightness fills my chest. A flicker of hope. Come to Cooper. Come on. Cooper Redmond. Cooper Redmond.

"And . . ." She gets the paper unfolded and reads. "Prudence Nash."

Damn it. It's like I'm sinking in quicksand and all my lifelines keep snapping.

Mrs. Turris smiles at Prudence. "There you go, dear. You can go see the nurse now."

"That's okay," Prudence says, tossing me a screw-you smirk. "I feel *much* better."

I wink at her to let her know I understand she's disappointed.

Prudence rolls her eyes.

It's the dance we do. Like birds before they mate. She hates me now, but someday soon, at some party or something, she'll succumb to the Cooper charm, and we'll fall into each other's arms, making out like a couple of horny cave people. We'll retreat to one of the bedrooms and chew and claw each other's clothes off. And then, finally, I'll get a full view of the serpent tattoo that snakes down the small of her back. The one I've only gotten teasing glances of when she squats to pick something up off the floor and her low-rise jeans ride just a little lower.

Mrs. Turris reads out Sam's and Prudence's topic but it doesn't register. I'm still stuck on Prudence's tattoo. I'm imagining what it will be like to spend the rest of my life examining every inch of it.

"This is so exciting." Mrs. Turris laughs. She's got the kind of round, trusting face you'd see on a pancake box. "I love placing things in Fate's hands. It always turns out for the best in the end, I think."

Okay, I may yurp.

I sigh loudly. Several of my comrades stifle chuckles.

Mrs. Turris pays no attention and grabs another slip of paper from her torture box.

I've pretty much given up trying to will the outcome of this. My Jedi mind control is obviously on the fritz today. I don't even care who I get twinned up with anymore. Like it even matters. It's just stupid Health. Sure I need to pass to graduate, but how hard is it going to be to swing a D-plus? Really. I'll even take Stoner Sneep. Bring it on. Give me the worst you've got, Mrs. Turris. Give me boogers-in-the-nose Gerald Tyrell. Toss me Tara ten-chins with the wandering eye and steel-wool mullet.

I breeze cheese in Fate's face. How do you like that, teach?

"Cooper Redmond . . ."

Here we go, people. I maintain my chillaxed pose: slouching posture, one arm dangling carelessly over the back of my chair.

Mrs. Turris does an on-purpose, anticipation-inducing, Academy Awards-y delay.

Whatever. Let her have her fun.

Nothing can faze me at this point.

"And Helen Harriwick."

Except.

Maybe.

That.

The class bursts with laughter.

Hot Dog Helen? Are you twisting me? I hadn't even considered this. I didn't even notice she was in the class. She makes herself that invisible.

My skin prickles with heat and my head swims, but I keep my face blank. Need to be caszh. Can't appear weak.

But come on! Jesus Christ!

Prudence has her hand clasped over her mouth. Her eyes dart over to me and they are filled with evil glee.

Matt and Sean have matching "yikes" expressions plastered on their mugs. They're trying to be all sympathetic, but I can see both of them stifling laughs.

I turn around and find Helen, who's skim-milk skin

has gone blotchy with clouds of pink. She is staring hard at her Health textbook, pretending the hysteria has nothing to do with the fact that she's the school's most taunted pariah.

Thanks a ton, Mrs. Turris. Fate can eat me. There is *no way* this is "for the best."

Okay. I need to breathe. To think. How can I get out of this? There has to be a way. I just need to concentrate.

Maybe Jell-O hawkin' Andy would be willing to flip stinky Nicky. But as soon as I think this, I see the mirthful tears coursing down his cheeks and I already know he'd never go for it.

Nothing could be worse than this.

Absolutely nothing.

"And your topic shall be . . ." Mrs. Turris announces like a judge handing down a life sentence. She has suddenly grown thirty feet tall, sprouted horns, and is engulfed in flames. Her voice is distorted and timpani-low as she reads my conviction. "Contraaaaceptioooon."

The room erupts in a nuclear explosion of whoops and howls. Gina and Kelly actually do a double fist bump, exploding their nugs in celebration.

I try to keep calm but my head is still spinning.

I swear I see Mrs. Turris look up to the heavens and cackle.

"The various forms of, including condoms, the pill, and diaphragm. Cost, reliability, effectiveness, ease of use . . ."

The desks, the chalkboard, the windows, the laughing

mouths of Kelly, Bronte, Prudence, and Gina all swirl around me. I can only catch snippets of their jeers: "field research . . .", "Corn Dog Coop . . .", "Put some *condom-ments* on that wiener. . . ."

The last thing I see is Helen, books clutched to her chest, fleeing the classroom.

And then the darkness collapses around me, and right before the world disappears, I hear Andy's voice calling out, "Theebedda—theebedda—theebedda—that's all folks!"

CHAPTER THREE

TOXIC

THAT WAS TOTALLY AWESOME," Sean says as we wait in the cafeteria line. "I've never seen anyone faint before. What was it like?"

"I didn't faint," I correct. "I just got dizzy for a second."

"Are you sure you're feeling okay?" Matt asks. "You still look sort of . . . pale."

"I'm fine. I just need some food. I haven't eaten much since lunch yesterday." Which is the truth. Mom was working late again, so dinner was a fend-for-yourself affair—which meant Pop-Tarts for *moi*—and I traded breakfast for three slaps at the snooze button.

"Uh-huh." Sean chortles. "That's funny. I thought you nearly fell out of your chair because you got stuck with Oscar Mayer Helen."

"Don't be such a tool, Sean," I say under my breath. "She's right there." Or at least, I think she is. At the front of the line. But I might be wrong. The lunchroom is crammed with bodies and faces, none of which I can bring into sharp focus.

"Like you never make fun of her," Sean says.

"Not when she can hear me, butt-wipe." My stomach is creaking doors. I grab a lukewarm, foil-wrapped donkey burger, a chocolate chip cookie, and an apple juice, and plunk them down on my green tray. The thick smell of the cafeteria—salami, pizza squares, and lunch lady BO—is not the fresh air I need to clear my head. "Christ. That circus in Health class today. I mean, *I* can take it. But what they were saying about Helen. That was some of the cruelest shit I've ever heard."

"Wasn't me," Matt says, sliding a chicken-finger- and french-fry boat onto his tray.

Sean says nothing, just pretends to be studying today's chow choices, which can lead to only one conclusion: he joined in on the verbal stoning.

He can't help it. Sean's a lemming sometimes. But he can also be a throw-himself-on-the-grenade-for-you friend, which are few and far between.

We pay for our meals and take up residence at the end of one of the metal-and-plastic picnic tables.

"What are you going to do?" Matt asks, sinking his teeth into a chicken strip.

"About what?" I unwrap my soggy burger, peel off the

top bun, and start squeezing ketchup pouches, drowning the gray patty. You know you're hungry when your mouth starts watering over crap like this.

"About having to work with Helen."

"I don't know. Drop out of school I guess."

"Now who's being cruel?" Sean says.

"I'm not being cruel, nutmeat. I'm being practical."

"Practical?" Sean smirks. "Right." He bites into his elephant-foot-trampled grilled cheese, which causes a trickle of oil to pitter-patter on the plastic it was once wrapped in. Even that looks good to me.

I start devouring my hamburger.

"Look at it this way. Helen's a brainiac," Matt says. "You'll get an A for sure."

"An A in exchange for a semester's worth of ridicule, torment, finger-pointing, and being called Corn Dog Cooper?" I say through a mouthful of burger. "No thanks. Besides, who knows how long the repercussions could last?"

Matt shrugs. "Maybe it won't be like that."

"Put it in your corn hole, Corn Dog!" someone shouts as a storm of buttery niblets rains down on my head, hurled from somewhere in the general direction of the wrestling team. Dean "the Machine" Scragliano and Frank Hurkle turn and roar at each other as they slam their chests together. Everyone in our corner of the lunchroom—except Sean and Matt, who just grimace—cracks up.

I could go over there and try to find out who chucked

the corn at me, but really, what am I going to do if I figure out who it is? Offer up my ass to be summarily kicked?

I grab a napkin and brush the kernels from my hair and clothes. I look at Matt accusingly. "You were saying?"

"It's today's news, that's all," Matt says. "I bet it dies down in a week when something else comes along."

"That's not how these things work, and you know it. It's been almost two years since Helen's hot dog habits were revealed. And that hasn't eased one bit." I look down at my T-shirt, which is now peppered with seed-sized grease stains. "If anything, it's gotten worse. You were in class. They were like a pack of hungry cheetahs on a downed ibex. And now I'm the ibex's partner. The rest of my high-school days are cursed."

"What's an ibex?" Sean asks.

"Look," I say. "It's not my fault about Helen, okay? Maybe the rumors are true. Maybe not. Maybe she saves abandoned kittens and spoon-feeds old people in her spare time. None of it matters, because if I'm seen hanging with Helen, or even *perceived* to be hanging with her, for *any* reason, my rep will be destroyed so fast I might as well find the nearest monkery and sign right up. Forget about tagging any bases; I won't even be warming the bench. Like it or not, how people see you is everything in this world. And once you're tainted, you're tainted for life." I take a swig of my juice. "You don't tie yourself to an anchor that's being thrown overboard. That's all I'm saying."

"So you're not going to do the project with her?" Matt asks.

"Hell no!" I say. "Do I look like an idiot?"

"Then what?" Sean says.

"We can just do our own thing. Split up the material and do two separate lessons. I'll tell her next time I see her."

"Yeah, well." Sean talks with a full mouth of sandwich. "You think you've got it bad? Guess who's in my Math class?"

"Oh, let me take a stab," I say. "Tianna?"

"Yeah. How'd you know?"

I roll my eyes. "I'm sorry, but having your ex-girlfriend in one of your classes doesn't even compare to my sitch."

"But I'm going to have to see her every day."

"It's not even close, Sean. My problem is a million times worse."

Valerie appears out of nowhere holding a tray loaded down with a salad, a brownie, a cinnamon bun, and lemon meringue pie. As if somehow the roughage balances out the desserts. How she manages to stay looking so skinny eating all the crap she does is amazing. If she were anyone else, I'd think she was yurking it all up, but Matt says her whole family's like that—her mom, dad, and her little brother, George—so it's got to be lucky genes, plain and simple.

Val sits down next to Matt. "Hey, guys," she says.

"What are we talking about?" I used to find that French accent of hers so hot, but now all it does is grate on me.

"Nothing," I say.

To which Matt adds, "Coop got paired with Helen Harriwick for a Health class project."

"Yeah." Valerie takes the lid off her salad. "I heard about that."

"*You* heard about it?" My stomach drops. "What's it on YouTube already?"

Valerie shrugs. "Kelly told me at our lockers."

"Oh, really?" I say. "Did she tell you how she and Gina did a touchdown celebration when it was announced?"

"You should be the one celebrating." Valerie gestures with her plastic fork. "Helen's on the honor roll every semester. It'll probably be the only A you get in your life."

"That's hysterious, Val," I say. "But you can stop talking now, because we've already heard everything you're going to say from your man-clone."

"What?" She looks confused.

"Don't listen to him," Matt says. "He's just ticked off because he thinks everyone's going to associate him with Helen for the rest of his life."

"I don't *think*. I *know*."

"Why do you even care about other people's opinions?" Valerie asks, setting her salad aside untouched and tucking into her pie.

I cock my head. "Why don't you ask my corn-covered

shirt? And while you're at it, maybe you should ask Helen that question, too. Then get back to me."

Matt suddenly looks down intently at his tray. "S-T-F-U," he mutters.

I turn to see Helen's ponytail-pulled moon face approaching. I'm hoping she'll just walk on by, but she stops right at the head of our table, her books hugged to her bulky sweatshirt-clad body. Her eyes are red-rimmed and puffy, like she's been crying all morning. Which she probably has.

"Here's your chance," Sean mutters.

Helen starts talking, her lips barely moving. It's impossible to make out what she's saying because she's talking so softly. Meaning I'll either have to lean in close to hear her, or ask her to repeat herself, both of which will draw more attention to her standing here.

I surreptitiously scan the cafeteria to see if anybody is catching this. Miraculously, everyone seems to be otherwise engaged. Could it be that the winds of luck have shifted since this morning?

"I'm sorry, what?" I say.

"We need to meet to talk about the Health project," she says a little louder, her eyes cast downward.

I'm tempted to point out that we could have done this during class if she hadn't ducked out, but I don't trust Sean not to pipe up about the fact that I passed out soon after.

"Oh, yeah." I cough. "About that . . ." *Go ahead, Coop,*

buddy. Kick her while she's down. Give her the old boot to the belly. Why should you have to suffer too?

I look into her swollen eyes. There's such sadness there. Aw, Christ. I take a breath. Close my eyes. Shake my head. "Let's, uh . . . How about . . . after school?"

"In the library?" Her voice is high and thin, like a badly played flute.

Maybe it's my imagination but she looks . . . What? Relieved? Which makes me feel like a prize jerk. I should just get this over with. Tell her we aren't going to work together. But I can't do it. Not here. Not now. "Uh, no. Not the library." Not here at school. Not at the mall. Nowhere we could possibly be seen by anyone we've ever known ever. "How about . . . Golf Town?"

"Golf Town?" She frowns.

"Yeah," I say. "It's a golf shop. Out on Douglas. Next to a plumbing supply place." The only reason I know this is because my father brought me to this strip of stores in the middle of nowhere to pick up some part for one of our sinks last year. "I have to buy a birthday present for my dad." He's never golfed in his life, but how would she know? "A club or a putter or something. Two birds with one stone, you know?"

"Sure. Okay," she says. "What time?"

"How about . . . five o'clock?" I say.

Helen writes it all down in her day planner. "All right. See you there." She turns and heads off, back to wherever she sits during lunch. The girls' bathroom, probably.

"What are you doing?" Sean asks. "I thought you were going to tell her—"

"She's been crying, dude. Not all of us are heartless bastards like you." But even as I say this, I'm trying to think of a million reasons why I can't be at Golf Town today at five o'clock.

"Hey, don't take your frustrations out on me." Sean points at me with his half-eaten lardwich. "I'm not the one who said he wouldn't work with her."

"Want to trade?"

"No."

"Thought so."

"Only because it's nice to see *you* squirm for a change. But if she was *my* partner, I'd deal with it."

"If she was *your* partner, it wouldn't mean anything. You're already a plebe. People like to see the greats fall. They don't try to topple the homeless."

"I'm not homeless."

"No, but you're clueless."

"Guys," Matt interrupts. "Enough already."

"Hey, I've got a thought," Valerie says as she cuts her brownie into quarters. She's already polished off her pie and her cinnamon bun.

Oh, great. This should be good.

"If it's so important to Coop"—she pushes the brownie pieces into the center of the table for everyone to share—"why don't *you* work with Helen, Matt? And Coop can work with Se—"

"No," Sean blurts. "That's a bad idea."

I scowl at Sean. "Hey. The lady was speaking."

Sean looks at Matt. "Please, Matt. Don't do it," he begs.

"Stay out of it," I say. "This doesn't affect you."

"Does too. Because you'll make me do all the work. Matt's at least fair."

I smile at Valerie. "Go on. You were saying?"

"I mean, *we* know it's not a big deal, right?" Val looks over at Matt. "But if it means that much to your friend, *pourquoi pas*?"

Matt's expression is priceless. He looks like he doesn't know whether to cry or text the pope. "I . . . um . . ."

It's a stellar plan, really. Matt's already got a wife. If all the other girls in the school think he's diseased, it shouldn't matter one pube to him.

"Yeah . . . um . . ." Matt stammers. "Yeah. No. It's, um . . . Yeah. Okay. Let's switch. It's a great idea, Val. I'll take Helen."

"See," Valerie says, taking a bite of brownie. *"Le problème a résolu."*

I toast the brilliant lady with my own piece of brownie. Maybe Matt being so whipped isn't such a bad thing after all.

⚡ CHAPTER FOUR ⚡

ROCK AND ROLL BAND

I'M TERRIBLY SORRY," Mrs. Turris says when me, Matt, and Sean stop by her classroom after lunch. "But Fate has made up Her mind. And I am not one to mess with Her. Unless Fate intervenes, the partnerships must remain as they are."

"This is Fate right here," I insist. "Intervening. Matt is desperate to work with Helen. What could be more fateful than that?"

Mrs. Turris smiles. "Fate is beyond our control. By choosing to change partners, you're trying to take back that control. I'm afraid I just can't let it happen. My decision is final. The partnerships will stand."

"Great," I say, when we're back in the hall. "Short of a miracle, I'm completely screwed."

"Well, we can't say we didn't try." Sean's got a bounce to his step and a big grin on his face.

"You shouldn't look so happy," I say. "This is going to have a trickle-down effect, just so you know. I was all ready to help you navigate the bases, Sean. But my bad luck is your bad luck."

Sean just shrugs. We walk in silence for a bit, dodging kids hurrying in the opposite direction.

"I really do think things will calm down after a few days," Matt offers.

"Crush the Corn Dog!" Dean the Machine shouts as he shoulder checks me into the wall. My cheek slams hard into a bulletin board, a red thumbtack barely missing my eye. Dean high-tens one of his wrestling buddies as they jog off down the hall to whoops and hollers.

"You okay?" Matt asks.

"I'm going to ask you to stop saying that you think the Hot Dog Helen thing will calm down, okay?" As I push myself away from the corkboard, a purple sheet of paper flutters right in front of my face. Some lame artist has drawn a guitar, a bass, keyboards, and a drum kit in badly skewed perspective. Above the instruments, inside a bullet-hole border, are the words:

BATTLE OF THE BANDS

DECEMBER 16TH

DEMO TAPES TO MR. GROSSMAN BY SEPT. 15TH

PLEASE INCLUDE TWO COVER SONGS AND ONE ORIGINAL SONG.

ONLY FOUR BANDS WILL QUALIFY.

I stare at the poster for a moment. Then something inside me clicks.

Here is my miracle. Win the battle of the bands and the Hot Dog Helen taint will be obliterated by my rock-and-roll awesomeness. And who gets to tag more bases than a rock god? No one.

"Guys, look at this."

Matt and Sean glance at the poster.

"Cool," Sean says. "They're doing a battle of the bands. I wonder who'll be playing?"

"We will," I say.

The guys look at me like I just told them we're going to try out for the football team.

"Our band." I smile. "Arnold Murphy's Bologna Dare. Remember?"

"Uh. Yeah," Matt says. "I know we came up with the name. But I'm also aware that we suck. Which means it's not going to be much of a battle."

"We've already done a million gigs on Rock Band," I say. "How much harder could it be?"

Sean backs away. "Are you nuts? Don't you remember when we tried to play in your basement last year? Your neighbor's dog started to howl in agony. And someone threw a brick through the window."

"We'll practice," I say. "We'll get better. All the best musicians were self-taught. Hendrix, Dylan, Van Halen, Eric Clapton, Jack White. We've got three months. It's a beautiful thing. Think of all the hot babes we'll get."

"Yeah." Matt rolls his eyes. "I'm sure Valerie will love that."

"Okay, so Sean and I will take your share of the groupies. But you can still ogle, can't you? When they take off their tops and toss their panties at us. Or did Valerie take your eyes along with your chestnuts?"

"Anyway," Matt says. "Even if we could cobble something together by December, it says we need a demo tape by this Friday. So, right there we're done."

"I'll figure something out," I say. "Trust me. Just say you'll do it. Think about it, dawgs. If we win this thing, we could become the most popular kids in the school."

And "Corn Dog Coop" will die a quick and painless death.

CHAPTER FIVE

SO WHAT

LOWER ROCKVILLE'S PUBLIC transportation system is a sackful of suckage. The number 66 bus, in particular, is a piece of crap on four wheels. The seats are cracked and wonky, the air stinks of asparagus-pee, and the windows are all carved up with things like "John Haz Sex With Gotes" and "Ubducted and Anully Probbed." If my English teacher, Mr. Metzendorf, ever rode this bus he'd go insane with all the spelling mistakes. I'm sitting at the back trying to avoid eye contact with the few wackos who are actually riding this rolling turd. We're heading down Douglas Street and it's 5:19 by my cell phone, which means I'm very late meeting Helen.

I hope that I haven't missed her, because this might be my only chance—away from school and all the prying eyes—to let her know that we won't be working together.

And if she has another breakdown, at least there won't be any Lower Rockville High witnesses.

Just for a precaution—in case someone happens to see us together—I'm wearing my father's grease-stained, blue coveralls, a MACHINISTS DO IT WITH LUBE baseball cap pulled down low, and a pair of someone's scratched-up old glasses I found in the junk drawer. The coveralls are a little long in the legs and sleeves, and the glasses make the world seem a little fuzzy, but I don't care. Nobody's going to recognize me. I'm just a dude coming home from work.

The bus pulls over to the curb across the street from the lonely strip mall. Apparently this isn't a real popular stop because I'm the only one who gets off. I misjudge the last step—stupid glasses—and stumble to the sidewalk.

The bus takes off, puking black smoke and filling my nostrils with the harsh stink of diesel. I look both ways and time the traffic before jogging across the four-lane road.

When I get to the other side, I peer over the top of my eyewear. And there she is, standing with her back to me, her hair down and out of her ponytail, wearing a zipped-up ski vest over a black long-sleeve sweater, a backpack slung over her shoulders. She's looking in the window of a school uniform shop, probably longing for a different life that includes private schools.

The chances of anyone I know being within ten miles of this place are pretty slim but still, I scope the surrounding area before I make my approach.

The coast is clear, so I stroll up to Helen. "'Sup?" I say.

She turns but obviously doesn't recognize me. Sweet.

"It's Coop."

"Oh," she says, blinking. "I didn't . . . your clothes . . ."

I look down at my outfit and laugh. "Oh, yeah. I help my dad out at his shop after school. That's why I was late. Sorry about that." No need to mention that my dad only works mornings now that his hours have been cut in half. Or the fact that I've never even *been* to his shop. I figure the less she knows about me, the easier it will be to get away with stuff.

"I didn't know you wore glasses."

"Yeah. I don't wear them at school 'cause they make me look like a royal dorkus. So, how do you want to do this?"

"Did you want to get your present first?"

"Present?"

"For your father."

Damn it. "Oh, yeah. Let's get that over with. It shouldn't take long."

I turn and make my way toward Golf Town, grab for the door handle and come up with a fistful of air. Real smooth. Okay, maybe the glasses were a poor choice.

I force a laugh. "Guess I need a stronger prescription."

On the second try I manage to grasp the handle and

hold the door open for Helen. Not cause I'm a gentleman—though I can be, if it means the chance to inspect a hot girl's boondocks—but because I don't want Helen blocking my escape route if by some odd chance I see someone from school in the store.

The place smells like old man. Everything is green and white and brown. There are three dudes—bald, balder, and comb-over—huddled around the cash register. They're all wearing lime-green Golf Town polos with name tags. They pay us absolutely no attention. Which is perfect, 'cause I'm not going to be buying anything anyway.

"What were you thinking of getting for him?" Helen asks.

"I have a few ideas." I've golfed a couple of times with Matt and his grandpa, and even though I totally suck, I'm pretty familiar with all the crap you can outfit yourself with, so I plan to make this a pretty convincing charade. I stroll over to the glove rack and spin it like I'm actually looking for something specific.

I wonder if my dad really would like golf? Maybe I ought to suggest it some time. I feel sort of bad for him. Coming home every day at noon with nothing to do but thumb through the classifieds looking for extra work. Might be good to get him out of the house once in awhile.

I take a step toward a hat display and my foot catches

on something. There's a clattering sound as I do a face-plant into the carpet. My glasses go flying, which makes it easier to see that I've just felled a row of putters.

Helen hurries over to me.

"Are you all right?" she asks, crouching down.

"Yeah. Sure." I get to my knees, rubbing my stinging palms. "Stupid golf clubs."

Helen retrieves my glasses and hands them to me. "Here you go."

"Thanks." I fold them and stick them in my pocket. That's enough of those. I hoist myself to my feet. The comb-over guy is frowning at me.

"Just look at what you've done." He starts collecting up the putters, all put out and annoyed, like I did it on purpose.

"Not injured," I say, brushing myself off. "Thanks for asking." The dude's name tag says JULES, which is totally fitting. He's wearing this heavy-duty knock-you-across-the-nose cologne that coats my sinuses with wet grass and low tide.

Jules lines the putters back up against the Peg-Board and crosses his arms. "Is there anything in particular you were looking for?"

"You mean before I nearly broke my neck?"

Jules says nothing, just raises his eyebrows.

"He's looking for a birthday present for his father," Helen interjects.

"Was there something *specific* your father was interested in?" Jules asks me, his voice laced with some major attitude, like he can smell my disinterest in everything golf above the stink of his perfume.

"I'm not exactly sure."

"Could we narrow it down a little, maybe?"

Could we tea-bag your semi-bald head, maybe? Fine. He wants to play with me. I'll play. "Yeah, okay," I answer. "Do you have, like, a portable ball washer?"

"As a matter of fact we do," Jules says, so smug and pleased with himself. "We have an automatic washer that you can attach to a golf cart. But it's fairly expensive. Maybe out of your price range?"

"Oh, I don't know, I've got a few Benjamins burning a hole in my pocket." I pat the breast pocket of my coveralls. "Besides, my dad could sure use one of those washers. His balls are always so dirty. I don't know how he does it, but every time he golfs, his balls get caked in mud."

I glance over at Helen, her eyes horrified, her mouth a perfect O. The look on her face is priceless—and almost as funny as how clueless Jules seems to be.

Jules nods. "That's what happens when you play on grass and dirt."

"I guess so." I shake my head. "Still, I don't think I've ever seen balls quite this soiled. Do your balls get that filthy?"

"Depends on how muddy the course is. Follow me. I'll show you the washer." Jules marches across the store.

Helen and me trail behind. Her brow is tightly knitted. "What are you doing?" she whispers angrily.

"Shopping," I say, waggling my eyebrows. "Come on, this should be fun."

"Cooper, knock it off."

But I pick up my pace, leaving Helen behind and joining Jules in aisle three.

"Here we are." Jules gestures at a fancy red ball washer like a game show host toward a fabulous prize. "It's forty-nine ninety-nine."

"Forty-nine ninety-nine?" I call over to Helen, who's hovering a few feet away. "That's not too bad, right?" I turn back to Jules. "It'd be totally worth it. My dad is always making my mom wash his balls in the kitchen sink. It's pretty gross."

Helen stares at the floor, her face all scrunched up, like this is causing her actual physical pain.

But Jules is oblivious. "Yes, well, this washer ought to—"

"Oh, wait. I know. The other night, my dad was saying that his driver was old and useless. Something about the, um . . . shaft being too flexible?"

Jules nods like he's known others with this particular problem. "Yes, that *can* pose some difficulty. It just so happens that I have a very nice driver with a fairly rigid shaft."

"Oh you do, do you?" I give Jules a conspiratorial wink. "But are you willing to sell it?"

Jules stares at me blankly. "Of course. If you can afford it."

Helen sighs and shifts her weight. Her neck and cheeks flaming.

"This wood of yours," I say. "Does it have one of those really big heads?"

Jules leans in. "It's not called Big Bertha for nothing."

"Big Bertha?" I give a low whistle. "You don't say."

I glance over at Helen. Surely she must find at least *this* much funny.

Apparently not. She's suddenly gotten very interested in the golf shoes.

"Would you like me to show it to you?" Jules asks.

I call out to Helen. "He wants to show us his Big Bertha, Helen. Aren't the salesmen here the friendliest you've ever seen?"

"Coop." Helen's voice is barely contained. "Why don't we just go look at the clubs by ourselves and let the salesman help someone else?"

"Because he's helping *me* right now." I look at Jules. "So, do you want to show it to us right here on the showroom floor? Or should we go in the back?"

Jules seems confused. "Um. No. Wait right here. I'll just go grab it."

He shuffles off, his pants sagging in the back like he's got a big old load weighing him down.

Helen storms over to me, her arms crossed, her jaw clenched. "This is *not* funny, Coop."

"What are you talking about?" I say, nearly losing it. "This is freakin' hilarious. The dude has no clue he's just offered to sell me his wang. What's funnier than that?"

"You're being mean."

"Here we go," Jules says, wielding a big fancy driver with an enormous silver head. He holds it out to me. "You wanted stiff. Take a feel of that."

I grab the club and hoist in the air, waving it around a bit. "Wow. That is a stiff one," I say. "I bet you could do some real damage with this."

Jules nods. "Your Dad unwraps that bad boy on his birthday and I guarantee it'll put a big smile on his face."

"Not to mention my Mom's," I say.

This makes Jules laugh, though I don't think he's sure why.

"What do you think, Helen?" I say turning toward her. But she's already stalking off toward the front door.

Jules watches her go, then looks back at me. "Is something wrong?"

I turn to see Helen shove open the front door and exit. "Her uncle was killed by a stray divot. Caught him right in the mouth. Choked to death. It was horrible." I hand the club back to him. "I better go comfort her."

I start to leave and Jules calls after me. "Do you want me to hold it for you?"

A thousand funny comebacks flip through my head.

But I let it go. "I'll think about it," I say as I head out of the store.

I approach Helen, who's standing at the bus stop. "What's your prob? I was just getting warmed up in there."

Her eyes won't meet mine. "I'm going home."

"What? Why? Don't we have to discuss our project?"

"I just . . ." Helen shakes her head. "You're really rude, you know that?"

"What? Me? That guy was a total dingus."

"He's just trying to do his job. He probably has kids to feed. You were wasting his time—*and* making fun of him."

"Big whoop. Like I care."

"You *should* care. He's a person. Just like you. How would you feel if someone said those things to you?"

"I'd think it was pretty damn funny. Hey, look, it wasn't like he was all, 'Let me help you up' or 'Are you hurt?' when I fell down. No, it was just, 'What do you want to buy?' People get what they deserve."

Helen looks down the street, like what she wants to say next is somewhere off in the distance. She turns back to me. "You weren't going to buy anything in there, were you? You just had us meet here so that nobody would see us together."

My pulse suddenly quickens. "What? No." There's a pounding in my ears. "I *was* going to buy something. But not after he started treating me like a tool."

"I bet you don't even work with your dad. I bet you put on that outfit to try to disguise yourself. Along with the glasses. Which you *don't* wear."

"How would you know?"

"Please, Cooper. You were stumbling around like a drunk. Besides. We've been going to school together since fourth grade. And I've never seen you wear glasses. *Ever.*"

"Look who's been keeping a close eye on me all these years. I don't know whether to be flattered or creeped out. Of course, who could blame you, but still . . ."

Helen's gaze flicks back down the road. A 66 bus is headed toward us. She hikes her backpack up. "Whatever. You don't want to work with me, obviously. And I'm happy not to work with you so, why don't we just go to Mrs. Turris tomorrow and ask if we can do projects on our own?"

"Works for me. If that's what you want. I don't know what your big ish is with me, but fine. I can take the rejection."

"Right. Put this on me. That way you don't have to feel bad about yourself."

"I *don't* feel bad about myself, okay? 'Cause I'm here. You're the one who's leaving."

The bus pulls up and opens its doors. "That's right. I *am* leaving. *Golf Town.* How could I have been so stupid?" And with that, she steps up onto the number 66.

She must know that I'm waiting for the 66 too, but I'll be damned if I'm going to ride the same bus as her. Better to wait the fifteen minutes and take the next one.

As the bus takes off, I stand there thinking how perfectly that all played out. It was actually way easier than I thought it was going to be. And tomorrow, I'll be free as a bird.

CHAPTER SIX

CAUGHT UP IN YOU

"ABSOLUTELY NOT," Mrs. Turris says, her chair creaking as she leans back. "It's out of the question."

Me and Helen are standing around the teacher's desk after class. I've got that tied-the-game-and-lost-it-in-overtime feeling in my chest. I knew that with all Mrs. Turris's talk about Fate that she wouldn't be easily convinced, but I was hoping that Helen's insistence might sway things in our favor.

"These projects aren't just about alcohol or drugs or contraception. They're about being able to work cooperatively. They're about interpersonal communication. Like it or not, there'll be times in life when you will have to work with somebody you don't get along with. And you won't be able to just give up."

Mrs. Turris starts organizing papers on her desk, clearly having rested her case. Time for me to step in and work some of my Cooper magic.

"Mrs. Turris," I say, giving her a chill, let's-talk-about-this smile. "It's not that we can't work together—"

"Good."

"It's just that we feel the topic you gave us is so . . . big, and . . . important, really, that it deserves two separate lessons. You know, one from the guy's point of view, and one from the girl's. We're just thinking of what's best for the class here. It has nothing to do with not wanting to work together. We're good friends, Helen and me." I sling my arm around her for emphasis. I feel her body go rigid, but she doesn't pull away. Instead she forces a smile. "We've been going to school together since fourth grade, for God's sake. That's not the ish here."

I let go of Helen's scarecrow-stiff shoulder. I don't want her frozen grin blowing our story.

Mrs. Turris studies me. She's not giving me anything by way of a clue. I can't tell if I've hooked this fish or if I'm going to come up empty-handed. She drums her fingers on her desk.

"Okay," she responds. "You've intrigued me. I like the idea of two lessons from the different perspectives."

"Great!" I say, letting out the breath I didn't even know I was holding. "You won't regret this."

A quick glance at Helen and, I don't know, but I think I see some newfound respect in her eyes.

"But . . ." Mrs. Turris says, the word like a sucker punch to my solar plexus. "Since you two are such great pals," she taps her salmon-painted lips with a pencil, "I don't see why you shouldn't work together on *both* lessons. You can present the male perspective on contraception one day and the female perspective the next. It's a fabulous suggestion, Cooper. It'll be more work, for sure—a great deal more actually—but two good friends like you should be able to get it done without a problem."

Helen glares at me.

"But that doesn't mean you have extra time," Mrs. Turris continues, an uppercut to the chin. "You two are really going to have to buckle down. Now, hurry along. You're already late for your next class."

Out in the nearly empty hall, I walk as quickly as I can without breaking into a full jog. But Helen catches up to me, matching my step no problem.

"Nice going," she says. "Now, not only do we have to work together, but we have to work together twice as much."

"Yeah, well, I didn't hear *you* chiming in with any brill ideas."

"Like I had time before you jammed your foot down your throat."

"It would have worked if you hadn't acted like I was a skeeve when I put my arm around you." This is not my normal pace, and I'm out of breath before we reach the stairs. But I force myself to keep my breathing even. I'm not about to let Helen sense any weakness. "She totally picked up on that."

"What do you expect?" Helen's not even huffing. "You

could have told me what you were going to say before we went up there to talk to her."

I stop at the bottom of the steps. For emphasis. But also to rest. "It's called improv, babe. I was working with the pitch we were thrown."

"Well I don't *do* improv. I need advanced notice before . . . things like that."

I hold my hands up. "You know what? Just stop. You have nothing to complain about. You're getting the better deal here. By *far*."

"Oh, really?" Helen snorts. "And how do you figure that?"

"Because you get to work with me."

Helen places her hand over her heart. "Oh, excuse me. I'm sorry. I must have missed the memo describing what a privilege that is. Remind me again what you bring to this project? Besides your *D* average?"

"Besides my D-*plus* average." I start up the stairs. Helen follows. "Let me think. Hmm. Oh, yeah. I also bring this." I reach into my pants pocket and pull out a big ol' bird which I brandish in front of Helen's eyes.

She nods. "Right. Maturity. That's what I figured."

"Okay, Miss Maturity." I stop on the landing. "Why don't you tell me what *you* bring to the table? I mean, other than your glowing reputation and wild popularity."

Helen glares at me, her eyes narrowed into little slits. "Screw you, Cooper." She shoves her face close to mine, which kind of surprises me. "You're a real prick, you know that?"

It throws me off my stride. Her vehemence. By the time I open my mouth to respond, she's already headed down the stairs.

"I'm sorry," I call after her, but she doesn't turn around. Just keeps going.

CHAPTER SEVEN

SOMETHING TO TALK ABOUT

WHY DON'T YOU GUYS just bring your instruments over this afternoon?" I say, shifting into a lower gear as Matt, Sean, and I cycle up Cardiac Hill. "We'll just lay down a few simple tracks and see how they sound."

Matt laughs. "Okay, what part of 'No, we aren't doing this' didn't you understand?"

"I just don't see the harm in giving it a shot."

"Because it's pointless, Coop," Sean says, huffing and puffing as we reach the steepest point of the climb. "Recording us playing is only going to confirm what we already know: we stink. And honestly, I don't see us getting any better in three months."

My thighs are burning from the slog of pedaling. I can hardly wait until I get a car and I never have to bike this stupid hill again. "Just for kicks, then," I wheeze out. "We don't have to . . . hand it in." My lungs scream for mercy. "We'll just . . . have some fun." I think I might hurl. "We can smooth the songs out with my computer and GarageBand."

"Forget it," Matt says, "I already told Valerie we'd watch a movie today."

"And I've got to Skype my Uncle Doug," Sean adds as we reach the top of the hill. "So he can do my Algebra homework for me."

"Fine, get all your stuff out of the way and we can do it after dinner," I say. "I'll be expecting you." I peel off and race down my street before they can protest.

Matt yells after me, "I'm not coming!"

"Me either!" Sean shouts.

"I can't hear you!" I call over my shoulder. "Seven o'clock! Don't be late! We have a lot of work to do!"

I coast up to my house, not entirely confident that Matt and Sean will feel guilty enough to show later. Still, I'm holding on to a tiny strand of hope.

I can hear Mom singing—or rather, butchering—the Beatles when I open the front door.

"She's got a chicken to ride. She's got a chicken to ri-hi-hide. She's got a chicken to ride. And she's not scared."

"Those aren't the words, Mom," I say as I step into the kitchen, heading straight for the cupboard to forage. "Not even close."

"What are you talking about?" she says, opening the freezer.

"It's a *ticket* to ride." I laugh, reaching past the already opened bag of Doritos and grabbing the brand new bag of Cheetos hiding in the back. "Not a chicken."

"Are you sure? I guess that does make more sense." She pulls out a Tupperware container with something beige in it. "Now what's this?"

Angela walks into the kitchen, blabbing on her cell phone. "I'm so sure," she says. "Like I even care."

"We're having an early dinner today. Are you feeling more Salisbury steak or pot pie?" Mom asks me, shoving the mystery food back into the freezer.

My stomach heaves. If I have to eat another cardboard encased microwave meal I may put myself up for adoption. "I'm leaning more toward homemade oven-fried chicken, roast potatoes, and corn on the cob," I say, tearing open the bag of Cheetos.

Mom laughs. "Right. And who's whipping *that* up in the next,"— she glances at the sunflower clock on the wall—"twenty minutes, before I have to be at Porterhouse Nick's?"

I groan. "Are we going to be eating frozen foods for the rest of our lives?"

"I don't want to reschedule, *Graham*!" Angela barks into her phone. "Oh, um, let me think. Maybe because we *already* rescheduled this week."

Mom sighs, her whole face looking weary. "You know the deal, Cooper. Once your father's back to regular hours at work, I won't have to—"

"I know, I know," I say, feeling like a dick for even bringing it up. "I'm sorry. Pot pie will be great."

Angela huffs. "Yeah, whatever. Have fun at the gym, asshole. I hope you strain your groin." She snaps her phone shut and tosses it onto the kitchen table.

"What's wrong?" Mom pulls a family pack of pot pies from the freezer and places it on the counter.

"He's going to break up with me. I know it." Angela flops down into a chair, the legs scraping on the floor. "And it's all because of my giant schnoz. I need a nose job."

"Don't talk like that," Mom says. "You're beautiful, honey. You're just coming into your own. You'll see. Six months from now you'll be beating the guys off with a stick."

"Yowch," I say, popping a handful of cheese puffs into my mouth. "Is that how you do it, Ang? No wonder guys keep breaking up with you."

Angela shoots me a double-barreled finger salute.

I laugh and start to make my escape with the Cheetos when Mom calls out, "Wait, Coop. Where are you going?"

"The basement."

"Your father wants to talk with you."

Oh, great. Just what I need right now. "About what?" I ask.

Mom blushes, then turns away. "Just . . . go into the family room." She starts fumbling with the box of pot pies. "It's important."

Okay, what the hell is going on?

Angela chortles. "Jesus, Coop. Are you failing out of tenth grade already?"

I flash her a screw-you glare, then turn back to Mom. "Can't I talk to him later? I have a lot of work to do."

"No." Mom drops one of the frozen pies and it slides into the sink. "Go. He's waiting."

CHAPTER EIGHT

PAPA'S GOT A BRAND NEW BAG

DAD'S SITTING ON THE COUCH watching Grand Prix darts and drinking a beer when I get to the family room. There are two empties already on the side table. For the last three years Mom's been pretty strict, rationing the beer because of Dad's diabetes, but he's been ignoring the rules lately.

"Mom said you wanted to see me?" I say, hovering in the doorway with my bag of Cheetos.

He looks over at me. "Oh, hey there, bud. You got to watch this." He gestures to the TV with his bottle, his dry and cracked fingers permanently grease-stained. "These guys are really good. I didn't even know they *had* dart championships, did you?"

"No." I want to get this over with as fast as possible. "So, um, Mom said you had something you wanted to tell me?"

“Come on. Have a seat.” Dad takes a tug on his beer and pats the couch beside him.

I glance over my shoulder, feeling more than a little uneasy. When Dad wants to talk to me, he just talks. It’s never been this kind of arranged-meeting sort of thing. Is he going to tell me Mom and him are getting a divorce? Or that we’re going to have to sell the house and move? Or that I’m going to have to get a job to help support the family? I don’t know if I could handle any of those situations.

“Get over here,” Dad says. “This is the grand finale. You don’t want to miss this.”

I drag myself away from the door and slog over to the couch. I place the Cheetos bag on the end table. Dad scoots over a little and I sit. He smells like a combination of beer and Old Spice.

“O’Shea is ahead right now,” he says. “But this Adams fella is coming on strong.”

On the TV, two beer-bellied dudes are chucking darts at a board.

“Wow, yeah, nice aim.”

“So, how’s tricks?” Dad asks, his eyes glued to the screen. Is it me, or is he acting really weird?

“What do you mean?”

He turns his head toward me. “What do I mean?” He cuffs the back of my head. “Girls, chucklenut. I’m starting to worry about you. Your two buds have dipped their toes in the hootchy pool. What about *my* boy? These are precious years you're letting slip by. High school is an all you can eat muffet. It's no time to be shy."

Is *this* what we're talking about? My opportunity to score with girls? I can't believe that this is Mom-sanctioned. "Yeah. It's chill, Dad. Seriously"

"I'm just sayin'." He takes another slug of his beer. "Anyway. So . . ." He clears his throat. "Your mother and I were wondering . . ." Why are his ears getting so red? "Your Mom and I felt that . . ." Dad rubs the back of his neck. Looks over at the door. "Maybe you should go close that."

I follow his gaze. "The door?"

"Yeah. So we're not disturbed."

"What the hell's going on, Dad?"

"Nothing's 'going on.' I just want to spend some man-time with my boy." He claps my shoulder awkwardly. "Everything's normal. This is normal. We're just a normal father and son here. Chatting about . . . normal guy things."

My skin suddenly feels too tight on my face. I lean away from him. "Okay, you're starting to freak me out."

"Look, just close the damn door and then we can talk in private. This is personal stuff."

I get up from the couch cautiously and make my way to the door, keeping my eyes on him the whole time. I pull the door shut, then walk back to the couch and sit at the far end.

"So . . ." Dad coughs. He won't meet my eyes. "Last

night, when I was in the garage . . . your mom came . . ." His Adam's apple bobs as he swallows hard.

A grossed-out chill rockets up my spine. "Okay, could you *please* finish that sentence."

"No, that's not . . ." He tilts his head, cracking his neck. "Listen. Your mom came out to the garage while I was working on one of my projects. You remember that massage chair I found by that dumpster a few weeks ago? I've almost got it fully functional. Except that it still sort of gooses you every once in a while. But I'm almost there."

"That's great, Dad. You were saying?"

"Right. Anyway. Your Mom said she found something when she was cleaning your room. Some papers. On contraception."

"Yeah? So? It's for Health class."

"That a fact?" He seems relieved by this. Hopeful, almost. But then his shoulders slump. "Well, that doesn't really change things. Your mother thinks that you might be . . ." Dad forces a laugh. "You know your mother. She's kind of naive about these sorts of things." His upper lip is beading with sweat.

My stomach flops over. I suddenly know exactly where this is heading.

"Look, Dad," I say, cutting him off at the pass. "I'm good. Don't worry. I've got it covered."

"I'm sure you do. I just . . . you know . . . we've never really had . . . 'The Talk,' you and me. You know. *Officially.*" He wipes the perspiration from his lip. Then takes another gulp of beer. "I mean, I figure you know a bit already. But do you have any questions? Are you familiar with all the, uh, details? The mechanics of things?"

"Dad. I'm fifteen. I've got a computer. What I know would probably make Mom cry. Can I go now?"

Dad takes a supremely deep breath. Then closes his eyes. "So, uh, then you . . . know how to put a condom on? I mean, have you . . . practiced?"

The air feels like it's all breathed up in here. "I can put together a BIONICLE blindfolded. I think I can handle a condom."

Dad leans back as he drags an aqua-blue box of Trojans from under the coffee table with his sock-clad big toe.

I turn away. "Oh, Jesus!"

"Your mother made me promise I'd show you how to put one on."

"No," I say, shooting to my feet. "Absolutely not."

"Sit down! Now!" He grabs my arm and yanks me back to the couch. "We're going to do this." He leans over and picks the box up off the floor. "Your mother's worried you'll wind up with some disease. Or get a girl pregnant or something. And then it'll be my fault for not showing you." He tears open the box and pulls out a long chain of condoms.

I shut my eyes. Hold up my hands. "Seriously, Dad. I'll wiki it. This is *not* cool."

"Come on. Open your eyes," he says. "You think this

is fun for me? It isn't. But if I don't do this, your mother's gonna lock the love trunk until I do. So let's just get this over with."

"Please, Dad." If a genie suddenly appeared and offered me one wish right now, I would ask to be made small enough so that I could crawl between the couch cushions.

"I said open your goddamn eyes." He cuffs my head again.

I open them partway, half-expecting to see him tugging his pants down and working up a proud one so he can perform his demonstration.

Instead, he drains his beer and places the empty bottle between his legs. Thank God for small favors. "This is important information. You do it wrong, you might as well not even be wearing one." He carefully tears one of the condom packets from the chain. "The first thing you want to do is check the expiration date. This isn't a 'Best Before' date. If it's expired, it's expired." All of a sudden he's gone from being completely embarrassed to totally practical, like we've dived into the ocean, and he's over the fact that it's freezing cold, and is now ready to bodysurf. "Then, you want to make sure the packet hasn't been compromised. It should feel like a little air pillow." He hands me the condom. "You feel that."

"Yeah, great." I hand it back. My eyes are trying to look at anything but his beer-bottle erection, which for some reason has become the only thing in the room. "Can you at least take the bottle out from between your legs?"

"No, I cannot. Because your champion isn't going to be sitting on a table, or next to you, or anywhere else but where it is. As a matter of fact . . ." Dad grabs one of his other empties, reaches over, and jams it between my legs.

My back shoots up straight. "Whoa. Hey now."

He rips another condom from the chain and tosses it to me.

"We're going to do this together," Dad says. "Because if you don't learn how to do it now, the right way, you sure as hell aren't going to be able to do it properly when it's dark and you're all hopped up in the back seat of a car. Now open your condom. But do it carefully. With your hands. Not your teeth. Believe me, I learned that one the hard way."

We go through the whole painful process. Step by agonizing step. Making sure it's not inside out. Pinching the tip to keep the air out in order to make a reservoir. Rolling it down to the base of our long necks.

"Good," Dad says, gesturing at his success. "Now that we're suitably sheathed, we can go about our business. Do you need me to go over that part with you?"

"I do not," I say.

"Okay." He nods. "So, let's say we've performed admirably. Everything has—you know—worked out the way it should. Now we have to remove the condom. And it's different than how we put it on."

All of a sudden, the door swings open and Angela pokes her head in. "Mom says dinner's going to be ready in fifteen . . . Ohmygod!" Angela blanches, her eyes bugging. "What the hell?"

Dad and I look over from the couch, our beer-bottle condom-sheathed wangs standing tall between our legs. The mixture of confusion, disgust, and complete horror on Angela's face is supreme. All of a sudden, this whole thing is worth it. I wish I had a camera.

"Do you mind, hon?" Dad says. "This is man talk. We're a little busy here."

"I hate this family!" Angela shouts as she turns on her heel and bolts from the room.

Dad and I look at each other for a second.

"Oops," he says.

And we both burst out laughing.

CHAPTER NINE

I STILL HAVEN'T FOUND WHAT I'M LOOKING FOR

I'M HUNCHED OVER my drums, staring at the posters on the wall. The Who. The White Stripes. The Beatles. Radiohead. Arctic Monkeys. All of them mocking me. My T-shirt is soaked through with sweat, my shoulders are in knots, and I have a blazing headache.

Five and a half hours. I've worked my ass off down in this basement for five and a half hours trying to cobble together a demo—pounding on my drum kit, figuring out how to work the software instruments in GarageBand, trying to lay down some passable tracks on my computer—and still I have dick to show for it.

Part of me wants to say screw it, but another part won't let it go.

I sit up. Set myself. Reach over to my laptop and press the trackpad with the tip of my drumstick to start a new recording. Count myself in, then beat out the intro to "Dani California."

"Coop, buddy!" Dad calls out over the drums as he clomps down the stairs.

I click off the recording. Damn it. That was sounding good, too.

"I love the dedication, bud," he says, as he makes his way toward my drums, "but there are three other people living in this house."

"This is for school, Dad. It's due tomorrow."

He recoils at the sight of me. "Jesus Christ, Coop. Are you okay? You're sweating like a nun in a cucumber patch."

"I'm fine," I say. "I just . . . need to do this."

He glances around at the mess on the floor: the crumpled Cheetos bag, the five empty Coke cans, the scattered pages of sheet music, the broken drumsticks. "This is some kind of homework, you say?"

"Yeah. Sort of."

Dad smirks and looks at me sideways. "Right. And a dog's breath smells like fresh baked bread. Come on. What's the poop and scuttle?" He flops down on the old gray sofa.

It's bizarre. I feel this welling up of emotion, like I might break down and cry. I force myself to hold it together. "It's the Battle of the Bands. I have to get in."

Dad raises his eyebrows as he pulls a packet of nicotine gum from his shirt pocket. "As a one-man band?"

"With Matt and Sean."

Dad scans the basement, like he's trying to find them.

I breathe deep and exhale. "The demo's due tomorrow. But the actual competition isn't for three months. They didn't think we could put together a CD in time to enter."

"Yeah, well, it looks like they were right." He pushes a piece of gum from the packet and pops it in his mouth.

"If we could just get in, I'm sure we could get good enough by December. I wanted to give it a shot." I shift on the drum stool, my butt sore from all the sitting.

Dad studies me for a long time, chawing his gum. "Nope. Sorry. You can't bullshit a bullshitter."

"What?"

"Look, no offense, Coop," Dad says, "but you're not the nose-to-the-grindstone type. The last time you put this much effort into something was when you were lobbying us to adopt the sorriest looking dog at the kennel so you could pretend to be a homeless kid and beg for change outside the PriceMark. So, what's the angle here?"

I feel my face flush. "There is no angle."

Dad peers at me, chewing loudly but saying nothing.

I try to stare him down but it doesn't take long before my resolve evaporates. "It's a girl," I say, putting my drumsticks aside and rubbing my aching hands.

He smiles. "Okay. So you're trying to impress the ladies."

"No. Well, yes, that. But . . . it's more complicated."

I don't know why my chest feels so constricted. Like I'm wearing a straightjacket or something. "There's this *other* girl. Who I've been saddled up with for a school project. Everyone at school hates her. So now I'm . . . reaping all the benefits of that."

"What do you mean 'everyone hates her'?"

"She's got a reputation. You know. There are all these rumors about her . . . and deli meats."

Dad tries not to laugh. He nods and says, "Hairy Mary."

"Excuse me?"

"It was Hairy Mary at my school. Mary, Mary, she's so hairy, yeasty, beasty, everywherey." He shrugs. "Anyway, go on."

"Yeah, well, being partners with this girl, now everyone's saying I'm *with* her. Which means my chances of hooking up with any of the girls in the school are less than zilch."

Dad lifts his chin. "So, you think being in the Battle of the Bands could help the situation?"

"I know it would. If we win, absolutely."

"Yeah," he says. "I can see that. Rock star trumps pretty much anything. It's too bad really. If you'd told me a few days ago I could have had your grandmother FedEx me my old band tapes. You could have floated one of those as your own until you guys got your act together."

"You were in a band?" My voice is thick with doubt.

Dad laughs. "Don't sound so surprised."

"No, I just . . . didn't know."

"We were damn good, too. The Spiroketes. Landed me a flock of squanch, I'll tell you that. Cindy Berman. Alison Hripsack. Kathryn Jaspers. Lynn Skayling. Wendy Figlia." He's got this far away, life-used-to-be-so-great expression on his face. He blinks hard, shaking off the memory. "Anyway, we tried to keep the band chugging after high school, but you know how things go." Dad taps his lips, the wheels turning behind his eyes. "Still, it's a shame about those tapes."

"Yeah, that would have been cool," I say. "I guess I'm just going to have to start looking into the priesthood."

"Hold on a second. Don't go hanging up the guns just yet." He stands and starts to pace. "Three months, huh? Three months. Yeah. We could get you sounding decent by then. But the demo. That's the rub. And if you can't use *my* high school band tapes, then what?" He stops. Runs his hand through his thick black hair. "Unless . . ."

"Unless what?"

"Okay, hear me out." Dad looks all excited, his fingers twitching. "This going to sound a lot like stealing. But really, I think we can justify it."

CHAPTER TEN

USE SOMEBODY

I DON'T KNOW," I say. "Maybe this isn't such a good idea after all."

"Look," Dad says, "when the situation is as dire as yours, you can't apply everyday morals and values. You gotta shove all that stuff to the side. And besides, technically, you'll just be borrowing the music. Ultimately, your band is going to have to live and die on its own."

We're hunched over my MacBook, scrolling through whacks and whacks of unsigned bands on MySpace, searching for someone I might be able to safely crib—I mean *borrow*—a few songs from for my demo.

The door to the basement squeaks open. *"Good night, yellow brick road,"* Mom sings down from the top of the stairs. "What do you say, Walter? You coming to bed?"

"It's *good-bye,* yellow brick road, hon." Dad looks up from my laptop. "And I can't come up right now. I'm helping Coop out with a school project."

"It's past midnight. Cooper, you should be in bed."

"I know, Mom," I say, my eyes burning from staring so long at the screen. "I have to finish this. It's due tomorrow."

"That's why you don't leave things to the last minute."

"We shouldn't be too much longer." Dad gestures at a band called Sinus Trouble.

"All right, but don't wake me up when you come to bed, Walter. I'm babysitting the Bermans' kids all day tomorrow. I need to have my wits about me." Mom shuts the basement door. Her footsteps *clip-clop* over our heads.

I click on the Sinus Trouble page and we take a listen. They sound like a mix between Linkin Park and Collective Soul. Not my particular bag of chips, but definitely polished.

"Forget it." Dad waves them off. "Too good. You'll get busted for sure."

I yawn and close my eyes. My head feels like it's filled with sand. I start to drift off.

"Right there," Dad says, jolting me awake. "Understain." He points at the screen. "They do covers and originals. They're unsigned. And they're from Canada. Even better. Click on them."

It turns out Understain does a pretty good rendition of "(Don't Fear) the Reaper." Good, but not great. They also play a passable "Paint It Black." One of their better original songs is some kind of meat protest anthem called "Grind the Rump Roast."

Again, it's decent, just not brilliant.

In other words, absolutely perfect.

Dad and I turn to each other.

"Can you download those?" Dad asks.

"Better if I blast them on my computer speakers and record them that way. Then, it'll actually sound like we were playing in the basement."

Dad points at me. "Good call. Now, when you hand this in to the teacher, you have to play it completely cucumber. Look him in the eyes. Keep it brief. If he asks you questions, don't go into long explanations. The best way to approach this is to keep telling yourself that this Mr. Grossman character is a jerk for not giving you more time to make a demo. It's his fault, really. He drove you to this."

"Thanks, Dad."

"Good luck." He stands and claps me on the shoulder. "You do know, though, that if the shit comes down, I'm gonna have to deny any knowledge of this. You're a kid. You'll recover. It won't be so easy for me. When you get to be my age people think you should know better."

"It's cool," I say. "I won't narc you out."

Dad smiles. "That's my boy. Now, let me know how it turns out. If you get in, we're gonna have a buttload of work to do."

CHAPTER ELEVEN

PARANOID ANDROID

MY CHEEKS AND NOSE are numbed by the damp air as I ride my bike through the mist that rises off the asphalt. I remember listening to the rain last night, in between bouts of fitful sleep, and praying that it would let up before I had to go to school this morning.

And while everything around me is wet, my mouth is as dry as an empty taco shell.

The pilfered demo whispers to me from my backpack. *"You are going to get expelled from school. This will go on your permanent record. You think babes are going to want to date a thief?"*

"Shut up!" I say. "I'm not stealing. I'm *borrowing.* There's a difference."

Okay. Be caszh. The demo isn't talking to me. That's ridiculous. I am the baron of bull. This is no big deal. I've been dishonest to teachers my entire life.

"But never on this scale before," the demo warns.

"I said, shut up!"

I take a deep breath. There's not a chance in hell Mr. Grossman will be able to tell that I jacked these songs. How could he? Does he spend his free time prowling MySpace and listening to mediocre unsigned Canadian bands? Doubtful. So just chillax.

I take the turn onto Division Avenue, my tires sloshing through a puddle.

I had to lie to Matt and Sean so they wouldn't be wondering why I couldn't ride to school with them today. I told them I had early detention. It's weird. I can't remember ever having actually flat-out lied to my buds before. I have to say, it didn't feel real good, but it had to be done. It's *their* fault I'm having to jump through all these hoops. If they'd showed up last night, like I asked, none of this subterfuge would be necessary.

The hallways are pretty barren when I step into the school. Just your early drop-offs and a few pre-caffeinated teachers wandering around like zombies. I adjust my backpack, get myself focused, and start toward the music department.

It's funny how long and bright the hallways seem when there aren't a billion kids jostling to get to class. And how you can hear your footsteps so much louder. And how everything smells like fresh pencil shavings and wet newspaper.

I'm hoping that Mr. Grossman won't be in the chorus

room, so I can slide the demo and entry form under the door without having to do a face-to-face.

But when I arrive, there he is, sitting at his piano, scribbling something on staff paper.

I stop in the doorway, a lump in my throat.

Okay. I either do this or I don't.

"Don't," the demo calls out from my backpack. *"Just throw me in the trash and we'll never speak of this again."*

"Get the hell in there, chucklenut," I hear Dad's voice in my head. *"Are you going to take advice from an inanimate object? Or from your dear old Dad?"*

The demo sighs. *"It's not too late. The teacher hasn't seen you yet. Just back away quietly—"*

"Mary, Mary, she's so hairy!" Dad sings loudly, drowning out the voice of the demo.

"Yes?" It's Mr. Grossman. Looking at me over his glasses with his squinty eyes. He's got this pinched-up look on his face, like he knows I've done something wrong but hasn't quite figured out what it is yet.

I swallow and step into the room. "I've got a demo for the Battle of the Bands." Keep it brief. Get in and get out.

"Very good," Mr. Grossman says. "Give it here." He gestures toward me. His hand looks enormous. Like it could reach out and snap my neck.

I swing my backpack around and dig out the CD. "Here." I pass the jewel case off to him, keeping my distance.

He looks at it and raises his eyebrows.

"What?" I say.

"Your entry form?"

"Oh, right." I pull the folded-up form—complete with Matt's and Sean's forged signatures—from my bag and give this to him as well.

Mr. Grossman unfolds the paper and studies it. "Arnold Murphy's Bologna Dare?" he says. "It sounds *lewd*. What does that mean?"

"Short and simple," I hear Dad whisper.

"It's not lewd. It's just an inside joke. From grade school."

Mr. Grossman levels his gaze on me. Waiting for me to elaborate.

"This kid," I say. "We dared him to eat an old boloney sandwich. Off the cafeteria floor. It's just . . . It's nothing. . . . He moved away. But not because of the sandwich. His father got transferred, I think. I'm not sure. . . ." I feel Dad giving me an internal head-cuffing. "Anyway. That's it."

I can tell by Mr. Grossman's curdled expression that he doesn't like my answer. "I don't recognize any of these names from our music program."

For a brief moment, I consider mentioning that Sean was in chorus for a few days last year, before Mr. Grossman kicked him out, but then think better of it. Instead I just say, "Nope."

"And why is that?" Mr. Grossman asks.

Yeah, why is that, Coop? Could it be the fact that the three of you are amazingly unmusical?

Shut up, shut up, shut up!

I shrug. "Don't know."

He sniffs. "Hmm. Curious."

What the hell does that mean?

"The committee will listen to the tapes over the weekend. Announcements will made Monday." Mr. Grossman places the demo and the entry form beside him on the piano bench, then returns his attention to his staff paper.

I guess . . . that's it.

I spin around and walk out of the room, feeling dizzy and sweaty all over, like I may chum the fish, even though my stomach is hollow from not eating this morning.

CHAPTER TWELVE

LUCKY MAN

YOU'RE IN LUCK," Mrs. Turris says after the bell rings and everyone settles down. "I'm going to let you use the class period today to get some work done on your projects."

She grabs a stack of papers from her desk and hands them to gerbil-cheeked Trina Boyle in the first row. Trina takes one and passes the stack behind her.

"Since this project is such a large undertaking," Mrs. Turris continues, "I've set a strict timeline to help you pace yourselves." The class lets out a collective groan, which causes Mrs. Turris to smirk. "These are hard deadlines that I expect you and your partner to meet without excuses. In two weeks, a basic summary of your lesson will be due. Two weeks after that, a first draft lesson plan. And the like. So keep these schedules handy. If you follow the plan, you should have no problem once it comes time to give your presentations."

I glance over at Helen, who is already taking notes. She's the only one moving her pen. I wonder if Mrs. Turris would notice if we worked on opposite sides of the room. Probably.

"Once you get your copy of the schedule, find your partner and get to work. There are reference materials in the bookshelves at the back of the room, and of course there's your Health text, which is a rich source of information."

Everyone's up and shuffling around. Matt and Sean scoot their desks together. They're already talking and laughing it up.

Jerks.

I stand and start across the room, only to be assaulted by the facial-hair-challenged Andy Bennett, who bumps my shoulder.

"Watch it, Corn Dog." He smirks.

"Is that you, Andy?" I say. "Oh, thank God. I knew that sphincters couldn't talk, but for a second there—"

Andy shoves me. "You want me to break your face, butthead?"

"Do I want you to give me head?" I say loudly. "No, Andy. I do not."

Several kids nearby laugh.

"That's it," Andy grabs two fistfuls of my shirt. "You're dead."

"Head? I already told you, Andy. I'm not interested. Read the poster on the wall, dude. *No* means *no*."

His face crimsons. He keeps hold of my shirt with one hand and cocks a fist with the other.

"Hello?" Mrs. Turris calls from the front of the room. "Do I need to send you two to the principal?"

Andy grits his teeth and pushes me away. "Watch your back, Corn Dog. 'Cause you'll never know when I'll be coming."

"On my back? Dude, no thanks."

"You're a real comedian. Just you wait." He makes an I'm-watching-you gesture before walking off.

What a dink.

I make my way over to the empty desk across the aisle from Helen, feeling an invisible noose tightening around my neck. She's already marking pages in her textbook with Post-its.

"So, whadda we got?" I say.

Helen looks up at me for a second, then goes back to her scribbling.

"That's cool. I'm down with that. We'll work on our own thing and compare notes later."

I slap my Health book on the desk and start flipping through it. I pretend to be looking stuff up but really my mind is bouncing around like a SuperBall. The Battle of the Bands. The songs we'll do if we get in. The Phenomenal Four wearing tight sweaters and dirty dancing to our music.

I glance over at Helen, swaddled in her thick, baggy gray sweatshirt, hunched over her book. I wonder what she's packing under all those clothes. You never know. Sometimes the biggest diamonds are buried below a ton of rock.

"What?" Helen's caught me looking at her.

"Nothing."

"You were staring at me."

"Was not."

"I'm not blind, Cooper."

"If I was going to stare at anyone it wouldn't be you, I can tell you that."

"Whatever. You're obviously getting a lot of work done there."

"As a matter of fact, I am." I tap my temple for emphasis. "Not all of us have to write every little thing down. Some of us use our brains to store the information for later retrieval."

"That would require you to actually *have* some brains."

"On your period much? I hope you're not going to be all raggy when we present our lessons, 'cause that's not going to score us any points with the teach."

"How's my wonder team getting on?" It's Mrs. Turris, the omnipresent-one herself. She grins down on us, hands on hips.

"Super." I plaster a big smile on my face. "We were just discussing the female menstrual cycle."

"I don't see how you can be discussing anything

when you're so far away from each other." Mrs. Turris grabs my desk and drags me right up next to Helen. Man is she strong. "There. That's better. Now you won't have to shout at each other across the aisle." She nods, satisfied with her work, and moves on.

It's impossible to miss the sniggers and jeers—"Bet she likes it *doggy* style," "Put your wiener between her buns," "Make her use her Cooper Scooper"—that flutter around the room like crickets.

"Quiet down," Mrs. Turris snaps, ignoring what's actually being said and instead focusing on the decibel level.

"So." I plant my feet and surreptitiously slide my desk a few inches away. "We're here. We might as well get something done."

"That's what I was *trying* to do," Helen says.

"Okay, fine, let's whip this puppy—I mean, *project*—out." Note to self: avoid all references to hot dogs, canines, and condiments when around Helen. "How long could it take, right? There's rubbers, the diaphragm, and the pill. Big deal."

Helen stares at me. "Coop, there are way more contraceptive methods than that. I've been counting them and so far I've got at least twenty different kinds."

"Jesus. Are you twisting me? Do we have to do them all?" My gut clenches thinking about having to stand in front of the whole class with Helen and talk about all this stuff. I can hear the taunts now; "Wrap up that corn dog, Coop, or she might have puppies!", "Give her the old cocktail weiner!", "STDs? You're more likely to get food poisoning!"

"I'm sure Mrs. Turris is going to want us to say something about each of them. Besides, we have two class periods to fill."

I flip through my Health text and find the list of contraceptive methods. "Alphabetical order. How convenient." I start to read them out loud. "Abstinence? What's that?"

"It means not having sex."

I laugh. "Like anyone is going to use *that* method."

"A lot of people do."

"Yeah, but not by choice." I scan down the list. "Birth control implant. Yikes. Don't like the sound of that. It's probably some kind of microchip they insert in your brain that sends out electric shocks every time you think about doing it."

"Somehow, I doubt it."

"Don't be so sure. There's some pretty sick stuff out there. I heard that Ernie Plingus's dad had this operation. They filleted his sack right open. Yanked his manstones out. Like what they do to animals." It makes my tool bag shrivel up just thinking about it.

Helen raises a skeptical eyebrow.

"It's true."

"Let's just stick to what it says in the book, okay?"

"I'm just saying. We could have some fun with this if we wanted to. Introduce some real-life examples and totally gross people out. Maybe even make Mrs. Turris hurl a crustless pizza on her desk. It'd serve her right. What do you think?"

"I think that we should stick to what's in the book."

I throw my hands up in surrender. "Whatever you say, Sister Helen."

Helen sighs and returns her focus to the textbook. "There's the birth control patch."

"Birth control patch? Isn't that what pirates use? Arrrr, I be horny lass, but I dasn't want t'get ye preggers."

Helen slams her textbook closed. "Coop! Enough! Knock it off."

I look around, feel the heat of people staring. "Jeez keep it down, would ya?"

"You're acting like an idiot."

"I'm just trying to make this a little less painful. But if you want to be all uptight about it, fine. We'll just do the most boring project in the history of the universe."

"Cooper. Helen. May I see you up here, please?" Mrs. Turris makes a come hither gesture with her finger. Her mouth a little annoyed dash on her face.

Helen scowls at me. I glare right back at her.

There are more chuckles and comments from the choir as we head up to the front of the room and stand at Mrs. Turris' desk. "Bad dog. Bad dog."

I flip the whole class off behind my back.

"Now, this is the last time I'm going to tell you, so listen closely. This project is as much about the relationship between the two of you as it is about the health topics you're researching."

"Um, we're not in a relationship, Mrs. Turris," I say.

"That's where you're wrong, Cooper. You are in a very close relationship. You're partners. And as partners, you have to be able to depend on each other. Trust each other."

Helen blows sarcastically through her lips.

"Excuse me?" Mrs. Turris says.

Helen crosses her arms. "How am I supposed to trust someone who doesn't even want to work with me?"

"Me not want to work with you?" I laugh. "That's funny. Because it was your idea to ditch me and work on separate projects."

"Yeah, right. You keep telling yourself that."

"I don't have to tell myself that because *you're* the one who told me. Outside Golf Town."

"Uh-huh. And why were we at Golf Town again?"

"Enough," Mrs. Turris says. Her jolly-round-Mrs.-Claus face is not jolly anymore. "I'm giving you one more chance to figure this out. But if you can't make it work on your own, trust me, I'll *make* it work for you. Do we understand each other?"

"Yes," Helen says.

I'm clenching my jaw so tight it's giving me a migraine.

Mrs. Turris turns to me. "Cooper?"

"Mm-hmm," I mutter.

"Good. Now, remember, you have *two* outlines due in two weeks. So, why don't you schedule a time when you can both get together this weekend."

Yeah, right. Like *that's* ever going to happen.

"Right now," Mrs. Turris demands.

I look at Helen and force a smile, pretending I'm willing to give this a shot. "When are you free?"

She sighs. "I have cross country practice from eleven to one on Saturday. But I can do it any other time."

"Well, Saturday at noon is the only time I can do it, so I guess we're out of luck."

"See?" Helen says to Mrs. Turris, like this explains everything.

"Cooper." Mrs. Turris glares at me.

"What? Our schedules don't mesh. Is that my fault?"

"I'll mesh them for you. Sunday from one to three. The Rockville Public Library. Be there, for the entire two hours. If either one of you doesn't show up, you'll both find yourselves with three months' worth of detention. Then, you'll have no choice but to work together. Are we clear?"

Aw, man. This blows. I was keeping the whole weekend clear to focus on Battle of the Bands stuff. There are set lists to be made. Rehearsal schedules to put together. Convincing arguments to be formulated in case Matt and Sean continue to be difficult.

And now this. A big boil on the beautiful boob of my Sunday—and just a preview of my life to come if we don't make it into the Battle of the Bands. I swear, if our names aren't announced on Monday, I'll be packing my bags and booking a one-way trip to Tibet.

CHAPTER THIRTEEN

WHAT I'VE DONE

We are very proud to announce the four bands that will be performing in Lower Rockville High's illustrious Battle of the Bands this year." Mr. Grossman's melodious commercial-ready voice pops and crackles over the school's cheap-ass PA system like he's speaking over a bowl of Rice Krispies.

I'm biting the hell out of my thumbnail as I sit on the edge of my seat in homeroom. There's the sting of a ripped cuticle and the aluminum-foil taste of blood on the tip of my tongue. This ought to be the danger sign that tells me to stop gnawing on myself, but it's been a pretty hang-cliff morning and I'm vibrating with nervous energy, so I just move on to another finger.

I skipped out on meeting Helen at the library on Sunday. Not on purpose. It just slipped my mind because I was so caught up in trying to learn to play our demo songs on the drums. They're not as easy as I thought they'd be. I started practicing right after my bowl of Chocolate Lucky Charms and didn't stop until after three. And by then, of course, it was too late. But it's chill. I know Helen won't narc me out, otherwise she risks getting us both three months of detention.

"First off, we'd like to thank all of the participants who entered a demonstration CD," Mr. Grossman continues. "We were quite impressed with the high caliber of the performances submitted. Although, in one particular band's case, we found their original song to be *not* so original, I'm afraid. I won't name names at the moment. But I can assure you, we will be conducting a thorough investigation into what appears to be a case of blatant plagiarism."

"Ooooooooh," the class collectively responds.

Fuuuuck me.

I break out in a cold full-body sweat. My ears *wah-wahing*.

"And now, onto the announcements." Mr. Grossman's voice sounds like it's echoing down a long tunnel. All of a sudden, I feel like Luke Skywalker trapped in the trash compactor. The walls closing in around me. "Our first band is an all-girl group, consisting of students Kelly West, Gina Lagotta, Bronte Hastings, and Prudence Nash. The Wicked."

There are loud catcalls and enthusiastic desk smackings from most of the guys in the room. At any other time in my life, the thought of those four gorgeous girls singing and gyrating onstage would be giving me a blue steeler. But right now, I feel like I've just come down with the world's worst flu.

"Our second band, whose members include Larry Fungfeld, Ernie Plingus, Greggory Zuzzansky, and Andrew Bennett, is Mjöllnir."

I barely register the names of some of the school's biggest losers. I can't breathe. I stare at the door to the classroom. How obvious would it seem if I bolted?

Just take a pill, Coop. There's no proof you stole those songs. They're just going ask some questions. If you play it chill, you'll glide right over this thing. You've done it before, you can do it again.

I look down and read the words DESK OF THE YEAR '06 that somebody shakily carved into my desktop a million years ago. Well, there now, see? I'm sitting at an award-winning desk. Things are looking up already.

"Our third band, comprised of students Justin Sneep, Lucas Izzi, and Brody Carson, is Cheeba Pet."

This gets a chuckle from about half the class. How did *that* get past the censors? Obviously, Mr. Grossman neglected to google "cheeba." And yet, he somehow managed to find Understain—the most obscure amateur Canadian band possible—on MySpace.

I lay my head down on the desk. The wood veneer is

cool on my cheek. I don't know why I thought that this would go my way. Tenth grade is obviously going to be my year of disgrace.

"And our fourth and final band that will be competing in December sixteenth's Battle of the Bands is . . ."

I wonder if I'll even be able to get into another school. And if I do, will I get to start off fresh? Or will my new Corn Dog reputation trail me there like a bad smell?

"Arnold Murphy's Bologna Dare!"

I guess I had to get called out someday. I mean, Christ, I've gotten away with so much stuff in my life already. It's just the odds, plain and simple.

"Featuring Cooper Redmond, Matthew Gratton, and Sean Hance."

Wait, did he just say . . . ? I bolt upright. Holy crap. He did. He said our names.

We're in.

We're *in*!

They bought it! Ha! I knew it would work.

A wave of pure relief washes over me.

Dean Scragliano beans me with his beaten-up copy of *Lord of Flies*. "Nice band name, Corn Dog. Bologna Dare?" He laughs. "Way to keep it in the meat family. You guys should play some Meat Puppets. Or Meat Loaf."

"Yeah, and you should go play your meat whistle," I say, suddenly feeling invincible. "I hear you've been practicing a lot on your wrestling buds."

Dean leaps to his feet just as the bell rings.

I'm out the door and lost in the crowd before he can come after me.

My phone vibrates. I grab it from my pants pocket and check the screen. A *wtf?* text from Sean and an *r u hI?* from Matt.

I text them both back: *mEt n hOl.*

I'm going to have to do a bit of explaining. And a lot of convincing.

This should be interesting.

CHAPTER FOURTEEN

MR. BRIGHTSIDE

LAST YEAR, ME, MATT, AND SEAN found an old storage room—the Hole—in the basement of the school that nobody seems to know about. Or at least, that no one uses much anymore. It's always unlocked and filled with old school furniture and moldy boxes of crap that look like they haven't been opened since the Civil War. It's the perfect hangout where we can play our PSPs and not be hassled by the Man. It's also the ideal location for spur-of-the-moment meetings like this one.

That's where I'm standing, watching a daddy longlegs climb a rusty file cabinet, when Sean storms through the door, his head and chest jutting forward like a cartoon wrestler going in for the kill. "You assbag!" he shouts.

He's all red-faced and googly-eyed. It's too funny. I know he's uber-pissed, but I can't help cracking up. It's my nerves as much as anything else. Still, it doesn't help the situation.

I clap my hand over my mouth but my body still shakes.

"You think this is *funny*? You think this is something to *laugh* about?"

"No," I say, laughing.

"You're a prick, you know that? A selfish, egotistical, narcissistic prick!"

I dodge the spittle that flies from his frothing mouth. "Jesus, did you get a thesaurus for your birthday, Sean?"

A moment later, Matt pushes open the storage room door, shaking his head and looking weary.

"Tell him, Matt," Sean says, swatting Matt's arm. "People congratulating us. Offering fist pounds. And us having to pretend like we were totally stoked. It was so freakin' humiliating."

"Look, I would have told you guys I was handing in a demo," I say, "but I wanted to keep you dawgs insulated in case anything went down. It was like a million-to-one shot. I didn't think it was actually going to be an ish."

"Yeah, well, it's a *major* ish now, buttleak!" Sean kicks one of the old stacked-up boxes, and his foot sinks deep into the cardboard. "How are we supposed to bail out now with everyone being all kudos and cheers?" He tries—and fails—to pull his foot free. "The whole school heard that announcement. We're gonna look like a bunch of tool bags." Sean's as angry as I've ever seen him, but I have to say, with him shaking his leg, struggling to extricate his foot from that box, it's hard to take him seriously.

"There's a simple answer to that. We don't bail."

Matt sits on an old wooden dugout bench. "How'd you do it? What'd you hand in?"

I shrug. Try to look caszh. "I jacked some songs off MySpace. Some nobody band. It's totally airtight."

"That's called plagiarism, idiot," Sean says, jerking his foot back hard from the box. "Could you be any stupider?" When his foot finally comes free, it does so without his sneaker. The sock that dangles there is gray and holey.

I bust up. "Dude."

"Dude yourself. You heard Mr. Grossman. They already called out one band that handed in a fake demo. When they find out you jacked those songs, we'll be expelled." He shoves his hand into the box and digs around for his shoe. "If you want to get yourself thrown out of school, be my guest. But do me a favor, huh? Leave me out of it."

"The band I cribbed is called Understain," I say. "You ever hear of them?" I don't bother waiting for an answer. "Neither has anyone else on the planet, except maybe their parents. Who, I'm assuming, live in *Canada*. Which is where they're from. So untwist your tighty-whities, Sean."

He wrenches his sneaker from the box. "*You* untwist them, Coop! How about that? Untwist them straight to hell." He hurls his shoe at me but misses by a good two feet.

"Jeez, do some yoga, dawg," I say.

"Don't tell me what to do! I've put up with all your idiot schemes in the past because at least you had the decency to tell us about them. But going behind our backs like this? That's totally screwed."

I look over at Matt, who shrugs like Sean's got a point here.

Sean retrieves his sneaker, then plops down on the dugout bench to pull it on.

I take a deep breath. "Okay. Look. Just hear me out for a sec. I'm totally sorry I wasn't upfront about this. Seriously. It was wrong. I know. And I'll never do it again. I promise. But you're looking at this the wrong way. We've been handed an opportunity to be rock stars in our school. I mean, look at the reaction you got just for getting into the Battle of the Bands." Of course, I don't mention the reaction I got from Dean Scragliano. But we can deal with that later. "Just think about all the babes who'll be hurling their thongs at us when we're rocking out onstage."

"Maybe just hurling," Matt says. "When they hear how bad we sound."

Matt seems way more chillaxed than Sean. Which is good. I think I can turn him. As long as Valerie doesn't get in the way. And if Matt signs on, Sean'll tag along.

"So what if we can't play right now?" I start to pace. "We'll get better. It's just gonna take some practice. My dad said he'd help us out. He had a band in high school and they were like superstars."

"No. I'm not listening to this. You're just doing your whoopty-doopty-loopty-doos again." Sean twirls his hands in the air like a crazy man. "Spinning things around. Making yourself come out all sweet and clean."

I keep my voice calm. "We've been presented with the chance of a lifetime here, boys. We talked about forming this band two years ago. But talk is cut-rate. I took action. That's what's so great about us being friends. I need your talent and smarts, and you need my good looks and screw-the-consequences attitude. Otherwise we'd never do anything. It's like you're little baby ducklings that I have to scoot into the water. Because *I* know you can swim. *I* have faith in your greatness, even if *you* don't have it in yourselves. I mean, think about all my other plum plans. You've never regretted joining in."

"Oh, no?" Matt says. "What about the time you convinced us to jack that coffin lid from the funeral home dumpster and use it as a toboggan?"

"Okay. So *one* time things didn't go . . . exactly as planned."

"Really?" Sean says, sarcastically. "How about when you had us jump off your roof using an umbrella as a parachute?"

"Christ! Are you guys gonna live in the past forever? I'm talking about the here and now."

Sean points at me. "And then there was that time

when we were six and you talked me into eating all that Play-Doh to see if my duke would come out different colors."

Matt and I glance at each other and bust up.

"Now *that* was dope," Matt snorts. "It came out like a rainbow roll."

Sean suppresses a smile. "More like a tie-dyed Pay-Day." His face isn't nearly as red as before. Which is good.

"Okay, look," I say, sitting down between Matt and Sean, one arm around each of them. "I'm gonna lay it on the line, dawgs. This Helen thing is going to kill me. Everyone calling me Corn Dog all the time. Getting slammed in the hallways. Doused in niblets. I mean, forget about rounding any bases, I just don't think I can handle this much longer. Mentally. I'm serious. I might even have to get my family to move. Which would totally suck, because I'd miss you guys."

Matt and Sean both look at me.

"I don't know what else to say. I'm begging you. If you won't do it for yourselves, then do it for me."

Sean takes a deep breath and lets it out loudly.

"Think about it," I continue. "If we win this thing, we instantly become the coolest kids in school. Nobody will be able to make fun of us. There won't be a party we won't be invited to. The hottest girls in the school will want to shack up with us, then steal our underwear and sell them on eBay. What's so bad about that?" I squeeze the backs of their necks. "And I promise, if any heat comes down about the demo, I'll take the full brunt. You know I will. But I'm telling you, if you bail on this you're going to regret it for the rest of your lives."

Silence. Sean's eyes flick over and find Matt's.

And there it is. The holy grail of white flags. The what-do-you-think? look. It's all over now but the "Okay, we'll try, as long as . . ." concessions. Just so that they don't feel like they've totally given it up without dinner and a movie.

"Ahhhhh." I feel myself grin. "You're gonna do it. You *guys*." I grab their shoulders tight and give them a little shake. "I love you, dawgs. You're the best friends ever. You won't be sorry. I promise. This is going to be epic."

CHAPTER FIFTEEN

WE CAN WORK IT OUT

I DON'T BEAT THE BELL to Health class but luckily I *do* beat Mrs. Turris. Everyone is busy doing what you do when the teacher's late—talking, listening to iPods, texting, reading magazines, chucking balls of paper at each other.

I flop down at my desk and hear a squish followed by some chuckles from Andy Bennett's corner of the room.

"Coop's got his period!" Andy calls out.

I look down and see the flattened ketchup packets that were placed under the legs of my chair. See the squiggles of red on the floor and the bottom of my pants.

I am in too good a mood to give Andy any kind of reaction. I just wipe the ketchup off with my sneaker and pretend it never happened. Andy's amateur hour. If he was really thinking, he would have put the packets on my seat. Gotten some tan paint from art class to camouflage them. Now *that* would have been a prank.

Prudence is at her desk, across the aisle from me, working the keyboard on her phone, looking like the perfect goddess she is. Her perky yabbos are doing a pretty good impression of a couple of Hostess Sno Balls below her form-fitting fuzzy pink sweater. My breath catches and my heart pounds out a thrash metal beat. I shake my head to break the spell, otherwise I might actually leap across the aisle and bury my face right into her marshmallowy goodness.

"Hey there, you," I say to her. "Kudos on getting into the Battle of the Bands, by the way. Looks like you and me have yet another thing in common."

Nothing. Which makes me smile. I like a challenge.

"So, who do you think our biggest competition is?" I ask.

"I don't care," Prudence says, her attention squarely on her phone.

"I bet Cheeba Pet is real good. At least, they look the part." I laugh.

Prudence sighs, her purple-polished fingernails clicking away on her phone's keyboard. Punching the letters harder than before.

"Of course, if you girls want to win, you're gonna have to get through us first. Which means you're gonna have to beat the Bologna. Is that something you think you can handle?"

She's ignoring me with a vengeance. I love it.

"Here's a thought," I say. "We should organize an

after party. Don't you think? With a theme. Like, I don't know, Garden of Eden or something. You, Gina, Bronte, and Kelly could come over to my house today and we could start planning it. We could all try on some fig leaves. Tempt each other with apples. It'll be dope. What do you say?"

Prudence slams her cell shut and turns on me. "God! How does it feel to be such an asshole all of the time?"

I smile, because now she's engaged. "This is crazy. When are we going to stop fooling ourselves and just admit that we both want to dance the rug rumba?"

"Right." Prudence snorts. "I'd rather have sex with a monkey."

"Whoa. Hello. She's gorgeous *and* a freak. I'm down with that. I mean, we couldn't ever tell anyone, 'cause most people wouldn't understand. But yeah, all right. You know anyone who's got a monkey?"

Prudence shakes her head. "I hate you." She flips her phone open again.

"You know what they say about the line between love and hate."

The door to the classroom flies open and Mrs. Turris enters, hefting a stack of books and papers and looking frazzled. "Sorry, sorry, sorry," she says, bustling over to her desk and dumping all her stuff.

Suddenly she stops and stares at us like she's just caught us whizzing all over the room. "Why aren't you with your partners already? Do I have to hold your hands every single day? Let's go. Up."

"Thank God." Prudence leaps to her feet, grabs her books, and moves across the room to Sam Shattenkirk's desk.

"Today's the last day I'm giving you class time for these projects," Mrs. Turris says. "So make good use of it."

The rest of the kids in the class grumble and take their sweet time getting together with their respective partners. The room fills with the cacophony of thirty people all talking to each other at once.

I look over at Helen, who's got her textbook open and her pen going a million miles an hour. *Again.* She doesn't even glance in my direction. She's probably still mad because I stood her up at the library. But it's cool. I'll get her to cover for me. She's got as much to lose as I do.

I drag myself over, pull a desk up close to Helen before Mrs. Turris does it for me. "So. What should I be doing?"

"That's a good question." Helen doesn't look up from her work. Yup, she's pissed.

"What's that supposed to mean?"

"Nothing."

"So, tell me what you want me to do."

"Same answer as before." She's gripping her pen so tightly her knuckles are turning white. She's not so much writing as carving letters into her notebook.

"You want me to do *nothing*?"

"It's what you're good at."

I feel my neck and cheeks flame. "Hey, look, I was going to come to the library, okay? I just lost track of time."

"I waited for you for nearly an hour."

"Well, I was really busy on Sunday. In case you didn't hear, my group just got accepted into the Battle of the Bands."

"Congratulations," she says flatly. "You must be really happy."

"I am, as a matter of fact. It's a pretty major accomplishment. I was rehearsing all weekend. And the library just . . . slipped my mind." I glance over at the teacher. "But if Mrs. T asks, we were both there the whole time, 'kay? Remember what she said about us both getting detention?"

"Great. Good. Fine," Helen says.

"Anyway, I'm here now," I say. "So let's put a dent in this bad boy."

Helen glares up at me from her notebook. She puts her pen down and rubs her hand. "Listen. I've decided I'm going to do our projects on my own."

"What? But Mrs. Turris said we—"

"Don't worry. We'll pretend like we did them together. In front of the class. In front of Mrs. Turris. You can sign your name to everything we have to hand in. It'll look like we're partners. I'm just sick and tired of waiting around, pretending like you're actually going to contribute anything. It's too frustrating. So, you'll get a good grade, and you won't have to do a thing for it. And I won't have to deal with your bullshit."

"Are you sure? I think I should do *something*." I say this, but of course I don't really mean it. Quite frankly, this is a dream come true. Helen doing all the work. Not having to spend any time with her. Getting an easy A. If she's serious about this, I might want to get someone to buy me a lottery ticket, because my fortunes have most definitely taken a turn for the better.

"You *think* you should do something. But let's be honest. You aren't *going* to do anything. Focus on your band if that's so important to you. Why are you arguing?"

"I'm not. I'm just . . . For reals?"

She nods.

"Okay. But I did have an idea for our presentation."

Helen scowls. "Oh. Is that so?"

"Don't sound so surprised. It's not like I haven't been thinking about the project." All right, so that's a total crock. I've barely given the actual project a second thought. But I did come up with this one thing while Dad was putting on his condom show.

"Okay. What is this brilliant idea?" Helen leans back and crosses her arms.

"You know what? People might like you a whole lot more if you weren't so sarcastic all the time."

"Yeah, well, I'm trying to think how people might

like you more, but that'd require an entire personality transplant."

"Mee-ouch." I laugh. "Good one. Anyway, what I was thinking was that we should get a whole whack of birth control stuff. You know. To have out on a table. Like a giant display or something. Then we can pass them around—condoms, diaphragms, pills, lubes—while we're giving our presentation. To keep everyone busy while we're up at the front of the room acting like we know what we're talking about."

Helen studies me. Then shrugs. "Why not? That can be your job. Get whatever you can and bring it in when we do our lesson."

"Hey now. I thought we agreed it was better if I didn't actually have to *do* anything."

"It's *your* idea."

"Right. I'm the ideas man. It's my strong suit."

"Well, I'm not about to go out and buy a whole bunch of contraceptives."

"Who said anything about *buying* them? Just collect up whatever you have around the house."

Helen looks like I just snapped her bra. Oh, crap. I just stepped in it. "What makes you think I have any of that stuff around my house?"

"I don't know." I shrug. "I just figured. Because . . . you know."

"No, Coop. I *don't* know. Why don't you explain it to me? Is it because you think I'm a slut, like everyone else does?" Helen's voice is a low, hissing whisper. "That I sleep around with anything and everything in the world? Is that it? Go ahead. Say it." Her ears are bright red. Her eyes are narrow, angry slits. "You think I give a shit what you think about me? What *anyone* thinks about me?"

"Eh hemmm." Mrs. Turris clears her throat. "Helen? Cooper? May I see you a moment?"

"Send them to the pound!" someone calls out, which makes the rest of the class crack up.

I feel all the blood rush to my face as I realize I'm not exactly out of the Hot Dog woods just yet.

CHAPTER SIXTEEN

POKER FACE

ME AND HELEN WALK UP the aisle toward the front of the room. Andy Bennett starts whistling the wedding march, which gets a big laugh from the class. It kills me that my sorry sitch has made this knuckle dragger a bona fide class clown.

"We need to chat," Mrs. Turris says to us when we arrive at her desk.

"Cool" I say. "What about?"

"You two seem to feel like you can afford to waste your class time today. You must have gotten a lot done at the library yesterday."

"Oh, yeah. For sure," I say. "Couldn't have gone better. Right?"

I glance at Helen, who stands stiffly. Her cheeks cherrying. I bet she's never had to lie to a teacher before.

Personally, I think it's healthy for her to expand her horizons a bit.

"Excellent." Mrs. Turris interlaces her fingers on her desk. "May I see what you accomplished?"

"Mmm," I say, the possible excuses ping-ponging around my skull. "Unfortunately, you can't."

"And why is that?"

"Well, because we had a brainstorming session, Mrs. Turris. We spitballed all these ideas around and then just scribbled them in a notebook so we could keep the juices flowing."

"All right. May I see the notebook, then?" Mrs. Turris looks straight at Helen when she asks this, like she knows where the weak link is.

"I . . . um . . ." Helen looks like she might pass out. "It's . . . um . . . I . . ." Poor girl. Can't even lie to save her own skin.

"It's not here," I leap in, rescuing her. "It's at home. I'm typing the ideas up on my computer. You know. Putting it into proper outline form. There's a lot of stuff there, Mrs. Turris. Pages and pages. It's going to take some time."

Mrs. Turris tents her fingers. "Okay. Let me make this easy for you. You weren't at the library yesterday."

"What?" I make an appropriately incensed expression. "Where do you think we had our brainstorming session?"

"Cooper." Mrs. Turris stares at me. "You didn't *have*

a brainstorming session because you didn't meet yesterday." She turns and peers at Helen. "Isn't that right, dear?"

Helen can't hold Mrs. Turris's gaze. She looks down at her feet. Goddamn her and her truthful ways.

Mrs. Turris turns back to me. "I happened to be at the library a little after two. I only live a couple of blocks away. I had some books I needed to return. So I popped in to drop them off and check up on you. And guess what? No Cooper and no Helen."

"You live near the Barrytown Library?" I say, feigning innocence.

Mrs. Turris laughs. "You're going to tell me that you went ten miles out of your way to the Barrytown Library? Instead of the Rockville Public Library, which is right in town? And where I told you to go?"

I shrug. "We prefer Barrytown, right?" I look at Helen to chime in with some support here. "They have better lighting."

"Coop, just stop," Helen says, defeated.

Oh, great. Sell me right out, why don't you? What happened to trusting the person you're supposed to be partners with?

Mrs. Turris's mouth is squinched up into a tight anus. "You've left me no choice, you two. I'm going to have to insist that you both report to the school library after dismissal two days a week until the project is completed. Shall we say, Mondays and Wednesdays?"

"I'm sorry. I can't do that," I say. "I've got band practice after school."

"And I've got cross-country," Helen adds.

"Okay. Let me clarify something for you." Mrs. Turris levels her gaze at us. "When I said 'insist' I *meant* 'insist.' So whatever your previous obligations are, they'll have to be rescheduled. And you'll want to make sure you sign in with Miss Jerooni, because I'll be checking in with her. If you skip even a single day, two projects will become three, will become four, will become five. And the like."

I exhale. "So, you're giving us detention?"

"More like *in*tention."

"I don't understand," I say.

"Oh, you will, Cooper." Mrs. Turris smiles. "You will most definitely understand before the end of the semester. I'll make sure of that."

CHAPTER SEVENTEEN

CLASSICAL GAS

I CAN'T GO WITH YOU GUYS," Matt says, placing his books into his locker.

"What are you talking about, dawg?" I dial the combination on my lock and snap it open. "The Corner Market at lunch. That was the deal. I've got detention with Helen today. I need your help with my plan."

"I just . . . can't." Matt won't meet my eyes. "I told Val I'd join chess club. She said it'd look good on my college applications."

"Chess club?" Sean laughs. "You don't even like chess."

Matt shrugs. "I don't hate it."

"No, but you like being a pawn." I peer at him. "Dude, isn't chess club, like, three days a week?"

"Just at lunchtime." He shuts his locker door. "I had no choice. It was either that or I couldn't do the band after school. I had to make a compromise. During school time in exchange for after school time."

I feel my eyes bulge to the point where if they weren't attached to my head they'd flop from my skull. "Okay. Are we going to have to do an intervention, Matthew? Because, seriously, it's hard to sit around and watch one of my best buds getting systematically castrated."

"Relationships are about give-and-take, Coop. Of course, you wouldn't know that, having never been in one."

"If that's what a relationship is, I'll never *be* in one." I flip through a notebook, looking for a paper I printed out in the computer lab. "Just wait. Ten years from now, you'll be the dude with the squawking, doughy wife and six barfing brats hanging on to your legs, and I'll be the happy bachelor, bouncing from growler to growler, feeling pity for you, but knowing that I told you so."

"Yeah, well, I happen to want to have kids someday," Matt says.

Which makes me laugh. "Ah, yes. Babies. The worst of the STDs. Make sure you and Sean address *that* in your Health report. It's the disease that keeps on growing and can't be cured with ointment." I find the page, fold it in half, and chuck the notebook back into my locker.

"Anyway," Matt says. "I'm doing this for you. You could show a little gratitude once in a while."

I get that dropping feeling in my gut, like maybe I've pushed this too far. "Okay, I'm sorry," I say. "I do appreciate it. I'm just used to the way things were before. The Three Musketeers, you know. It's totally cool. Sean and me will hit the store on our own. We'll catch you later."

It's a five-minute bike ride up to the Corner Market, which, oddly enough, isn't even on a corner. The store sells pretty much all the basics—candy, chips, soda, Twinkies—as well as a decent selection of vegetables, cold cuts, milk, cheese, and canned goods.

"So," Sean says, looking around. "What are we getting?"

I pull the folded-up paper from my back pocket, the results of my research during study hall.

"All right." I unfold the page and scan the article on flatulence. "I want some heavy duty gas producers. Radishes, celery, prunes. Beans, of course."

"Of course," Sean echoes.

"But what I really need is some serious stink." I run my finger down the page and find what I'm looking for. "Here." I read, *"Foods that are thought to produce excessive flatulence include cabbage, broccoli, kale, and other vegetables belonging to the cabbage family. These foods will also have a tendency to intensify the pungency of the flatus."*

Sean smiles. "That sounds like something out of World of Warcraft." He makes his voice deep. "You have been granted the pungency of the flatus, my son. Go forth and use it well."

"Oh, yes," I say. "I will wield the flatus with deathly precision. And shall lay waste to mine enemy."

CHAPTER EIGHTEEN

SMELLS LIKE TEEN SPIRIT

I CONVINCE SEAN TO SKIP eighth period shop class and hang with me in the Hole as I attack the fart food with a plastic fork and knife. The cashier dude at the market was dope enough to open my can of beans, but I had to be super careful carrying it back to school, storing it on the top shelf of my locker until I was ready to feast.

"I'm still not sure I get this plan," Sean says, cringing as I chew a broccoli stalk with my mouth wide open. The farticle I read stated specifically that eating with your mouth open and swallowing air as you go will create the mightiest explosions.

"It's simple," I say. "Until I can figure out a way to get Mrs. Turris to split us up—and I will—I don't want anyone seeing me and Helen in close proximity. If I start ripping noxious ass blasters, you can be damn sure Helen's going to want to work at separate ends of the library. And who knows—if it's bad enough, she might just run screaming from the room."

I shove a heaping forkful of coleslaw into my mouth. When you're on a mission to save yourself, you'd be surprised how much raw broccoli, raw cauliflower, cold baked beans, prunes, celery, radishes, and cabbagey coleslaw you can choke down.

"I'm glad *I'm* not going to be in that library," Sean says, pulling the leaves off the celery for me. "Your regular H-bombs could clear a circus tent. I hate to think what kind of stench all this fuel is going to create."

"You want me to crack you off a taster?" I say.

"Hell no!"

"Too late." I smile, popping a cauliflower floret.

Sean reels back as he's smacked in the face with my silent sampler. It's a fine bouquet laced with the smell of rotten eggs, runny cheese, dead skunk, and just a hint of pruney sweetness. "Whoalee crap!" He screws up his face, covering his nose and mouth with the crook of his elbow. "You bastard!" He starts to gag and laugh at the same time. "That's worse than a Saint Bernard beefer."

"Thanks," I say. Coming from Sean, that's a major compliment, his house being the orphanage for every stray pet in Lower Rockville. "And that was just a gentle breeze. Imagine what the full tropical storm'll smell like."

"No thanks." Sean's eyes are watering. "Jesus Christ." He rubs his nose hard. "And it's got a long finish, too. Poor Helen. She's going to be knocked unconscious."

Miss Jerooni is sitting at her desk when I arrive at the library. She's reading some beat-to-hell paperback, her tiny face nearly swallowed up by the giant gray frizz that surrounds her head. If a chipmunk suddenly poked its nose out of all that fuzz, you wouldn't be surprised. You'd be like, "Oh, huh. Miss Jerooni has a chipmunk living in her hair."

"Hi, Miss Jerooni," I say, bending over her desk to autograph the sign-in sheet. I can feel the squeezing and grumbling in my gut as the vicious vegetable-bean brew percolates.

Miss Jerooni glances over her book, nods acknowledgment, but says nothing. The only sound in the library are her lovebirds, Fanny and Alexander, gently peeping in their cage behind her.

I smile, then turn away and squeak out a little gurker for Miss Jerooni's sniffing pleasure.

Helen's already here, of course. Planted right in front, where every cheerleader and jock in the school can see us sitting together as they pass by in the hall on their way to and from practice.

She's piled a stack of books on the table and is busy marking them up with her limitless supply of Post-its, when I pull up a chair.

"Hi," she says coldly.

There's no time to waste. I have to jam the stink wedge between us immediately.

"Good afternoon," I reply, relaxing my ass gasket and bearing down. I lift my right butt cheek a bit and . . .

BRRRRROOFFF.

It's not the lion's roar I wanted but it was definitely audible.

Helen's gaze shoots up from her book, her eyes wide.

The desired tangy stench follows almost immediately. Wow. Now that's some concentrated evil. My eyes start to burn.

Helen wrinkles up her nose, the smell obviously having made the short journey over to her.

"Sorry. My stomach's been acting a little funny since lunch." It's hard to keep a straight face—even harder than keeping reign over my bowels. That sucking-lemons expression she's making is hysterious. "So, how do you want to organize this? Should we just go alphabetically, like in the book? Or by effectiveness?"

Helen clears her throat. "I was thinking . . ." She raises her hand to her nose, all nonchalant, pretending she's not trying to block my zesty odor. "There's a chart here that breaks them down by types, convenience, availability, protection against STDs . . ." She reaches for one of the books with her free hand, keeping the other close to her nostrils.

I contract my stomach muscles, giving a nice forceful push.

THRRRRAAAAP!

Yes! Now that's what I'm talking about. That one actually caused my chair to rattle.

"Cooper, what the hell?" Helen shoots me a wave of hate.

The smell rapes my nose. Holy crap, that is *nasty.* Talk about the pungency of the flatus.

Miss Jerooni looks up from her book. "Is everything okay over there?"

"Yeah." I nod. "I think I just had some bad ham at lunch."

Miss Jerooni's whole face suddenly shudders, my foul fog having floated to the front of the room. "My goodness," she says, then rushes over to crack open a window.

Helen stares at me, looking none too pleased.

"What?" I say. "You think this is fun for me? It *hurts.*"

I'm going to have to remember this trick next time Sean and Matt sleep over.

Helen shakes her head, then casually lifts her shirt over her nose and mouth to use as a respirator.

"Look," I say. "If it's bothering you so much, move to another table. You said you were going to do all the work on your own anyway."

"That deal was off as soon as we got detention," Helen replies. "If Mrs. Turris finds out I'm doing everything, I don't even want to imagine the trouble we'll get into."

"Well, then, just tell me what you want me to do and then you can move."

"No. It's fine," she says, her voice all nasal. "Let's just keep working. We'll start off with the barrier methods."

I'm afraid the barrier method won't work in this particular situation, Helen.

I execute another hard internal thrust, my eyes rolling back into my head as I give in to the nearly orgasmic release of the wonder wind.

RUM-BUM-BUM-BUM-BUM-BUM.

It's like the sound of a sputtering boat engine.

"Jesus Christ," Helen says.

"Oh, God. I'm really sorry. This is so embarrassing." I swear, the air around us is turning a greenish yellow.

Miss Jerooni makes a little retching sound. "Young man. Please control yourself." She bolts up and opens another window. "Perhaps you should visit the lavatory."

"No." I hold up my hand. "I'm feeling better. I think the worst part has passed."

Miss Jerooni harrumphs. She's about to sit at her desk again, but then thinks better of it and grabs her book, retreating to the safety of her glassed-in office and shutting the door behind her.

"You think I can sue the school for food poisoning?" I ask Helen before unleashing another violent buttquake. "I think it's causing serious damage down there."

Fanny and Alexander are fluttering around their cage like mad, slamming into each other, their feathers flying as they look for some escape from the onslaught. But there's nowhere to go. And Miss Jerooni doesn't look like she's coming out of her office to save them anytime soon.

"Here," Helen says, breathing through her shirt and shoving several books toward me. "Just find all the pros and cons of the various contraceptive methods and write them down. I'm going to do some research on the Internet."

"Wait," I say, trying not to bust up. "I had a question."

Helen's already standing. "What?"

BRRRRAAAAP! I launch another thundering boomer. Then sniff the air.

"Does that smell like ham to you? 'Cause I'm thinking now it might have been the Italian Dunkers."

Helen groans and races off toward the open window and the computer in the corner.

There's a real sense of satisfaction when you put a plan into action and it all charts out exactly how you thought it would. I lean back in my chair, breathing in the sweet smell of success—which, in this case, has a slight elephanty odor to it—when I hear some girls laughing in the hallway.

I'm enjoying my victory too much for it to really register at first.

Until I see three of the Phenomenal Four step into the library.

It takes half a second for the odorama to make an impression on Prudence, Bronte, and Gina.

And the remaining portion of that very same second for me to realize that I have beefed myself into a corner.

CHAPTER NINETEEN

BLOWIN' IN THE WIND

ALL THREE GIRLS STOP DEAD, like they've run into a concrete wall, their hands shooting up to cover their noses.

"Holy crap" Prudence makes a face. "Who opened a grave in here?"

Think! Quick!

I make eye contact with the girls, then point surreptitiously toward the librarian in her glass-enclosed office. "Miss Jerooni's been floating air bagels ever since we got here," I say. "It got so bad we finally had to ask her to go sit in her office."

"I thought this was the library, not the bathroom," Bronte says through her cupped hand.

"Prudence." Gina pinches her nose and looks like she might cry. "I think I'm going to puke. Literally."

Prudence rolls her eyes. "Like that would be so bad for you."

Gina looks mortified. "What are you saying?"

"I'm saying, just shut up and go find the dress pattern books."

"I hate smelly smells," Gina whimpers nasally.

Prudence clenches her jaw and hisses through her teeth, "Then stop wasting time and go get the goddamn books. Both of you." She shoos them away.

Bronte and Gina scurry off, huddled close together like scolded children.

Prudence sighs, then looks and me. "Why would you stay and wallow in this stink?"

"I don't have a choice." I gesture toward Helen sitting at the computer in the back of the room. "I tried to ditch Helen as my partner. All I got was detention."

She glances at Helen. "Ew. *She's* here?" Prudence makes a face. "I don't know how you can work with *it*. I wouldn't be able to."

"Yeah, well, Fate screwed me," I say. This is good. We both feel bad for me. People have leaped into the sack with much less in common. "Seems like the harder I try to get out of it, the more time I end up having to spend with her."

Prudence's eyes slide back to me. Then to Helen. Then to me again. "Maybe you just haven't tried the right thing."

"What do you mean?"

Prudence gestures with her head toward the door. "Take a break. In the hall."

Most people would worry that, with a gut full of gas, they might end up carving off a hunk of havarti right in front of one of the hottest girls in the entire school. But I'm not most people. I have near-superhuman control over my sphinc. I once bet Matt and Sean that I could beef out the first verse of "Amazing Grace." It was the easiest ten bucks I ever made.

Prudence lures me through the door and into the hall, her body looking assassin in a lion-print top and hip-clinging jeans. The serpent tattoo on the bull's-eye of her lower back just barely visible.

Oh, God. If I could just spend one night with her, running around and around the bases, it'd totally be worth dying for. Because, really, after that, what would you have to look forward to?

Well, unless of course you could get her friends to join the baseball game for a seventh-inning stretch. Now *that* would be worth sticking around for.

Prudence turns and flashes a sex kitten grin at me. "She's been slagging you, you know? I mean, you've probably already heard, but just in case you hadn't, I thought you should know."

"Helen? Really?" My stomach gurgles its displeasure. I clear my throat to try to mask the sound. "What's she been saying?"

"Talking smack. What else? For one, she says you've been coming on to her—"

"That's bullshit." I'm so surprised that a breezer nearly takes flight without authority from air traffic control. But I clench my butt cheeks right quick and abort the launch.

"She said you asked her to the movies. And that you tried to make out with her."

I shake my head. "Are you for serial? Why would she say that?"

"Pfff." Prudence smirks. "Because that's who she is. Why do you think everyone hates her so much? She's a liar. And a bitch. You don't get that despised for no reason, right?"

I glance toward the library. "Yeah, I guess."

Prudence leans in close, the warm peach smell of her breath on my cheek. "So, do you want to hear my plan?"

"Got 'em," Bronte says, stepping from the library and waving a couple of dress pattern books in the air.

Gina lets out the breath she's obviously been holding this whole time. She gasps. "I swear. I literally almost *died* in there. *Literally.* Who knew Miss Jerooni was such a stanky skank?"

Prudence looks at her friends. "I've just be telling Cutie Coop here what the Sausage Queen's been saying about him around school."

Cutie Coop? Whoa. Did I miss something? When did we start referring to each other by endearing pet names? Not that I'm complaining. Sure, it's not the butchest nickname in the world, but coming from the lips of such a hottie, I kind of love it!

Bronte looks momentarily confused, then grins. "Oh, yeah. The rumors. They're pretty bad."

"I hate false rumors," Gina says, looking at her fingernails. "Especially when they're not even true."

"You guys heard Helen talking about me?"

"Totally." Bronte laughs. "Everyone's heard." She glances at Prudence, who starts circling me.

Prudence plays with the gold necklace that dangles around her cleavage. "What do you think, girls? Shall we help the poor lamb?"

Gina tilts her head, giggling. "He does kind of look like a lamb. Like the cute little chubby one I sleep with every night."

I'd offer to be her cute chubby lamb, but I'm starting to feel like the shock of Prudence's revelation may have compromised my sphincter seal. I'm going to have to end this conversation before my unsteady bowels end it for me. "Can we talk about this later? I should probably get back in there before—"

"Helen's been threatening to transfer to Our Lady of Mercy for two years now," Prudence says, completely ignoring me. "Frankly, we're all getting a little sick of hearing about it."

Someone's coming down the hall. It's Andy Bennett. Perfect timing.

Now, generally, Andy is the last person in the world I want to see. But right here, and right now, there isn't another person I'd rather have approaching us.

"I'm thinking that maybe we could just help Helen make up her mind," Prudence continues. "You know, give her a bit more incentive to transfer to a new school. You think you'd be up for that, Coopee?"

"Sure," I say, but my mind is too preoccupied with my immediate plans to be paying close attention.

"Well, well, well." Andy and his walrus whiskers step up beside me. "What are you beauties doing wasting your time with this beast?"

He claps me on the shoulder and I give him a big grin as I ease out a nice long-drawn-out S.B.D.

The moist-manure stench is almost instantaneous.

"Jesus Christ, Andy!" I leap away from him. "What the hell? Were you eating lunch with Miss Jerooni today?"

Andy freezes, completely confused. Until, all of a sudden, he's blinking hard.

The girls shriek, clapping their hands over their noses and backing away from him.

"What the fuck's wrong with you, Andy?" Bronte shouts through her hand.

"That wasn't me!" Andy's head swivels like crazy. "I swear."

I point at him. "He who denied it, supplied it." I take off down the hall before the girls have time to put all the pieces together. “Run for your life!” I call over my shoulder. “Before he sneaks off another one.”

The girls squeal and scatter in the other direction, leaving Andy alone, confused, red-faced, and holding the beef bag.

CHAPTER TWENTY

ICKY THUMP

I HAMMER MY CYMBALS, Sean rakes his hands up and down the keys on his Casio, and Matt thrashes like crazy on a three-quarter-size Torino Red Squier Mini guitar, as we bring our very first song to a hard-driving ecstatic conclusion.

"Yes!" Sean shouts, thrusting his fist in the air.

Valerie and Dad sit side by side on the old gray sofa with stunned looks on their faces. Completely silent.

Were we *that* good?

Or were we that bad?

My drums were pretty loud, so I had a hard time hearing the other instruments. But it *felt* good.

Dad finally blinks. "Wow," he says. "That was . . ." He blinks again. "Wow."

A burst of laughter escapes from Valerie's lips.

Oh, crap. So we sucked.

Valerie buries her face in her hands. "Oh, my god. *Désolé! Désolé!* I'm sorry!" God, that accent can be so grating sometimes. She tries to hold in her laughter for a second, but then rolls over on the couch and starts cracking up.

My skin prickles with embarrassment. Why'd she have to come here, anyway? I thought they made a deal. Chess club for girlfriend-free afternoons.

"That was *awesome,*" Sean crows with a big clueless grin on his face. "Did we not rock the hell out of that, or what?"

"Muzzle it, Sean," I say, my cheeks flaming. "We were crap."

Sean looks suddenly bitch-slapped. He glances at Matt for confirmation of my assessment but Matt just stares at the floor.

"No, no." Dad stands and runs his hand down his face. "This was . . . um." He starts to pace. "This was a starting point." He scratches his head. "I mean, yes, we have some work to do—"

This sends Valerie—who'd finally begun to compose herself—back into fits. "I'm sorry. Seriously, I just . . . Didn't you guys have to hand in a demo? I mean, what was on that?"

Dad and me lock eyes.

"It was an older recording," I say. "We haven't played together in a while."

Dad raises his hand. "Let's not lose our heads here.

There were a lot of positives. I mean, Coop, you were giving it your all. And Matt, you were, you know, showing some real energy there." Dad strums an air guitar furiously. "And Sean. You definitely . . . were standing up straight and tall." Dad's eyes slide off to the side. "I just . . . I don't think you guys are as bad as you sound."

Oh, God. I want to crawl inside my bass drum.

Valerie wipes the tears from her eyes. "No. He's right. Absolutely. There were moments I could almost tell what song you were playing." Her body shudders with suppressed laughter. "What song *were* you playing?"

" 'Satisfaction,' " Sean blurts.

" 'Twist and Shout,' " I correct.

"But I thought"—Sean shuffles the sheet music on the ironing board he's using as a keyboard stand—"Didn't we say . . . ?"

"The Beatles." Matt sighs.

"Oh." Sean lowers his head. "I knew we should have had someone sing."

"So, you guys weren't even playing the same song?" Valerie busts up again. "Now *that's* funny."

"Matt," I growl through clenched teeth. I feel an angry vein pulsing in my temple. "Can you *do* something about her?"

Matt gives Valerie a please-honey look. Not really what I had in mind, but there you go.

Valerie waves her hands in the air. "Sorry, sorry. I'll be quiet." She reaches into her purse and pulls out a travel guide to China. Hopefully, she's planning on *moving* there.

"No, no." Dad gestures with his finger. "Now that explains a lot. And I'll tell you what. It shows character. You know how many people would have cut the song off? But you guys acted like *pros.* You played the whole song straight through."

"*Two* whole songs." Valerie looks up from her book and laughs, then pretends to zip up her lips and throw away the key. If only it were that easy.

"The bottom line is," Dad points at us, "you persevered. *That's* the mark of a true professional. Because if you stop in the middle of a song, it sounds bad."

"Or," Matt says, "if you just plain blow, it sounds bad."

"Okay." Dad gestures at Matt. "Give me that guitar. I'm gonna show you how it's done."

Matt lifts his guitar off and hands it to Dad, who looks at it like the pathetic thing it is. Dad slips the strap over his head, does some fine-tuning of the strings, and cranks up all the dials on Matt's Rocktron Velocity amplifier.

"You guys just started with something too difficult," Dad says.

The speaker on Matt's amp buzzes like it's filled with wasps. The feedback squeaking and squealing.

"Um." Matt looks concerned. "Isn't that going to damage the, uhh . . ."

Dad glances back at Matt's amp. "Nah. These bastards

are built like brick shithouses. You could throw it off the roof and it wouldn't break."

Dad strikes a pose and hits a power chord with authority.

Matt's amplifier makes a loud *POP!,* and smoke starts to billow from the back. He looks over at Valerie, who grimaces.

"Ah, crap," Dad says. "All right. Don't worry. I can fix that." He unplugs Matt's guitar from the smoking amp and plugs it into the secondary input on Sean's.

"That's my Uncle Doug's amplifier." Sean gulps. "He said if I break it he'd beat the piss out of me with a tire iron."

"And well he should," Dad says. "Because this is a real nice Mesa/Boogie. I don't even know why the hell he'd loan it to you in the first place." He dials all the knobs up to ten. Now it's Sean's speaker that starts hissing and feeding back. "Okay, we're going to play one of the easiest rock songs in the world: 'Paranoid' by Black Sabbath."

"Cool," I say. "We know that song. We've done it on Rock Band."

"Good. Then you know the timing." Dad grabs the microphone stand and drags it over to Sean. "You're going to be our lead singer."

Sean recoils. "What? Me? No!"

"What? You? Yes!" Dad says. "You've got the girliest voice. It's perfect."

Me, Matt, and Valerie laugh.

"I don't have a girly voice," Sean squeaks.

"Did I say girly?" Dad coughs into his hand. "I meant musical. Don't worry. You'll be great. Besides, the lead singer's the front man. He gets the lion's share of the muttonchops."

Sean ponders this a moment. Then shrugs. "Fine. I'll give it a shot. But don't blame me if I'm not any good."

"You don't have to be good," Dad says. "You just have to be loud. Now, the most important thing to remember is to bring the energy. Rock is all about passion. You want to play straight from your lamb fries." He sniffs loudly. "Okay. The chords are simple. It's E minor, D, G, D, E minor. Over and over again. I'll start us off."

Dad does a colossally loud pick drag and then rips up the intro.

God*damn*. He sounds really good. Way better than I expected. His guitar riff sends an excited chill skittering up my arms.

I look over at Sean and Matt. They seem impressed, too. Although Sean keeps glancing at his uncle's amplifier to make sure it isn't smoking.

Dad looks over at me. Then nods. I dive in with a driving drumbeat. It takes Sean a second to catch up, but he's with us by the time he starts screaming out the lyrics.

Now, I won't say that we sound great. Because we don't. Even though Dad is totally dope on the guitar, Sean has a hard time playing and singing at the same time, and my drumming is anything but stellar.

But I will say that it beats the hell out of our last tune.

And when Dad tears into the guitar solo, his fingers flying up and down the fret board, I feel the tiniest glimmer of hope. Like, maybe, with his help, and if we practice every day, and if all the stars align . . . maybe we won't get completely laughed off the stage come December.

CHAPTER TWENTY-ONE

TWO OF US

YOUR DAD'S A KICK-ASS GUITAR PLAYER," Sean says as we trudge up the stairs toward our lockers.

"Yeah," Matt adds. "I wish *I* could play that well."

I clap them both on the shoulders. "We've just got to give it some time, dawgs. We'll get there. My dad promised he'd make us better. I mean, we were already sounding halfway decent by the end of our first rehearsal, right?" Halfway decent might be a bit of an exaggeration. On a scale from one to ten I'd give us a one and a half. But it's definitely better than the negative eighteen we started out with. "Imagine what we'll sound like after a month of rehearsals."

"Speaking of rehearsals," Matt says. "Can we do it after dinner tonight?"

"What? Why?"

"Valerie's coming over for dinner. She wants to hang out before."

I glare at him. "That's so lame, dude."

"I'm okay to do it tonight," Sean says.

"That's not the point." I run my hand through my hair. "She's trying to sabotage the band. You realize that, don't you?"

"What?" Matt shakes his head. "No. It's not like that. It's just . . . she's going through a hard time right now. Kelly barely even talks to her anymore. It's like they were best friends one day, and the next, Kelly's spending all her time with Prudence."

"Well, they are in a band together, dawg. They're probably *rehearsing*."

"It's *all* the time. In school and after school. And Val's really upset about it, okay? Kelly's one of her best friends. Look, it's not like I'm canceling practice. I just want to move it."

Well, that explains why she's been hanging around us all the time. And clinging to Matt like a koala to a eucalyptus tree. Still, this could become a major ish down the road if I don't play this right.

"Okay," I say. "After dinner. But don't you bail on us."

"I won't," Matt says. "But she might be coming with me again."

A surge of anger swells inside me. But I force myself to think about how bad it would suck to lose your best bud like that. And suddenly I feel kind of sorry for Val.

I take a breath. Let it out slowly. "Fine. Just . . . ask her to keep her yap shut, okay?"

We reach the second floor and head down the hall. It's chock with the usual crowd of kids hurrying to get to next period, but there seem to be a few people lingering by our lockers.

Some douche bag approaches me, laughing. "You and Helen make a cute couple, Corn Dog." He gives a few hip thrusts before taking off.

"Screw off," I say, flipping him the finger.

We push through the small group of people laughing and pointing until we reach our lockers.

"Hey, it's the man of the hour," somebody calls out, causing a ripple of laughter to sweep through the hall.

And that's when I see the photograph on my locker.

Someone has Photoshopped Helen's and my ninth grade yearbook headshots onto an eight-by-ten picture of a couple on a beach in bathing suits, holding each other in a loving embrace. It's pretty crudely done—and made even less effective by the fact that our heads are facing the camera instead of each other—but still, it gets the message across. One that fills my gut with acid.

"Assholes," Sean says, ripping the picture off and throwing it on the ground.

There's a disappointed groan, and the onlookers disperse.

"Aw, I think it's kind of romantic." I turn around to see Prudence laughing and picking the picture up off the floor. She's flanked by Kelly on one side and Bronte and Gina on the other. "Personally, I'd recommend a biohazard suit the next time you're going to hug the unwashed."

The girls snicker. My ears get hot.

"Hey, Kell," Matt says.

Kelly smiles, unwrapping a Tootsie Pop. The grape smell of it wafts over to me. She gestures at the photo with her lollipop. "That is just mean."

"They sure were kind to Helen, though," Bronte says. "I mean, where's the cellulite? And the belly rolls?"

"And the herpes sores?" Gina giggles as she films the whole thing with her purple paisley Flip Video camera.

"This is getting really serious, Coop." Prudence looks at me sympathetically. "We'd better talk." She lets the picture float to the floor. "Come on. Walk with us." She turns and starts down the hall, her friends following.

Um . . . okay, I'm confused. Have I read this whole situation completely wrong? Could this Helen mess actually be the thing that gets me up to bat with Prudence?

"What's that all about?" Sean asks.

"I'm not sure," I say. "But I'm going to find out. I'll catch up with you later."

I take off after the girls and reach them just before they turn the corner.

"It's starting to reach epidemic proportions, Coop," Prudence says as I walk in step with her. "Between all of

Helen's gossiping and what everyone's starting to say about you and her hooking up. I felt bad for you before, but this. It's the kind of thing that could ruin you for life."

I glance at the other girls. They nod in agreement.

"I mean, yeah," Prudence continues, "we haven't always seen eye-to-eye you and me, but honestly," she laughs shyly, "I always thought you were kind of cute. I'd hate to see this thing completely destroy you."

Whoa. Yes. I like how this is going. Nightmare turns to dream-come-true. I feel myself walking a little taller.

"Outside the library," I say, "you mentioned you had some kind of plan?"

"I do, but we're going to have to work really fast." Prudence produces some papers from a notebook and holds them out to me. "We need to fill this out."

I take the pages and look at them. "What is it?"

"It's an application form for Our Lady of Mercy," Bronte says. "I picked it up on my way to school today. If Helen's going to transfer schools, we have to get the process started for her."

"We want to make it as painless as possible," Gina adds, her video camera still going. "*Literally.* If the paperwork is done for her, all she has to do is go."

Kelly tugs the lollipop from her mouth. "It'll be good for you both, really. She gets a fresh start. And hopefully all these rumors about you and her fade away."

"We're going to have to do some detective work," Prudence says. "And fast, because the deadline for second semester is November seventh. We filled out what we know already. But you're going to have to get some of the more confidential information. We figure, since you're working with her all the time, you'll be able to find these things out. And then, of course, you're going to have to get her mother to sign it. Which will be an entirely different kind of challenge." She smiles. "But we think you're up to it."

"I don't get it." I flip through the pages. "Why would Helen transfer to another school just because we fill out the forms for her?"

The bell rings and the hall starts to clear. Prudence stops walking and turns to me. Her friends do the same.

"That's just phase one, Coop," Prudence says, touching my arm. Sending a shiver all over my body. "Laying the groundwork. But phase two—offering encouragement—is the most important part."

Bronte steps up close to me. Her breasts brushing my shoulder. Oh, God. "And that's where we're *really* going to need your help."

My jeans start to feel tight. My knees want to buckle. Must stay focused. "What—My breath hitching in my throat. "What . . . do you need me to do?"

CHAPTER TWENTY-TWO

HOUND DOG

WE'VE FINISHED ALL OUR WORK in Math class with five minutes to spare before the end of the day. Which means only one thing.

Mr. Spassnick is going to tell us a joke.

"So, these two guys are out hunting moose," Mr. Spassnick says, sitting behind his desk, grabbing a New York Mets hat from one of the desk drawers and tugging it on. "And they're both staring down the sights of their rifles, scanning the trees." He mimes sighting down a rifle.

I glance up at the clock. The second hand ticks off the time ever so slowly. My books are all stacked up and I'm poised to bolt once the dismissal bell rings. It's crucial that I meet Helen at her locker before she heads up to the library for detention.

"There doesn't appear to be anything out in the woods." Mr. Spassnick grabs his briefcase and places it on top of his desk. He pops it open and starts putting papers inside. "And then, both of the guys hear a rustling sound in the bushes."

Prudence promised me that nothing really bad would happen to Helen. But that life would have to be made uncomfortable for her if we really wanted her to transfer to a new school. Honestly, though, it was pretty difficult to concentrate on what she was saying at the time. After Prudence touched my arm and Bronte brushed me with her breasts, I just kept imagining all four girls naked and rubbing me down with oil on the couch in my basement. Gina filming the whole thing with her little camera. The five of us spending an entire night tagging all the bases known to God or man and then, when we'd exhausted those, making up entirely new never-before-imagined ones.

"All of a sudden," Mr. Spassnick shouts, slamming his briefcase shut and springing to his feet, "this guy leaps out from behind a tree and yells 'Don't shoot, I'm not a moose!' Hearing this, one of the hunters—BANG!—shoots the guy dead."

"Cool," Justin Sneep calls out.

Mr. Spassnick smiles. "So his friend turns to him and says, 'What the heck are you doing? Why'd you shoot that guy?' And the second hunter slaps his forehead." Mr. Spassnick demonstrates the action. "And says, 'Oh, dang it. I thought he said he *was* a moose.'"

There are a couple of embarrassed chuckles around

the room. But certainly not the reaction Mr. Spassnick was probably hoping for.

"Don't you get it?" He gestures at us. "Let me try that again. 'I thought he said he *was* a moose.' Huh? No? Okay. I thought for sure *that* one would get you guys. Guess we'll have to try again tomorrow."

"Please don't," someone groans from the back of the room, getting a much bigger laugh than Mr. Spassnick has ever gotten from any of his jokes.

"Who said that?" Mr. Spassnick scans the crowd, but the dismissal bell rings and everyone is up and out of their seats before he can pinpoint the heckler.

I'm first out the door, racing down the hallway, trying to dodge all the bodies streaming from the classrooms. Math is on the third floor. Helen's locker is on the first, all the way at the end of the art annex. I've tried a number of times to get there before her, but each time I've been too late.

I am built for comfort, not for speed, so it's a challenge to run this obstacle course of bodies and backpacks and AV carts and stairs at any kind of high velocity. I am sweating and sucking wind by the time I get to the art wing.

Helen is just stepping up to her locker when I arrive.

"Hey," I say, huffing and panting. "How's it going?"

She looks at me as she grabs her lock. "Why are you so out of breath?"

"Oh. I, uh, I just wanted to . . ." Whoa. Lightheaded. I lean my hand up against the locker next to hers. "I wanted to make sure . . . you brought your Health textbook . . . to the library. . . . Because I left mine at home."

"Of course I'm going to bring my Health text." She starts to dial her combination.

I glance down and catch the first number: 32.

"The question is," she continues, "do I need to bring a gas mask?"

I force a laugh and grab my stomach. "Yeah, no. I'm steering clear of cafeteria food for a while."

"That's probably a good idea." She dials the second number: 8.

All of a sudden I'm feeling a buzz of shame in my chest. I start to look away, but then I think of the picture on my locker this morning. And the rain of corn niblets in the lunchroom. And all the whispering behind my back. Not to mention the things Helen has been saying about me.

"Are you going to head straight up?" I say, glancing down at her hand and catching the last number—14—before she snicks the lock open. "'Cause I was thinking of grabbing a soda. Could you tell Jerooni I'll be there in a minute?" Thirty-two, eight, fourteen. Thirty-two, eight, fourteen.

"Yeah. Fine. Go ahead." Helen opens her locker door and starts putting her stuff away. "I'll meet you up there." Her locker's kind of a holy mess. It's not what I expected, actually. It could rival mine for the amount of junk inside. She's got all sorts of family pictures, poems, and quotes taped to the inside of the door.

"Cool," I say. Thirty-two, eight, fourteen. "You want one?" I don't know why I offered. Easing my guilt, maybe? "If we sit near the back of the library, we can sneak-drink them."

"Yeah, okay. Get me a Dr Pepper." She digs some change from the sweatshirt she's got hanging in her locker, then counts it out. "Never mind. I don't have enough."

"No sweat." I wave her off. "I got it."

I got it? Coop, dude, you are totally going to blow your cover here.

"I mean . . ." I say, "you can get me next time. See you up there." I turn and go before I swallow any more of my foot.

I round the corner and am texting Prudence with Helen's locker combo before I forget it, and before I chicken out. I don't really have a choice in the matter. This is self-preservation we're talking about. And since Helen doesn't seem to feel too bad spreading lies about me, why should I feel sorry about sacrificing her to save my own ass?

I stare at Helen's locker combination on my screen, feeling slightly nauseous, like I've eaten one too many bags of Funyuns.

Before I can talk myself out of it, I hit the "send" button. There. It's done. I can't take it back now. Better to just keep moving forward. Focus on the next task at hand: getting all the information we'll need to fill out the Our Lady of Mercy admissions form.

CHAPTER TWENTY-THREE

YOU CAN'T ALWAYS GET WHAT YOU WANT

I GLANCE OVER THE SCHOOL APPLICATION form again before I enter the library. The girls have already filled in all the easy stuff—first and last name, phone number, home address, date of birth—and left all the doozies for me. Schools attended shouldn't be too hard, but how am I supposed to get her to tell me what her parents' work numbers and email addresses are, or if she's ever been tested for special education needs, or where the hell she was baptized?

And then there's a stupid student questionnaire that has to be filled out. What are your hobbies? Your extracurricular activities? Books you've read lately? Plans for college?

Christ, this feels a lot like homework.

I tuck the form in my back pocket, so it's handy in case I need to refer to it. I hoist up my backpack with the contraband soda—Dr Pepper for Helen, Mountain Dew for me—and step into the library.

Miss Jerooni looks up from her newspaper when she hears my footsteps. She recoils slightly, like she can still smell the beef bombs I let off in here Monday. Fanny and Alexander must remember me too, because they suddenly start flapping violently around their cage like they've just seen a cougar.

I smile big at Miss Jerooni as I sign in. She snaps her newspaper and goes back to reading. If I could work up a nice tooter right now, I'd hound one out loud and clear just to see the expression on her ferrety face.

Helen has taken up residence at one of the tables in the far corner of the library, just as instructed. I hadn't actually planned the whole surreptitious-sodas-in-the-back-of-the-room thing, but it works out perfectly, because it puts us out of the sight lines of anyone passing in the halls.

I swing off my backpack and pop a squat. "Hey," I say, digging the sodas out and stealthily handing Helen hers beneath the table. She examines the can, looking at the top, the bottom, the sides.

"What?" I say.

"Nothing." She studies the soda can again. "You didn't shake this up, did you?"

"Why would I do that?"

"To make me look stupid. To get me in trouble for having soda in the library. I don't know."

"Look, if your soda explodes it narcs me out as much as you, so chillax." I grab a textbook from my backpack, open it up, balance it like a screen on the table, and place my soda behind my impromptu shield. Helen does the same with her Social Studies text, hiding her Dr Pepper.

I glance up at Miss Jerooni, then look back at Helen. "Get ready to open. On three. One. Two. Three."

I cough loudly to mask the spritzing sound as Helen and I simultaneously crack open our cans. Miss Jerooni turns the page of her newspaper, completely clueless.

Helen—looking relieved—takes a quick sip and smiles at me, like we're brothers-in-arms or something. Then she stares at my balancing book with a funny expression.

At first, I think that my fortress of soda-tude might be falling down. But it's holding firm.

"I thought you said you forgot your Health text?" Helen says.

Oh, crap. Not cool, Coop. You can't be slipping up like that.

"Huh. Look at that. Hiding in plain sight." I laugh. "I can't tell you how many times I rifled through my back-pack. And my locker. I even asked Mrs. Turris if I'd left it in her classroom. Funny how you can search the same place over and over and still not find what you're looking for. Even though it's right there the whole time."

"Less is more, fella," I hear Dad whispering in my ear.

"Yeah, I do that all the time," Helen says. "Sometimes I'll be looking for my house keys for hours and then, when I finally give up, I'll find them, like, right there on my dresser."

Bingo. Opportunity knocks. It's a stretch, but if I don't start ticking off the boxes on this form, I'll never get everything I need.

"My parents won't even *give* me house keys anymore," I say. "I've lost them probably ten times. It's a good thing my mom doesn't work, so there's always someone home." Okay, so my mother works *now*. But she didn't used to. "How about your parents? Do they both work?"

"Yeah." Helen opens her notebook and starts flipping pages

Damn it. That's no help. I need details.

"My dad's a machinist," I say. "He wants me to go to trade school so that we can open a business some day. Redmond & Son. Or something like that. But I don't know. It's not really my thing. What about you? You think you'll do what your parents do?"

"No way," Helen says. "I hate math, even though I'm okay at it. And teeth gross me out."

All right. We're getting closer. Math? Math could be anything. But teeth? That's a dentist, right? What else could it be? Oral surgeon, I guess. Christ, this is a pain in the ass.

"Teeth, huh?" I say. "So, who's the dentist?"

"My mom's a dental hygienist."

"Really? That's weird, because my family's looking for a new dentist. Where does she work?"

"Bayview Dental." Helen looks at me warily. "What's with all the questions, Coop?"

I glance around, feigning innocence. "Questions? Was I asking questions? No, I was just . . . talking." Bayview Dental. Bayview Dental. That's easy. Because it rhymes with . . . what? Gray screw rental? That doesn't help.

Helen pulls out a sheet of printer paper. "So, I found this interesting Web site where they talk about all the tests they have to do to make sure that condoms are effective."

"Really?" I lean over and pretend to look at the page. I better leave her dad's occupation alone for now. Move on to something else. "That's fascinating. Wow, they really put those condoms through the ringer. You know what all those tests remind me of? The time when my sister was in elementary school and they did all these evaluations on her. You know. To find out if she had special needs. They said she didn't have them, but I still have my doubts." I laugh.

Helen glances at me sideways. "Huh."

"So, uh, you ever have to do that kind of thing? You know, testing for special needs?"

She turns on me, her eyes narrowed to slits. "What the hell's that supposed to mean?"

I reel back. "It doesn't mean anything. Geez. I was just . . . making conversation."

"Oh, yeah, right. Casual conversation about my 'special needs.' Real funny." She looks pissed. "And here I was thinking we were getting past all that immature crap. Stupid me."

Okay, so does that mean she *has* special needs and is sensitive about it? Or that she *doesn't* have special needs and is mad at me for implying she does?

"I'm sorry," I say. "That didn't come out right. I wasn't making fun of you. I was just . . . trying to get to know you better. I mean, if we're going to be partners and all, I figured . . . I don't know. I guess I'm not very good at this 'get to know you' stuff."

Helen regards me suspiciously. "You expect me to believe that?"

"Believe whatever you want. Honestly. I don't care if you have special needs or not."

"I *don't* have special needs, Coop."

Ka-*ching*! Another one bites the dust.

"Well, good," I say. "I'm glad. But if you did, it wouldn't be the end of the world. I mean, John Lennon was dyslexic for Christ's sake. Albert Einstein. Orlando Bloom."

The only reason I know all this is because in seventh grade, when I was failing all of my classes, my mother was convinced I had a learning challenge. She did all this research and would rattle off the names of every famous person who ever overcame any kind of educational disability. Apparently, it never crossed her mind that I was just lazy and rarely handed in my assignments. All it took was her threatening to send me to a special school for me to pick up the slack and maintain a healthy D average.

"Anyway," I say. "If I had to guess, I would have pegged you as one of those kids who skipped a grade."

Helen's face softens a little, which is good. "No. I never skipped."

No grades skipped. Check.

"I was supposed to repeat third," I offer up. "But Ms. Wade passed me anyway because she was afraid she'd end up having to teach me again." I laugh. "What about you? Ever have to do a grade over again?"

Helen stares me down. "Okay, now I get it."

My heart rockets into my throat. "Get what?"

"You don't want to work. So, you're trying to distract me. With all the questions and the chatting. Nice try."

"No," I say, able to breathe again. "This *is* working. We're following Mrs. Turris's advice. We're establishing our relationship."

"In other words, procrastinating. Come on. Let's just get this done with so we can go home." She looks down at the condom article and runs her finger along the page. "Okay, so, even though they test the condoms, they're still not a hundred percent reliable."

Damn. This is going to be even harder than I thought.

I have to weave the questions in smoother, so it's not so obvious. Otherwise, there's no way I'm going to be able to get all the answers by the November deadline—and all the rock-and-roll glory in the world won't be enough to save my demolished reputation.

CHAPTER TWENTY-FOUR

JUNK

WE'VE GOT TO BRING ALL THIS CRAP down into the basement," Dad says, opening the back of the station wagon. The entire car is crammed full of boxes and guitar cases and amplifiers and stereo equipment. "I drove over to your grandmother's and picked up all my old music stuff."

"Cool," I say, feeling a rush of excitement as Matt, Sean, and me run over to the car. It's Friday night and I've convinced the guys to sleep over so we can have an extra long practice tonight and then pick it up again tomorrow morning.

Mom stands in the doorway, wearing her pink cowgirl apron. "Well, that explains where you were all afternoon." She holds the door open as Dad lugs his Fender amplifier up to the house. "Guess that means no job hunting, huh?"

"Parenting's a job, hon. I'm helping the Coopster out." Dad steps up onto the stoop. "I'll get back on it tomorrow. I promise." He gives her a kiss on the cheek as he enters the house.

"Whoa, look at all this stuff!" Sean shouts, pulling an opened box of record albums from the car. "It's like he robbed a retro store."

"Take a gander at these speakers." Matt laughs as he wrestles a giant walnut-encased speaker tower from the backseat. "Holy crap, it weighs a ton." He staggers under the weight of it as he lifts the behemoth from the car.

I grab Dad's ancient turntable—the thick dust on the plastic lid flying up and tickling my nose—and follow the guys into the house.

We're like a colony of ants, carrying Dad's stuff in single file down to the basement, then returning to the station wagon to load up again.

Sean stumbles up the steps of the stoop and nearly drops the Roland synthesizer.

"Whoa!" Dad calls out. "Careful with that there."

On our third trip from the car—Dad grabbing the guitar cases, Matt taking a box of videotapes, Sean snatching up a bag of cords and effects boxes, and me hefting the other speaker tower—Angela's pristine Toyota pulls up to the curb. She steps out and strides over to Mom, who's still manning the door.

"What's going on?" Angela asks.

"Your father's helping the boys out with their band," Mom says.

"I hope he's got a miracle in one of those boxes," Angela says with a snort. "Because that's what it's going to take for them sound any good."

"I'm surprised you wouldn't want the miracle for yourself," I manage to wheeze, barely able to keep my grip on the ridiculously heavy speaker. "So that you could—"

"I wouldn't finish that sentence if I were you, Coop." Angela tails me to the basement door. "Unless you want me to let it slip at school just how bad you guys suck."

"I love you, sis," I say, laboring down the stairs, peeking around the speaker to see where each next step is. Looks like I'm going to have to curtail my natural instinct to rank on Angela for the next few months. I don't like it, but it's all for a good cause.

It takes us an hour to get everything out of the car and set up down in the basement. It almost looks like an antique recording studio that you might see in a museum somewhere. With the old stereo and guitars and amplifiers and 4-track recorder.

We have a quick dinner of microwaved Swedish meatballs and fettuccine before Dad, Matt, Sean, and me reconvene in the basement.

"All right." Dad paces around feverishly. He runs his hand through his hair. "First things first. All these albums. All these concert tapes. You need to study them. They are a master class in how to rock out with your jock out. The Who. KISS. Talking Heads. The Rolling Stones. Jimi Hendrix. These guys knew how to put on a show. Not like these candy asses today. I mean, we're talking crazy outfits, blowing up their instruments, running around like men possessed by demons, lighting their guitars on fire, spewing blood from their mouths. You name it. Each and every one of them knew how put on the flash. And if anyone's going to sit up and take notice of you fellas," Dad points at us, "that's what *you've* got to do. *Capisce*?"

Matt waves his hands in the air. "Wait, wait, wait. Are you saying you want us to play our instruments *and* do other stuff on top of that? There's no way."

Dad gives Matt a stern look. "I don't like that attitude, Guitars. There's always a way. This past week we've learned a few songs. And that's good. But it's not going to mean squat if you're as boring as a narcoleptic whore. That's why we're going to start on this now. Today." Dad claps his hands and rubs them together. "Okay. So now I think we should start with a rock-and-roll staple. The big junk stroll. Who wants to go first?"

Nobody moves.

"All right, Keyboards. You're up." Dad motions with his hand. "Walk to the far wall and back."

"Why?" Sean asks.

"Just do it. There'll be time for questions later."

Dad takes a seat and presses his palms together. "Go on. Just walk."

Sean shrugs and starts walking.

Dad studies him for a second, then slaps his knee and cracks up. "That's hilarious. What do you got hanging between your legs? A couple of raisins and a twist tie?"

Sean stops, a confused expression on his face. "What? You told me to walk."

"Yeah, walk. Not mince." Dad stands and mimics Sean's walk, his legs pressed together, his feet shuffling across the floor. "Are you in a rock band or a baroque quartet?"

"I don't know," Sean says.

"Yeah, well, that's your first problem. Look, you've got to stroll onstage like you're king of the world." He straightens up, his shoulders back, and starts strutting around the room with his legs slightly bowed. "Like you're straddling something elephantine. See the difference?" Dad takes his seat again. "All right. Give'er another try."

Sean looks at me for some help but I've got nothing for him. He takes a deep breath, widens his stance, and starts walking like he's astride a bull.

Dad laughs. "That's a bit better, except now you look like you just spent the summer on Brokeback Mountain."

Matt and me bust up.

Dad whips around and points his finger at us. "Hey,

chuckleheads, keep it down." He turns back to Sean. "Just rein it in a little, pal. You're doing great."

Sean pulls his legs in a bit and strides back and forth. He still looks like an idiot but Dad's not laughing anymore. And Sean seems to be enjoying his new swagger.

"Perfecto," Dad says. "You saunter onstage like that, my friend, and you won't have to play note one before the ladies start screaming their lungs out." He turns to Matt and me. "All right, peanut gallery. Who's next?"

CHAPTER TWENTY-FIVE

ROCK AND ROLL ALL NITE

THAT'S THE KIND OF THING WE NEED," I say, pointing to the television screen. Sean, Matt, and me are watching a KISS concert in my bedroom. Well, actually, Sean and me are watching. Matt's been unconscious ever since he sprawled out on his sleeping bag with the excuse that he was "just going to rest his eyes for a minute."

It's one of the concert videos Dad brought back from Grandma's. The band members are all decked out in costumes and makeup. There are huge towers of smoke billowing up at both ends of the stage. A ton of confetti floats down on the audience, and bright colored lights flash all over the place.

"We can't afford those kinds of effects," Sean says.

"Not the effects," I say. "Although, that would be nice. I'm talking about the outfits. We should come up with something cool that we could all wear onstage."

Sean looks dubious. "I don't know. Maybe if we were really kick-ass musicians we could pull something like that off. But what if we don't get much better? Aren't costumes just going to draw even more attention to us?"

"We *want* to stand out, Sean-o. Everyone else is going to be lame and boring. We want people to remember Arnold Murphy's Bologna Dare long after we leave the stage."

"Like, with makeup and everything?" He grimaces. "People will laugh."

"Maybe not makeup. Unless we come up with something really dope. Like skull faces or something. Let's ask Matt what he thinks." I move over to our sleeping friend, who's lying on his back with his mouth hanging open. "Matt," I whisper. "What do you think about dressing up like skeletons for the Battle of the Bands?"

Matt just snores.

I glance over at Sean. "Do you think that was a yes or a no?"

Sean laughs. "I'm gonna say that was a definite no."

"Look at him," I say. "He's like an old woman."

"Your dad *did* work him over pretty good tonight. Making him do all those skip-kicks and air splits again and again."

"Yeah, or it could have been the three hour 'I miss you,' 'I miss you, too' chitty-chat with the wife. I don't know what's going on with him anymore. He's gone all soft on us." I lift the lid on the minicooler under my desk and grab a can of Mountain Dew. "How are we supposed to have band meetings if he's going to be falling asleep on the job all the time? I mean, we have important things to discuss here."

"We could wake him up," Sean says.

"Good idea." I crouch down and open the soda can right by Matt's ear. It makes a *pop* and *fizz,* spraying a fine mist onto his cheek. Matt gives a quick snorting grunt but doesn't stir. "Looks like we've got a heavy sleeper on our hands."

"Just give him a shake."

"Where's the fun in that?" I take a sip of the Mountain Dew and then put the can on my dresser. "I think we should try something a bit more . . . invigorating." I yank one of my stinky socks off my feet and waft it in front of Matt's nose. "Oh, Matt. Mattington. It's time to wake up and smell the sockee." I lower the nasty sock and let it brush his lips.

Sean cracks up. "You're a sick bastard."

"Here, watch this." I pick up one of my sneakers, shove the old sock inside it, and tap Matt on the shoulder. "Hey, buddy. Wake up. Valerie's on the phone."

Matt's eyes flicker open. He sits up, all groggy. "Huh. What? Valerie?"

"Yeah. Here. Take it. It's long distance."

"Long distance?" he says, all confused. He grabs my Nike and holds it up to his ear. "Hello? Valerie? Where are you?" Matt scrunches up his nose. "Jesus, dude, your phone stinks. Hello? Hello? There's no one there."

"That's 'cause you're holding it upside down." I grab the shoe, spin it around, and hand it back to Matt.

"Valerie?" Matt says into the sneaker.

Sean doubles over, cracking up.

Finally, Matt's awake enough to realize he's holding a sneaker instead of a phone. "You ass," he says, throwing the shoe on the floor. "What's your problem?"

"My problem is you falling asleep, dude," I say. "Sean and I are trying to figure out what kind of outfits we should wear for the Battle of the Bands. We'd appreciate your fully conscious input."

"Outfits?" Matt rubs his eyes. "Why would we wear outfits?"

"Because it's rock and roll." I point to the KISS concert on the television just as one of the costumed dudes is spewing blood out of his mouth.

Matt shakes his head. "Dude. I don't think so."

"Look," I say. "We can't just get up there in jeans and T-shirts. We'll look like a bunch of tool bags. Like everyone else. I mean, if it was only me, I've got my own edgy look going, but you two are, I don't know, sort of . . . vanilla. No offense."

"Vanilla?" Sean says.

"I'm not saying there's anything wrong with vanilla.

It's the perfect base for everything. We just need to dress it up a little. Throw in some chocolate. Nuts. Marshmallow. Graham crackers."

"You want to make us Rocky Road?" Matt asks.

"Something like that. So the band has a rock-and-roll personality."

"I don't get it," Sean says.

"It's simple, dude." I start to pace. "We come up with a theme. And then we all dress up in that theme. It'll help with the stage fright, too. 'Cause you'll be pretending to be someone else."

"Like ninjas?" Matt asks.

I teeter-totter my head. "I don't know about that, but—"

"Or pirates!" Sean shouts.

Matt glares at him. "Oh, Jesus. Don't start that stupid debate again, Sean."

"Why? Because you don't want me to prove you wrong? *Again?*"

"Look, there is no way a pirate could kick a ninja's ass. Just because you keep saying it over and over again, doesn't make it true."

"I don't just *say* it. I state the facts." Sean grabs a candy bar from our stash on the nightstand and tears it open. "Pirates are cunning. Pirates have swords. Pirates have muskets. One shot and the ninja is dead." He takes a bite of his candy bar for emphasis.

"I have two words for you." Matt gets to his feet

and snags a bag of barbecue potato chips. "*Training* and *stealth*. It wouldn't even be a fight."

"Who gives a crap?" I say. "We're not dressing up as pirates *or* ninjas. We want to look cool. Not like we should be working in a comic book shop."

"That's where you're wrong." Sean points at me. "Pirates *are* cool. Way cooler than ninjas. I think we might want to consider a pirate theme."

"What about a vampire?" Matt asks. "They're cooler than pirates."

"That's true," Sean says. "And girls dig vampires."

"All right, look," I say, not wanting to quell their enthusiasm, but not about to agree to dress up like a vampire. "We don't have to discount anything right now. We'll go to the Salvation Army when we have some time and have a look around. Then we can decide what works and what doesn't."

I look over at the TV where KISS is doing their big finale. A wall of flames surrounds the entire band as they're lifted off the stage on a riser. Sparks pinwheel everywhere, fireworks rocket into the air, and the crowd goes absolutely berserk.

An excited buzz fills my chest. Those cheers and screams. All those girls going crazy, wanting to rush the stage and tear off their clothes.

Pretty soon, that's all going to be for us.

CHAPTER TWENTY-SIX

TRY A LITTLE TENDERNESS

THERE'S A FAINT VINEGARY SMELL in the air as I take a seat next to Helen in the library. Must be some new cleaner the custodian is using. Or maybe it's Miss Jerooni's attempt at masking any flatus she thinks I might produce.

"Hey," I say, placing my backpack on the floor. I'm hoping to make some real progress today on the Our Lady of Mercy form so I can put this thing to bed and get it off my vaguely guilty conscience ASAP. "How's it going?"

"Fine." Helen flips a page in her Health text so violently it tears the paper.

Someone's in a mood. But I can't let it derail me. I've got a ton of blanks left to fill out before this baby's done.

"So," I say, trying to work Helen's school disciplinary record into the conversation. "Is this, like, the first time you ever got detention or what?"

Helen's mouth is pinched up. "Can we skip the chit-chat and just do our work today?" She flips another page, and the sharp vinegar smell wafts up at me.

I sniff the air. "What *is* that? It's not me this time, I swear. It smells sort of like—"

"Sauerkraut," Helen says.

"Yeah, that's it. Sauerkraut. Good call. Where do you think it's coming from?" I rock my chair back, looking under the table.

"My books. My backpack. My sweatshirt."

I stare at her, confused.

"Some idiot got into my locker and dumped it all over my stuff."

"Oh." A surge of seasickness rises up inside me. *What did you expect, Coop? That they were going to go in there and neaten everything up?* "Jesus, I'm sorry."

Helen shrugs. "Not your fault."

"No, I know, it's just . . ." My palms are clammy. Play it cool. Technically, she's right. It's not like *I* put the sauerkraut in her locker.

"Are you okay?" Helen asks. "You don't look well."

"What? Yeah, I'm okay. Why wouldn't I be okay?" My mouth is cottony. "Of course I'm okay. It's just, you know, I just . . . don't get why anyone would do that."

"Someone's warped idea of fun. Anyway, I'd rather not talk about it anymore."

"Sure. No. Yeah. So, uh . . ." I lean over, glancing at her book. "Where'd we leave off the other day?"

"Birth control pill." Helen finds a paragraph in the Health book and starts to read. *"The birth control pill can have certain side effects like bleeding in between periods, nausea and vomiting, breast tenderness—"*

"Whoa. Wait a second. Maybe we should leave that part out."

"What part?"

"Breast tenderness. It might give certain people, I don't know, the wrong idea."

"What are you talking about?"

"I'm just saying, if you get up in front of everyone . . . and mention . . . breast tenderness. I don't know. Don't you think that everybody's going to be picturing your breasts? And that they're tender?"

Helen glares at me.

"No?" I ask. "Because that's what I'm thinking. And I don't even want to. Honestly."

"Are you done?"

"I'm worried, that's all. It's like if I say, 'Don't think of an elephant,' right? I mean, you said breast tenderness, and the first thing that jumped into my head was your breasts and their tenderness."

"Right. And what about the bleeding and the vomiting? Of course, *that* didn't jump to mind. Just the breasts. Which tells us a lot about where your mind is."

"Okay. Fair enough. But if I said testicle tenderness, wouldn't you be thinking about my testicles?"

"Eww. No. Never. *Ever.*"

"So you're not imagining my testicles right now? Even when I say 'testicle tenderness'?"

"No! Absolutely not!" Helen huffs. "If you want to know the truth, I'm thinking about this guy on television."

"Same difference. So you're thinking about some guy on TV's testicles."

"*No*. I'm thinking about what he *ate* on his show."

"He ate his testicles?" I feel my tool bag shrink up.

"*Yak* testicles." Helen smirks.

I wince. "Dude. Are you kidding me? Yak goolies? Sick. Why the hell would he do that?"

"I don't know. He goes around the world and eats bizarre foods. It's his show. *Weird Cuisine*. I guess he gets paid a lot of money."

"You couldn't pay me enough to eat yak's testicles."

"Right. You wouldn't eat them for a million dollars?"

This stops me. A million bucks? Now we're getting into interesting territory. "Do I get it all at once? Or do they pay me like the lottery? Over twenty years."

"All at once. But you have to eat both of them. And you have to chew them"—Helen looks skyward, thinking—"eighteen times each." She laughs.

I cringe. "Aw, man. That's vile." Helen's got this happy twinkle in her eye that I haven't seen before. "Did the guy say what they tasted like?"

"Like a combination of liver and oysters. But more

gristly." She raises her eyebrows. "Sounds appetizing, huh?"

I feel my stomach clench. "And you *watch* this show?"

"Every week. So? Would you do it?"

"For a million bucks? Yes. I would."

"On national TV?"

"Hold the phone. You didn't say that."

"That's the deal. Take it or leave it."

I think it over a moment. I'd get major crap from everyone at school, but so what? I'd be a millionaire. I could just flash my mud flaps at them from my limo. "Yes. On national television. What about you?"

She laughs "*No* way."

"Why not?" I say.

"Because they're yak testicles. And the whole world would see me eating them."

"So? I mean, seriously. At this point, does it really matter?"

The words are barely out of my mouth when Helen's face shuts. It's like this curtain blew aside for a few moments, and now she's grabbed it and drawn it tight.

I feel my entire body flush. "I didn't mean that. I just—"

"Whatever," Helen says. "Forget it." She glances at the clock. "Damn it. We're never going to finish our lesson plans for this week." She closes her eyes for a second. Takes a breath. Then opens them and looks at me. "Look, you probably don't want to but . . ." Helen's neck goes pink. "would you maybe be able to meet tomorrow after my cross-country practice? Just for an hour or two?"

I look into her deep hazel eyes and open my mouth to tell her no. That I couldn't possibly do it. That there's no way.

So I'm completely floored when what comes out is, "Sure. Okay. Can we meet at your house?"

CHAPTER TWENTY-SEVEN

I GOTTA FEELING

SEAN BOUNCES UP TO MY LOCKER. "Hey, look what I found." He reaches into his pants pocket, pulls out a stack of old Pokémon cards, and starts shuffling through them with a dumb smile on his face. "Dragonite. Mewtwo. Charizard. Remember how we used to go nuts for these things?"

"Dude, what the hell are you doing? Put those back in your pocket." I turn away from him fast, chuck my stuff into my locker, and take a furtive glance around to make sure no one is witnessing this. Thankfully, there's nobody directly beside us, and everyone in the halls seems to be in their own worlds.

"Why?" he says, still holding the cards.

"You don't bring that stuff to school, dawg." I keep my voice low. "Not if you want the babes to take you seriously." I shut my locker door and start walking.

Sean tails me. "Okay, Mr. Know-Everything. Then why did me and Gina Lagotta have, like, a forty-five minute conversation about Pokémon in Biology today when she's never even given me the time of day before?"

My stomach drops. "Do not tell me you were showing those cards around school."

"So what if I was? It's not like I'm the only one who ever collected Pokémon stuff. Gina still has her Pikachu doll."

I pick up the pace as we make our way down the stairs. I can't get out of this school and away from any prying ears fast enough. "Jesus, Sean, don't you get it? It's okay for her, because she's a *girl*. She's *wants* people to think she's cute. Exactly what you *don't* want her to think about you. Girls aren't attracted to little baby boys, Sean. They want mature cool dudes. Why do you think all the hot babes date guys in college? You've got to get with the program, dawg, or you'll never attain rock god status."

"Look, I'm not going to pretend to be someone I'm not, okay?"

"I'm not saying to pretend to be someone else. Just a cooler version of yourself." I burst through the first set of doors we come to. Sean trots to keep up. "Haven't you been listening to my dad? We have to present a rock-and-roll attitude. Pokémon is *not* rock and roll."

Sean stares at the cards he's still holding in his hands. There's a wistful look in his eyes. "I thought he was just talking about when we were onstage."

Because we came out the front, we have to walk all the way around the school to the bike racks at the back. "Look. Okay. It's like, say you had a Lamborghini."

"I'm never going to have a Lamborghini. My mom says it sends a bad message. Girls like you for the wrong reasons."

"Yeah, right, whatever. Listen to your mom's advice on women. Good idea. Anyway, just *say* you had one. For the purpose of this example. And it's got some, you know, Pampers advertisement painted on the doors."

He looks perplexed. "Why would it have a Pampers advertisement on the doors?"

"I don't know. The dude who owned it before you was strapped for cash. Who cares? The point is, it's on there. You wouldn't pick a babe up in that car until you repainted it, right? It's the same machine underneath. The same engine. Same doors. Same interior. But now it's got a nice, shiny new paint job. It makes all the difference. And it's the same with us. We have to maintain an attractive external persona. And, you know, later on, like fifteen years from now, when you're married, you can laugh and tell your wife that your car used to have a diapers advertisement on the side. Right now you've got to front, man. It's just as important as us learning the songs."

"Fine. Geez. I won't talk about Pokémon with anyone anymore. Being cool is almost too much work." He pockets the cards and stops walking.

"What are you doing?" I ask.

"I didn't ride to school today, remember?" He motions toward the street. "My mom's picking me up. I've got a dentist appointment."

"Oh, right," I say. "Well, don't let him numb your mouth. You've got to sing later."

Sean laughs. "I'd do a lot of things for you, Coop, but getting fillings without Novocain is not one of them. I'm sure it'll wear off by tonight. See ya."

He peels off and heads toward the road.

I continue on around the school. Past the baseball field and tennis courts.

Just as I am cutting toward the football field, Helen rounds the corner of the rust-colored track. Her hair is pulled back and her cheeks are rosy. She's breathing heavy but smoothly and her eyes are super-focused on where she's headed.

And Oh. My. God. Helen Harriwick is totally stacked. I never would have guessed it from all the baggy sweat-shirts she's always wearing, but the tight white T-shirt she's got on now makes it abundantly clear. And her legs are long and toned, looking damn fine in those tiny running shorts. Who knew she was packing a swimsuit model's body underneath all those clothes?

As she passes by, my eyes follow the bouncing balls, and I have to say, it sends an electric charge all over my body.

She stops by a bench to grab a water bottle. For a moment, I am in complete awe. I watch her take a drink.

Spray some water on her face. I want to move toward her. Feel myself take a step in her direction.

And then, suddenly, a shudder courses through me. A voice in my head, *For Christ's sake, Coop, shake it off. That's Helen Harriwick, dude. What the hell are you thinking?*

I clench my eyes shut tight. Try to erase the image of Helen as a hot girl from my mind. But it lingers there. Like a camera flash. Almost brighter, more intense with my eyes closed.

I open my eyes to try and focus on something—*anything*—else. But all I see is Helen. Running again. Her butt ticktocking so wonderfully in her shorts.

Oh, jeez.

Go! the voice in my head shouts. *Get out of here! Before it's too late!*

I turn quickly and walk off. Flipping the channels in my brain. Battle of the Bands. Prudence. Dad. Miss Jerooni.

Helen.

Helen running.

Helen running in tiny shorts and a tight T-shirt.

Oh, no. No, no, no. This is not good.

This is not good at all.

CHAPTER TWENTY-EIGHT

STEADY, AS SHE GOES

THERE'S AN HOUR TO KILL before I have to head over to Helen's house, so I grab a couple of slabs at Napoliano's. I've got the place pretty much to myself, save for the apron-clad man-of-few-grunts Arturo and the occasional dude or dudette coming in to pick up an order.

I'm sitting in one of the three plastic orange booths by the faded framed posters of Italy. I glance down at my grease-stained paper plate and realize that I've already consumed a slice and a half of my pizza and haven't tasted a bite of it.

The image of Helen running on the track keeps badgering me.

I lift the remains of my second slice and take a bite. This time, I savor the sweet tang of tomato sauce, the salt of the cheese. But only for a second before my mind wanders off again like an idiot child attracted to something shiny.

Helen Harriwick is *hot.*

The thought sticks in my brain like a burr. One that I am going to have to dislodge before I see her this afternoon. I do not need anything clouding my judgment. I have way too many questions to get answered for the school form, and I am not going to waste this prime opportunity.

I look at the Parmesan-wheel clock on the wall. Forty minutes have evaporated and it's time to head out. I clear my plate and leave.

It takes me way less time to get to Helen's than I thought it would. I'm ten minutes early as I coast up to her smallish two-story house, the aluminum siding painted a faded brick red. The front yard is neat and tidy. Three metal numbers—687—have been nailed to the post by the front door and are canted a little, like they're sledding down a steep slope.

I'm not sure where to put my bike. Somebody might jack it if I leave it out here. Locking it up to the post by the front stoop would probably seem weird. Maybe Helen'll let me put it in her backyard. That way, if anyone I know passes by, they won't see my wheels and put two and two together and get sixty-nine.

An image pops into my mind. *No, no, no! Do not go there! Not with Helen!*

I shake the thought from my skull, then lay my bike on the slate path leading to Helen's front door, bound up the three concrete steps to the porch in one stride, and ring the doorbell. It makes a metallic *BING-BONG* sound.

The red wooden door opens and a warm clean-laundry smell wafts out. Helen is wearing formfitting powder-blue sweats. It's weird seeing her away from school like this. Standing there, head tilted to the side, her body framed in the door.

The same electric chill I got at the track dances across my skin, traveling up my back and down my arms.

"Hey," she says with a smile. "You're early."

"Yeah, sorry. Do you want me to come back later?"

"No, it's fine. I just got back from cross-country, though. I need to take a shower. Would you like some juice while you wait?"

I zero in on her full, moist lips. Watch them form each one of the words.

My breath is shaky. *Okay, what the* hell's *going on? Get a hold of yourself, dude. You are after bigger game here. Prudence is the prize. Prudence and her hot-as-hell friends. Let's not forget that.*

"Sure. That'd be great," I say.

"Come on in." She steps aside.

"My bike." I gesture behind me.

"Oh." Helen glances past me. "The garage is unlocked."

I wheel my bike over the lawn, by the windows that look into the kitchen, and lift the heavy garage door. Helen's got the cleanest garage in the universe. Everything's in order. Rakes and shovels leaned up against the back wall. Clay pots stacked in the corner. Garden hose perfectly wound and hung on a hook. Makes my garage look like a junkyard.

Normally I'd just drop my bike on the floor, but a garage this clean calls for use of the kickstand, for sure.

I return to the front porch and follow Helen inside. Everything's just as spotless as the garage.

"My mom wants to meet you," Helen says.

Cool. Her mom's around. This could turn out well, actually. I need her e-mail address and signature. They're two of the biggest hurdles I have to leap. If I can knock those out this afternoon and get a few more questions answered, I'll be golden.

"You're the first boy I've ever brought home," Helen continues as we make our way through the kitchen. "She's excited. But don't worry. I told her not to be."

Never brought a boy home? Really?

"Hi, Mom," Helen calls out as we walk down the hall.

We enter the showroom-ready den and there's Mrs. Harriwick, sitting on the couch, a laptop on her legs, wearing jeans and a button-up man's shirt. She looks way younger than my mom. Hair short, blonde-streaked, cut in a swoop across her forehead. Hazel eyes just like her daughter's.

"Well, hello there." Mrs. Harriwick looks up from her computer. "You must be Cooper," she says with a half smile. "Just give me a second here while I finish this up." She peers at her computer, her fingers flying across the keys. "I'm afraid I'm a bit of a World of Warcraft addict."

Helen looks at the floor.

Mrs. Harriwick laughs, a few more clicks on the keyboard. "Could be worse things, right? Passes the time. Do you play, Cooper?"

"No. My friend Sean does, though. Apparently he's like some kind of level eighty Dwarf Warrior with a ton of gold and legendary items."

"Really?" She sits up straighter, excited. Like I just told her they both have the same birthday. "What's his game name?"

"I don't remember. Dorfwit or Hoofchomp or something."

Mrs. Harriwick places her computer, still open and running, on a side table. "Well, tell him if he ever wants to join up for a quest, I'm Pacheleine, a level seventy Night Elf Hunter."

"Sure. Okay." I glance over at Helen, who is blushing.

Mrs. Harriwick pats the couch next to her. "Would you like to have a seat?"

Helen shakes her head. "We have to get to work, Mom."

Mrs. Harriwick smiles. "Ah, yes. Helen tells me you two are working together on a Health project."

"Yeah," I say. "We have to present a lesson to the class

in a couple of months. Thanks for letting us get together at your house."

"Please." She brushes my thank you aside with her hand. "It's nice to have some male energy around for a change. We're all girls here. Helen, me, and the cat. So, what's your project on? Maybe I can help. I don't know if Helen told you or not, but I'm a dental hygienist. I know a few things about health."

"It's . . . um . . ." I feel my face get hot. I look over at Helen for some help. Then back to Mrs. Harriwick. "We didn't get to choose or anything."

"Birth control," Helen says, saving me. "We have to discuss the different kinds and their effectiveness."

Mrs. Harriwick nods approvingly. "Now *that* is something I wish they'd have taught *us* in high school. Not that I don't love my girl. God knows, I don't have a clue what I'd do without her. She keeps the house so clean. And she's become quite the little chef since I haven't been able to do much cooking. But she was an accident. There's no denying that." She laughs wistfully, staring off into what I assume is the past.

I look over at Helen, her cheeks flushing even more than before.

Mrs. Harriwick shakes off the memories and smiles. "A *happy* accident, of course. Just one I wish I could have pushed back a few years. You know. Until I'd sowed a few more oats." She exhales loudly. "No regrets, right? Anyway. Nice to meet you, Cooper. Help yourself to whatever's in the fridge. There's not much, I'm sorry to say. Haven't been able to get to the market the last little while. But if it's there, it's yours."

She grabs her laptop and adjusts the screen again as Helen and me take our leave.

CHAPTER TWENTY-NINE

THE PRETENDER

"SORRY," HELEN SAYS SOFTLY as we enter the kitchen, her cheeks and neck patchy with pink.

"For what?" I remove my backpack and lay it on the floor. Helen's already got her schoolbooks on the table, so I figure this is where we'll be working.

"My mom's . . . I don't know. She just blurts stuff out like that sometimes." Helen goes to the cupboard and takes out two glasses. "She hardly ever leaves the house anymore. I think she's, like, lost her social skills or something."

"Is she okay?"

Helen moves to the fridge and grabs a carton of Tropicana. "Oh, sure. She just . . . had to take some time off work. On stress leave. I don't know. She's a little weird."

"I didn't notice," I say, even though I totally did. I pull out one of the wooden chairs and sit. "I thought she was nice. It's sort of cool that she likes computer games."

Helen smiles. "I don't get you sometimes."

"What?"

She holds up the carton. "Juice?"

"Sure."

"I don't know," she continues. "It's like . . . you're this bizarre contradiction."

"I've been called a lot of things before. But that's a first."

She laughs and starts pouring the juice. "No. I just mean that . . . sometimes you're like this guy, you know. Like a lot of other guys. Kind of obnoxious. Sort of egotistical. Really crude."

"All this flattery's going to go to my head."

She laughs again. "Let me finish," she says handing me a glass. "Then there's this other side of you that's totally unexpected. Like . . . an empathetic side."

"I don't know what that means." I take a drink of my juice. "But I'll take it as a compliment."

"You should." Helen returns the carton to the fridge. She grabs her glass and leans against the kitchen counter. Her neck swoops so nicely into her shoulder. I get a flash of me kissing her right there. At that exact spot.

Jesus, Coop. What the hell are you thinking? Are you trying to make the rumors Helen's been spreading true? I mean, maybe if you *want to transfer to Our Lady of Mercy, sure, go ahead. Otherwise you're talking social suicide.*

I give myself an internal slap to the face.

"It's like the other day. When I didn't have enough money, and you bought me a soda." Helen's still talking. Thank God. It means she didn't notice my neck lust. "Or just now. You knew I was embarrassed about my mother but instead of making me feel worse about it you said something sweet."

"I hate to dump on your donut," I say, feeling a slight stab of guilt. "But you're giving me way more credit than I deserve."

"Okay, well." Helen shrugs. "You may not want to believe that you have a soft side but it's there. No matter how much you'd like to bury it under dumb jokes and crudeness." She drains her glass and puts it in the sink. "Anyway, I'm going to run upstairs and take a quick shower. I'll just be a few minutes."

In the porn version that instantly starts playing in my head, Helen asks me to join her and we stumble up the stairs, tearing off our clothes, and step into the shower as Mrs. Harriwick cluelessly plays on her computer in the family room.

"Coop?" Helen says. "Did you hear me?"

"What? Oh, yeah. Sure. Go ahead. I'll, uh, start doing . . . something."

"I'll be fast." She heads off, out of the kitchen.

I sit there for a moment, the image of water cascading down Helen's naked body in the shower mesmerizing me.

Until a voice in my head shakes me from the fantasy.

"Would you rather see her in the shower or me?" It's Prudence, and she sounds a little ticked off. *"This is your chance, Coop. Maybe your only one. Go get Mrs. Harriwick's e-mail and signature. Find out what church they attend. Save yourself. Your reputation is on the line."*

CHAPTER THIRTY

WON'T GET FOOLED AGAIN

MRS. HARRIWICK DOESN'T SEE ME standing in the doorway to the den. Her eyes have a slight unfocused look as she stares at the screen of her laptop. The only sounds I can hear over the heartbeat in my ears are the *clickety-clack* of the computer keys and the shower water running through the pipes in the walls.

I don't want to do this. My insides are a tortured cocktail of guilt, dread, self-loathing, and desperation. I envy the Vulcans, even though they don't really exist. What I wouldn't give right now for the ability to completely suppress my emotions and work on pure logic. Because, logically, Prudence is right. I may never get another opportunity like this.

"Oh, really?" Mrs. Harriwick says, startling me, until I realize she's just talking to her computer screen. "I don't think so, Snarkbone. That's just another dead end you want us to go down."

The rolled-up school form in my hand absorbs the sweat from my palm. If this goes wrong, I don't even want to think about the repercussions. And if it goes right, well, I kind of don't want to think about that either.

I take a deep breath and enter the room. "Hi, Mrs. Harriwick." My voice cracks. I clear my throat.

She looks up at me and flashes the very same vague smile she gave me before. "What is it, hon? Where's Helen?"

"I, um . . . She's taking a shower."

Mrs. Harriwick gestures at her computer. "Should I shut this down?"

"No, I uh . . . I just . . . I texted my friend, Sean. He said he'd love to do a quest with you. If you could give me your e-mail, I could pass it on to him so you guys could, you know, coordinate all that."

"Great. You have a pen?"

I walk over to the couch and hand her a piece of notebook paper and a pen. I didn't notice it before, but Mrs. Harriwick is wearing some seriously chunky perfume. It's like someone shoved rotten roses up my nose. It's odd that she would even be wearing perfume, considering Helen says she rarely leaves the house. Who is she trying to smell nice for, I wonder?

Mrs. Harriwick scribbles something down on the page, her hand shaking a little as she writes. Like she's forty years older than she actually is. When she's done, she passes the paper and pen back to me. "Make sure he mentions you or Helen in the subject line or I'll think it's spam."

"Sure," I say, trying to work up some kind of saliva in my mouth. "There's, um, something else."

The water upstairs shuts off with a clunk and a rattle of the pipes. How much time will it take Helen to dry off and get dressed? All of a sudden, the image of her stepping naked from the shower ambushes me. It occurs to me and my stirring divining rod that at this very moment Helen is upstairs, with no clothes on, probably toweling off her round breasts and her—

"Yes?" Helen's mother says.

"Yes, what?"

"You said there was something else?"

I blink, bringing myself back. "Right. Yeah. Our Health teacher, Mrs. Turris . . . She requires some kind of documentation every time Helen and I meet." I'm starting to feel light-headed. Have to get this over with fast. "So, usually Miss Jerooni, the librarian, signs our confirmation slip. But, since we're meeting here . . . I'm sort of in charge of getting the signatures and . . . I was wondering . . . if you could sign it for us today?" Oh, Jesus, there it is. I've done it. Could I sink any lower?

"Of course." Mrs. Harriwick laughs. "The way you were acting I thought you were going to tell me you got Helen pregnant or something."

"No!" I say. "We're not even . . . no!"

"Okay, sure, whatever. You're not even. Until you are." She gestures at me. "Give me that pen back."

I hand her the pen and present the school form, which I keep a tight grip on. I've folded down the page so only the signature line is visible. "Right here," I say, indicating where I scribbled a star.

I hold my breath and pray.

Mrs. Harriwick barely even glances at the paper as she scrawls her name. Her eyes half on her computer screen. "No, no, no," she says, passing the pen back to me. "What are you doing? You idiot." She looks up at me and smiles sheepishly. "Sorry. I just get so involved in this thing."

"It's okay. I understand." I start to leave, then remember the baptism question and figure I might as well go for broke. "Oh, yeah, I almost forgot." I turn back and see Mrs. Harriwick with one eye on me, and the other on her laptop screen. "I'm doing this survey for my World Religions class. Would you mind telling me what religion your family is? It's completely anonymous, don't worry."

"Oh, I don't care about that," she says, typing something on her keyboard. "Technically, we're Methodists. Though, to be honest, I can't remember the last time I was at church."

I scribble *Methodist* down on the notebook paper like I'm writing down the survey answers. Though I don't think Mrs. Harriwick even notices. "And, um . . . was Helen baptized?"

"She was. That was Stephen's idea. My ex-husband.

Back in Baltimore. He was the devout one. When it was convenient." More typing on the laptop.

I draw a few squiggles on my page to show I'm taking this all down. "And do you remember the name of the church?"

"Goring United. We used to call it *Boring* United." She laughs. "Obviously, you can tell I'm a faithful follower."

"No. That's cool. Not too many people in the class are very religious either. That's sort of why we're doing this survey." I quickly write the name of the church. "That's, um, everything, I think. Thanks. I appreciate it."

"Any time." Mrs. Harriwick returns her full attention to the computer.

"Any time, what?" I hear Helen say as she comes down the stairs, all freshly cleaned and showered.

Oh, crap. A jolt of adrenaline surges through my veins and I freeze. How am I going to explain this one?

CHAPTER THIRTY-ONE

AMERICAN IDIOT

"YOUR MOM WAS KEEPING ME COMPANY," I say, stealthily tucking the school form and notebook page into my pocket. "She gave me her e-mail to pass along to Sean so they could play World of Warcraft together." I force a laugh. "So, should we get to work?"

Helen glances at her mom, who's completely focused on her computer again. "Okay, sure," she says.

And that's that, thank God. A little bit of truth to hide the iceberg of lies.

Everything inside me trembles with the aftershocks of almost being caught. I feel slightly dizzy.

Once we're in the kitchen it takes me a few minutes to come down from the anxiety rush. I attempt to focus on our work, all the while trying not to let my shakiness show as I turn the pages in the Health text.

"So," Helen says. "We should figure out who's going to talk about what. I was thinking—now that we're working so well together—we could probably convince Mrs. Turris to let us do your 'He said, She said' thing, but do it all in one lesson instead of two. What do you think?"

"Yeah. Good plan." My internal gauges are starting to level out. Dodged a major duker there. "You think she'll go for it?"

"If we hand in a rock-solid lesson plan, maybe. It's worth a shot, right?"

"Hey, you know me. I'm all about having to do less work."

Helen smiles. "I don't know how much less work it'll be. But at least we won't have to spread it out over two days."

As we lay out our Health paperwork, my thoughts shift back to the application form in my pocket. I am so ready to be done with this stupid school form it's ridiculous. It weighs on me like a sumo wrestler. There's still so much left to find out. I flip through the questions in my head and decide to start with one of the easier ones. "You're really good at all this stuff," I say. "You're so focused. I mean, with cross-country, and your schoolwork. You probably have it all figured out, what you're going to do after high school, huh?"

Helen shuffles through some of her papers, looking for something. "I don't know. I kind of have this fantasy of being a pilot." She laughs self-consciously. "It's silly, I guess. There's something about flying, though.

I think I must have been a bird in a past life. But I'll probably go to college first. Get some kind of business degree or something. If I can get the scholarships. How about you?"

Oh, man, I've tapped a gold mine here. This conversation could provide a whole slew of answers. I'm not about to throw us off track by talking about me. "I haven't really decided yet." I shrug. "Do they *have* cross-country scholarships?" I ask.

"Sure. They have scholarships for everything."

"Ah, so, that's why you run. I was wondering. I mean, it seems likes so much work for something nobody even watches."

"What are you talking about? Cross-country's thrilling. We have tons of fans. And cheerleaders, too."

I look at her doubtfully. "Really?"

"No." She chuckles. "Of course not. It's totally boring unless you're doing it. I started running a couple of years ago, when things . . . weren't going so great at school. It's like a release. I get in this zone. It's hard to explain. And besides, I can just do it, right? I don't need any equipment or to count on anyone else."

"That's cool. It keeps you out of trouble. I can see that. Not that you ever get into trouble, right?"

"Actually, I got detention twice last year. For cutting Home Ec."

"Seriously? I never would have guessed that."

Helen laughs. Then pauses, regarding me for a second. "It's funny. You talk more than some girls I know."

"Do I? Really? Huh. I don't know. I guess I just . . . find people interesting." Oh, God, I'm going straight to the fiery pits when I die.

"It's nice, actually," Helen says. "Most guys don't want to take the time to get to know you. It's more like, 'Hi, want to go to bed?' "

I laugh. Maybe a bit too hard. "Yeah, most guys are dogs. Only one thing on their minds. Although, don't get me wrong, I'd be lying if I said that kind of thing doesn't flit through my brain every now and then. But what's the point of it all if you don't get to know the person inside, right?" *What the* fuck *are you talking about, Coop? Are you high?* "I mean, personally, I hope the girl I finally end up with . . . in that way . . . I just hope we're friends first."

Hello? You just *admitted you're a virgin to Helen Harriwick!*

Oh, my god. I did.

And what *is all that other crap? You don't honestly believe that stuff, do you?*

Oh, my god. Do I?

Helen looks at me. She smiles.

"We're wasting time again," she says. "If we keep this up we're going to have to meet after school every day."

Maybe I'm just hearing things, but it sounds like there's a quiet hopefulness in her words. Like maybe she would really like that.

I wait for the clenching in my gut. The internal recoiling. But nothing comes.

Okay, seriously, did someone put an alien pod under my bed? Have I been body-snatched?

Because something is *not* right here.

CHAPTER THIRTY-TWO

KEEP THE CAR RUNNING

HEY, BUD." DAD SMACKS ME on the back of the head as he walks by the couch. "Turn off the idiot box, we're going to the hardware store to pick up some supplies for our light show."

I kill the TV and get to my feet. "Let me grab a sweatshirt."

This weekend could not have come any sooner for me. I am wiped. Helen and I have met at her house five times in the last seven days—and that's on top of our two detention afternoons. Supposedly we were meeting so we could put together a kick-ass lesson plan—one Mrs. Turris would be so impressed with that she would let us off the hook of having to do two presentations.

But honestly, I've been pushing for the meetings in order to get this stupid school form completed. Once I got Helen's mom's signature and e-mail, I thought I'd be able to wrap it up pretty quickly, but it took way longer to finish than I ever imagined.

In the end, though, I think it will be worth all the work. And I'm pretty certain Helen is going to welcome the change of scenery. I can't imagine she isn't fed up with the increasing torment that's been going on at school lately: The BIOHAZARD signs stuck to her back, the mayonnaise on her seat, the Krazy Glue on her lock, her notebooks getting stolen, the chewed gum in her ponytail, and the dissected frog she found in her lunch bag.

But for some reason, now that the application is finally filled out, I can't seem to bring myself to hand it over. So it sits on the top shelf of my locker, tucked inside my History textbook, harassing me every time I open the door.

"Hurry it up, bumblescrew," Dad calls out, "before your mother comes home and puts the kibosh on."

We're out the door and headed toward the station wagon when I notice Dad's wearing a black satin bowling shirt with a flaming skull on the back and a red do-rag on his head.

"Uh, Dad," I say. "What's with the outfit?"

"What?" He glances down at himself. "You don't like my polish?"

"It's . . . um . . . why are you wearing that?"

"I'm just trying to get into the rock-and-roll headspace. I can't ask you guys to do something I'm not willing to do myself."

Oh, Jesus. I really don't want to be seen driving around town with Dad looking so ridic.

Unless, of course, it's *me* who's doing the driving. Then anyone who saw me might think I picked up a hitchhiker or something.

"Hey, Dad," I say. "Can I drive?"

He stops by the driver's side door and studies me over the roof. "Have you gotten your Learner's yet?"

"No. But it's just a stupid written test. It's not like it's going to help me drive any better. Besides, by the time I get around to it, you'll be back at work again. And I'd much rather have you teach me how to drive than Mom."

Dad considers this a moment. "That's a good point." He jiggles the car keys in his hand. "All right. But you listen to everything I say."

"Of course."

"And we keep this on the q.t."

"Absolutely."

"Okay, let's do it." He underhands the keys to me.

"Cool," I say, catching them. They feel heavy in my hand. There's an excited thrumming filling my chest as I walk around the car, open the driver's side door, and slide onto the cracked pleather seat.

I don't know if the stale smell of our car is stronger than usual, or if my senses have just become hyperaware now that I'm behind the wheel, but even the fat deck of pine tree air fresheners hanging from the stereo dial does nothing to mask the heavy scent of old coffee and mildew that permeates the air.

I slide the key into the ignition and am about to start up the wagon when Dad swats my arm with the back of his hand.

"Hey, hickoryhead," he says. "You want to maybe pull your seat up so you can reach the pedals? Or strap on your safety belt? Adjust your mirrors, perhaps?"

"Oh, sure." I slide the seat closer to the wheel. Check that my feet can work the gas and brake. Pull on my seat belt. Tilt the mirrors to make sure I can see behind me. Then start the car and crank up the tunes on the stereo.

"Yeah. I don't think so." Dad clicks off the music. "Listen to me. Learning to drive is a privilege. Not a right. But it's a privilege that comes with many benefits. Not the least of which is exponentially increasing your chances of putting the candle in the cupcake. So pay attention." Dad gestures toward the floor. "You know which one is your brake and which one is the gas?"

"I've won the NASCAR Sprint Cup on my Xbox like a million times, Dad. I got it covered."

"This isn't a video game, fella. You crash in real life, you don't get to press the restart button."

"I'm not an idiot."

"Yeah, well, the jury's still out on that one." He gestures at the steering column. "You know what all the letters stand for? P, R, N, D?"

"Park, reverse, neutral, drive."

"Good." Dad twists and looks over his shoulder. "Okay. So now the first thing you want to do is check your surroundings. Get the lay of the land. What's the traffic like in the street? Are there any kids playing nearby? Any sue-happy old ladies that might dive onto your bumper so she can help fund her retirement account?"

I glance around. "Looks all clear."

"Fine. Now put your foot on the brake, shift her into reverse, and ease down the driveway."

I grab the gearshift and notch it down to R. It takes me a second to get the feel of the brakes. The car jerks a bit as we move into the street.

"Take it easy, now," Dad says. "I don't need you putting my back out."

I coast us safely into the road, then stop and shift the car into drive.

"Okay, so, you want to go easy on the gas as you—"

I press down the gas and we jolt forward.

"Hey!" Dad smacks my shoulder. "I said *easy*."

"Sorry."

"Think gradual. Everything is measured. Speeding up. Slowing down. Give yourself enough time to start and stop so you can do it *gradually*."

"Okay."

I start down our street, trying to keep things smooth. I can actually feel the weight of the car. The power of the engine. There's an exhilarating rush about it, but also a dizzying terror. The idea that if I hit someone I could actually kill them. It's almost like what I'd imagine holding a gun for the first time would feel like.

"You're doing good," Dad says. "Keep a steady speed. No more than thirty."

Dad has me make a couple of turns, though I hit my wipers both times instead of my signal, and I keep swinging wider than I should. Luckily, there aren't too many other cars on the road.

The wind picks up, blowing dried leaves across the street. Several houses we pass are decorated for Halloween.

As I approach a couple of kids on their bikes, my whole body tenses up.

"It's okay," Dad says, noticing my anxiousness. "Just give them a little room."

I steer around them—giving them a wide berth—and breathe easier once we're past.

"So, I've been listening to the tapes we made," Dad says. "And I've come to the realization that your friend Sean can't sing to save his sandbag. Take a right up here." He points at the next intersection.

I slow down, clicking the correct control for my signal this time, and turn the corner.

"I thought we could get away with it, but he sounds like a cat getting a colonoscopy. We're definitely going to need somebody else." He adjusts the bandanna on his head. "What about Matt? You think he has any pipes?"

"Forget it. He goes off-key singing 'Happy Birthday.'"

"How about his girlfriend?"

"No. She's not going to be in the band. It's bad enough she shows up to most of our rehearsals already."

"That's my point. She's already there. Why not utilize her?"

"Because. It's not going to happen." I feel myself getting irritated. Like Dad's trying to stuff me into a pair of wool boxers. I can see it now. Valerie taking over the band. Making us change our name. Probably to something *French*. Deciding what songs we should play.

"Well, you're going to have to find *somebody*. And soon." Dad gestures to the green pickup truck heading toward us. "Now be careful. Watch this guy. You're hogging the middle of the street. You want to ease over a little so he has plenty of room to pass."

Suddenly, I get a surge of panic. "What about the cars parked on the side of the road?"

"Obviously you don't want to hit those. Just slow down."

But I can't. I'm frozen. "There isn't enough room," I say. I see it all unfolding in front of me as the truck closes in on us. The head-on collision. The crunch of metal.

"Slow down, Coop. Ease over to the side."

The truck bears down on us.

"Jesus Christ!" Dad shouts.

He grabs the wheel, pulling it down just as I wrench it to the right, causing us to careen off the road. Somehow, instead of slowing down, we speed up. The car bucks and lurches as we thump over the curb, onto a lawn, and into the midst of someone's elaborate Halloween display. Tombstones and haystacks and skeletons and pumpkins and vampires are sent hurtling through the air before the station wagon finally stalls out with a violent shudder and a great big belch.

The bed-sheet remains of a ghost flutter down onto the windshield, blocking out the light.

My heart is doing gymnastics in my chest.

"Are you okay?" Dad asks.

"Yeah, I'm fine," I say, my hands strangling the steering wheel.

"Good. 'Cause I'm gonna beat the crap out of you when we get home. What the *hell* were you thinking?"

"I don't know, I just . . . I got scared all of a sudden—"

"Come on. Move!" He's already unbuckled his seat belt and is clambering over to the driver's seat. "Switch. Let's go. If we get caught, I'm gonna lose my freakin' license."

I unstrap my seat belt and struggle to climb under him into the passenger seat. Our limbs tangle as we try to change places. I get a whiff of his Old Spice cologne underscored by the sweaty smell of panic.

"Ow!" Dad hollers. "Goddamn it. You nutted me."

"Sorry," I say.

When we've finally changed positions, Dad starts up the car.

I glance back at the road. Apparently the truck didn't

stop to see if we were okay. But an old man has just come out of one of the neighboring houses and is tottering over to us.

Dad rolls down his window, reaches out, and yanks the sheet off the windshield. "Buckle up."

I've barely clicked my seat belt in when he throws the car into gear and guns it. We're off the lawn and back into the street in no time. He peels out around a corner, sending my shoulder hard into the door and leaving a smoky trail of burning rubber behind.

"Shouldn't we wait?" I ask. "Or leave a note or something?"

"Right. That's just what I need." Dad glances in the rearview mirror. "They'll make me pay for all that stupid foam and cardboard. Probably jack up the price so they make a tidy profit. Your mom'll have my prunes."

"But isn't that, like, a hit and run or something?"

"Who did we hit? Dracula?" Dad makes a face. "He's already dead." He looks in the mirror again. "You think that geezer got our license plate?"

"No way. His glasses were thicker than Grandma's."

"Good. Then we have no witnesses. We're in the clear. But you don't mention this to anyone, you understand? Not even your buds."

"Sure, Dad," I say. "It'll be our little secret."

CHAPTER THIRTY-THREE

GO YOUR OWN WAY

ARE YOU KIDDING ME?" Sean howls. "That's awesome!"

Matt's eyes are wide. "Did you total your car?"

"Nah, it's fine," I say. "It just took a little while to pull out all the hay and pumpkin pulp from the grill when we got to the hardware store."

"Oh, man." Sean beams. "I wish I could have been there."

"Yeah, it was pretty epic," I say. "Now, remember. This stays between us. And don't go mentioning it when we're at my house."

The three of us just finished the Saturday lunch special at Mr. Poon's Chinese Restaurant and are walking over to the thrift shop to scout for band outfits.

Matt cracks open a fortune cookie and pulls out the little slip of paper. "Okay, are you ready to hear some ancient Chinese wisdom?" He pops a piece of cookie into his mouth.

"Don't forget to add 'in your pants,'" I say.

"Yeah, yeah. Here we go. *Constant grinding,*" he reads, "*can turn an iron rod into a needle* . . . in your pants."

"Whoa!" Sean laughs.

"That's good advice there, Mattie," I say. "You do realize that means you're going to have to find a new hobby, but still."

Matt makes a wanking gesture.

"I said a *new* hobby, Matt."

Sean and I crack up.

"I'm next." Sean breaks open a cookie and pulls out the slip. *"Special times are created when an unconventional person comes—"*

"In your pants!" I shout, pointing both my index fingers at him.

Matt socks Sean in the shoulder. "That's totally gay, dude. But not unexpected."

Sean flips Matt the bird, then turns to me. "All right, Coop. Your turn. I'm dying to see what's going on in your pants these days."

Bits of fortune cookie spray out of Matt's mouth.

I give Sean a do-I-even-have-to-respond-to-that look.

I snap open a cookie, pull out the fortune, and read it to myself. Uh-oh. Gonna have to do a little editing here. "Yup. Here we go. *You possess the key to unlimited satisfaction* . . . in your pants." I nod. "Guess that about sums it up."

"I'm so sure." Matt rips the fortune from my fingers. I try to grab it back but he dodges me and reads it. "Uh-huh. Like I thought. *A member of your family will soon do something that makes you very happy* . . . in your pants."

Sean and Matt bust up.

Matt rolls up the fortune and flicks it at me. "Sick. But also, not surprising."

"I think you misread that, dawg," I say. "It must have said 'a member of *Matt's* family.' Because I've got that date with your mamma tonight."

Matt grins. "That's totally weird, cause I've got a date with yours. *And* your sister. They want to show me something called 'The Cincinnati Sandwich.' I don't know, have you ever heard of that?"

"No, I haven't, Matt. But I'll be sure to ask your mom tonight. Although she might be too polite to talk with her mouth full."

"Oh, yeah?" Matt grabs me in a headlock and drills a killer noogie into my scalp.

"Ow. Jesus."

"*What* are you doing tonight?" he says, laughing and boring his knuckles into my skull.

"Nothing." I laugh through the pain. "Unless your mom really wants to."

Matt leans on me and we fall on someone's front lawn.

My hand finds the waistband of Matt's boxers and I give a hefty yank. There's a ripping sound I didn't expect.

"Goddamn it!" Matt cries, releasing me, scrambling to his feet and working his underwear from his crack. "A wedgie? How old are you?"

I get up and brush myself off. "Rock beats scissors. Wedgie beats noogie. It's the rules of the jungle, dawg."

"Are you two finished?" Sean asks. "It's like I'm babysitting my five-year-old nephews."

Me and Matt share a look.

A silent agreement.

And then we lunge for Sean. Who bolts.

We chase him for five blocks, all the way up to the Salvation Army.

"Truce," Sean calls as he grabs the door handle, like we're playing tag and he's touching base.

"Truce?" I laugh, sucking wind, sweat trickling down my cheek. "Now who's the five-year-old?"

Sean gestures through the window. "I'm just saying. There's old people in there. We don't want to give any of them heart attacks."

"All right, truce," Matt says. "For now."

Sean pulls open the door and we enter.

It smells like a mix between a urine-hosed back alley and mothballs in here.

But it's the perfect place to find some awesome retro gear for our band attire.

We cruise the clothing aisles searching for hidden treasure.

"Now just think about the image we want to portray." I pick up a plaid sports jacket on a hanger. "Right here. Maybe we should go old school and wear something like this with a Gatsby hat."

"Yeah. All you'd need is a colostomy bag and you'd be set." Matt laughs.

"It's called uncool-cool, douche wipe."

"I still don't understand," Sean says, unenthusiastically flipping through the clothes on the rack, "why we have to wear costumes. What are we trying to prove?"

"We're trying to entertain," I say. "That's why they call it show business. You're putting on a show. And don't think of it as a costume. Think of it more as a persona."

Matt grabs a long white lab coat from the rack and laughs. "Okay. Here's mine."

"A lab coat?" Sean asks dubiously.

"That's right." Matt threads his arms into the sleeves and bobs his head. "Oh, yeah. That's what I'm talking about."

I glare at him. "You look like a doink."

"No way. I'm uncool-cool, man." He smiles big, playing air guitar and doing a skip-kick. "You can call me The Doctor."

"Dr. Doink." Sean laughs. "That could be your stage name. Like The Edge or Sting."

"Okay. Hold on a second," I say. "I like the idea of stage names, but we're not all going to wear lab coats."

"Who said anything about *you* guys wearing them?" Matt struts off toward the mirror. "I've gotta see how I look in this."

Sean shakes his head. "I'm not going on stage dressed as a doctor."

"Don't worry. We won't. But at least Matt's getting into the spirit. We have to think about what's gonna make us stand out."

Sean glances despondently at the clothes on the rack. "I still think costumes—I mean *personas*—are a bad idea."

"Well, you're wrong," I say. "It'll totally work. But only if we present something cohesive. And really sell it. If you're all shy about it, then yeah, you'll look like a dumbass. But if you're like 'Yeah, that's right, I'm The Doctor,' or whatever we decide to be, everyone'll have fun with it."

"I don't know."

"Sure you do. Think about the Beatles when they all wore black turtlenecks. Or suits and ties. Or on the cover of *Sergeant Pepper*." I pull a faux-fur coat from the rack. "Here. Try this on."

He recoils. "No way."

"Come on. We can be pimp daddies. We'll get some big rings, sunglasses. Maybe some hats. It'll be sweet."

Matt comes back grinning, his hair disheveled, the collar of the lab coat upturned, and a stethoscope around his neck. "Hey, look what I found." He waggles the stethoscope. "Isn't this cool. You know what? I think I can actually pull this off. I'm gonna do it. I'm going to be The Doctor. And it's perfect, because Valerie wants to be a doctor, so it'll be like a dedication to her. I think with a little gel I can get my hair to—"

"Sure, Matt. That's a thought," I say, though I'll never let it happen. "We'll keep it on the back burner. Sean and I were thinking maybe we should be pimp daddies."

"That was *your* idea," Sean says.

Matt shrugs. "You guys can be whatever you want. But I'm The Doctor."

I scowl at him. "We can't be different things. We don't have to dress exactly alike but we have to pick a theme."

"Why?" Matt asks.

"Because otherwise we'll look like a bunch of numbwads." I hold the fur coat out to Sean. "Come on. Try this on." I stare at him and grit my teeth. "It's better than being doctors."

Sean sighs. "This is so stupid." He stands there as I drape the coat over his shoulders.

"Look at you," I say. "You're pimped out, dude."

"No." Sean shrugs the coat off. "It smells like a wet hamster cage. I can't do it."

I pick the fur off the floor, shake it out, and slip it on. Hold my arms out to the sides, admiring myself. "Come on. You have to admit I look dope. Think about it. We could dye our hair green. Maybe get some ink on our skin. A few dozen gold chains. Look out, Snoop Dogg, there's a new pimp in town. Coop Daddy."

"No. No, no, no." Sean shakes his head. "The Doctor and Coop Daddy? It sounds like a bad seventies sitcom. I can't be a part of this."

"Matt's not going to be The Doctor," I say. "We're *all* gonna be pimp daddies."

Matt crosses his arms. "I'm going to be The Doctor or I'm not going to play."

"The whole thing is just so stu—" Sean's eyes suddenly light on something across the store. His face brightens as he makes a beeline for the hat section. "Okay, well," he calls over his shoulder, "if Matt gets to be The Doctor, then I'm having my own persona."

Sean leaps up to a high shelf and snags a big black sombrero with silver trim. He places it on his head—even though it's two sizes too big—and beams. Then he does a little two-step and stomps his foot loudly on the floor. "You can call me *El Mariachi*." His head swivels around before he's off again, attacking another rack. "There's got to be a poncho around here somewhere. Maybe some toy guns and a holster."

I rub my face. Everything's become completely unglued.

"Ah-ha!" Sean yanks off the hat, pulls a red-and-orange poncho over his head, replaces the sombrero, then walks over to the mirror at the end of the aisle to take himself in. "Ohhhh yeah. Totally mysterious. Totally cool. How hot are the babes gonna get when they see me singing onstage looking all Antonio Banderas-sexy? Tianna will be kicking herself for cutting this *primero pescado* loose."

I haven't had the heart to tell Sean he's no longer going to be our lead singer. He's been getting so into it lately, full of the idea that he's going to bag all the hottest babes. I figure I'll let Dad drop the bomb. So it's coming from someone outside the band.

"Okay," I say, suddenly feeling bad for Sean. "What if we're all mariachis? That could work."

"No way," Sean protests. "I'm *El Mariachi*. There can be only one."

"And I'm The Doctor," Matt announces, smoothing his hands down his lab coat.

Oh, God. I run my hand through my hair. Breathe deep. "All right. I think we might want to reconsider the whole costume thing. Maybe it's not the direction we want to go."

"Screw that. I love my outfit." Sean puts his hands on his hips, gives a little Elvis lip snarl at his reflection. "Joo want some of dees, chica?" he says.

I glance at Matt.

We share an incredulous look.

And then . . .

The three of us collapse in hysterics.

The Doctor, Coop Daddy, and *El Mariachi.*

"Look at us," I sputter, gesturing at the mirror. "Do we not look completely ridic?"

"Yeah," Matt says. "But in a weird way, also totally brilliant."

"Joo can't say we will not capture dee full attention of dee audience. No?" Sean does another bullfighter dance, stomping his foot for emphasis. *"Si! ¿Donde está el baño?"*

Seeing the jaunty expressions on my friends' faces, it hits me that this is *exactly* what we need. Something that helps us have fun while we're playing. Something that helps us relax onstage.

And even though it's not exactly how I pictured it—not even *close* to how I pictured it, actually—these personas will definitely make us stand out from the crowd, and hopefully give us the confidence to put on a really kick-ass show.

CHAPTER THIRTY-FOUR

SULTANS OF SWING

WE ENTER THE BASEMENT wearing our new duds. Dad is hunched over the coffee table, half-moon glasses perched on his nose, stringing several light sockets along a wire. He's dressed in his skull shirt and bandanna and is sporting what looks like the beginnings of a goatee and sideburns.

"What do you think?" I say, lifting the collar on my fur coat and adjusting the purple Stetson I found jammed at the bottom of a box filled with ladies' hats.

Dad peers up from his work. He slowly removes his glasses and puts down the needle-nose pliers. "Have you guys been smoking the Mary Jane? I thought you said you were going out to get some band outfits?"

"We did."

"Those aren't band outfits. Jesus Christ, Coop, you look like castoffs from a Mexican soap opera!"

"What are you talking about?" Sean tilts back his sombrero. "We look good. We got clothes that express our individual personalities."

"Enlighten me." Dad sits back on the sofa and gestures at Sean. "What exactly are you *expressing* here with this costume of yours?"

"It's not a costume. It's a *persona*! I'm *El Mariachi.* And I'm expressing my love of all things southwestern."

"And I'm The Doctor," Matt says, with a hint of uncertainty. "Handing out . . . prescriptions to rock."

Dad levels his gaze at me. "And you are?"

"Coop Daddy. The badass pimp what wears a coat made of chimps."

"Right." Dad slaps his thighs and stands. "So this is all a big joke now, is it?"

"No," Sean mutters. "It's better than what you're wearing."

"Excuse me?" Dad gets right up in Sean's grill. "These happen to be classic rock-and-roll togs. Ripped jeans. A flaming skull shirt. And a Little Steven head adornment. Bold but not overstated. You guys are just a hodgepodge of . . ." He blinks and sniffs the air. "What the hell is that stink?"

Matt glances over at me. "It's Coop's coat of many ferrets."

"Chimps," I correct, starting to roast in my faux fur.

"I told you it smelled like a petting zoo," Sean says.

Dad rubs his cheek. The movement of his calloused

hand on his stubble makes a scratching sound. "All right. No. This is my fault. When you told me the idea, I thought it could work. But of course. You guys are rock-and-roll rookies. I have to keep reminding myself of that. We'll just go back to the store and exchange all of . . . this." He makes a sweeping gesture with his hand.

I glance over at my buds. They look like wilting sunflowers.

I take a step forward, spinning the giant fake ruby ring on my finger. "Listen, Dad. I know it seems sort of . . . random."

"*Sort* of random?" He snorts.

"But we put a lot of thought into these personas," I continue. "We worked hard putting them together and—"

"No, no, no. It's too disjointed. We need to mesh," he says, interlacing his fingers. "There's no meshing going on here. I'm sorry." He laughs. "We'll do costumes, but we'll do them right."

"No," I say, feeling my jaw set. "We're keeping these, Dad."

Sean steps up beside me. "We like what we came up with. It's interesting. And confusing. Just like our band name."

"Yeah, I was gonna get to that eventually," Dad says. "Arnold Murphy's Bologna Dare is kind of a mouthful, don't you think? How would you feel about shortening it to something simpler. Like, The Dare?"

"We're not changing our name." I glance over at the guys. "And we're not changing our personas. It's *our* band, Dad. It has to reflect who we are."

He studies Matt and Sean. "Is that how you two feel?"

They nod their heads tentatively.

"All right." Dad throws his hands in the air. "I don't get it, but what do I know? I'm just the guy who's band was asked to play Spring Fling. Whatever. Maybe I'm out of touch. We'll keep the costumes. For now. Let's see how they look while you're playing."

We run through the first few songs that Dad has chosen for our final set list. "The perfect mix of timeless classic-rock tunes and audience pleasers," he insists.

At first, the music is cautious and timid and sloppy, but then, in the middle of "Back in Black," something happens. It's like the three of us finally settle into our personas and just let loose. The energy builds and builds until you can feel it filling the basement. It's weird, because we don't sound a whole lot better. It just *feels* a whole lot better. And that makes all the difference.

When we finish, the sweat is pouring off of my forehead, *pitter-pattering* on my snare drum.

"Okay," Dad says, sitting on the couch, nodding his head slowly. "I'm sensing something here. A shift." He stands and starts pacing around. "This is pretty good. You guys have kicked it up a notch in the attitude department.

If it's the costumes doing that, then they've got my vote. Sure, people might say, 'What the hell?' But, so what? We keep them on edge, right? They'll be all, 'What's going on here?' 'What's it all mean?' And we'll be like, 'Fuck you! What's a goddamn Jackson Pollock painting mean?'"

Dad's fingers start wiggling like they do when he's excited. "The audience'll think we're crazy. Capable of anything. And just when their heads are ready to explode from the confusion of it all . . . BAM! We blast them with our flash pots." He gestures emphatically at the light socket contraption on the coffee table. "It's attention grabber after attention grabber after attention grabber. Of course, we still have to do something about the singing."

"What?" Sean looks around, bewildered. "Wasn't I loud enough?"

"You were plenty loud, Sanchez," Dad says, flinging his arm around Sean. Leaning in confidentially. "But it's not making up for the fact that you sound like Yoko Ono on helium. I'm sorry, but we need a new singer."

"But . . ." Sean blinks like he's been hit over the head with a two-by-four. "What about all the hot babes?"

"Trust me," Dad says. "You'll get way more girls if you keep your mouth shut."

"But I thought—"

"Uh-uh." Dad holds his hand up like a traffic cop. "I compromised on the costumes and the band name. This, we can't afford to waver on. End of story. You're going to have to start asking at school. Hang around outside the chorus room. Put an add in the school newspaper. It's top priority right now. I don't care how you do it but we *have* to find someone who can carry a tune."

"Hello?" A girl's voice coming down the steps. At first I think it's Valerie, but it doesn't sound like her.

A second later, Helen appears from around the stairwell, wearing a zipped-up pink hoodie and tight jeans, looking adorable and slightly uncertain. It's amazing how much more attractive Helen is when she's out of the shadow of school. "Hi. Your mom let me in. We said four o'clock, right?"

Oh, crap. I completely forgot I invited her over to work on the project during our last detention. In a moment of weakness—when she was gazing at me and giving me that cute little half smile—the unwanted words just flopped from my lips, like they seem to be doing with disconcerting regularity lately.

"Cool outfits," she says, tucking her hands in her back pockets.

Sean straightens up a bit. "Thanks."

"Hi, Helen." Matt gives a small wave.

"Sorry," I say. "Rehearsal's running late. We can reschedule if you want." I'd like to get her out of here before she fully comprehends that it's my dad who's wearing the do-rag and burning-skull shirt.

"That's okay. I can wait." Helen leans against the wall. "Is it all right if I watch?"

"It's not only all right," Dad says, shooting me a

where-have-you-been-hiding-this-hottie look as he steps up to her. "We absolutely insist." He holds out his hand. "Walter Redmond."

Great. Just great.

"Helen Harriwick," she says, shaking his hand. If she thinks he looks weird, she has a damn good poker face.

"Let me ask you something, Missy," Dad says, circling her. "You look like the type of girl who can belt out a tune. Am I right, or am I right?"

CHAPTER THIRTY-FIVE

REVOLUTION

DAD!" I CHOKE OUT, my stomach free-falling. I try desperately to think of a way to signal him that this is the school pariah I was telling him about. I clear my throat, make an X with my drumsticks, hum "Hairy Mary."

But he stares me down, oblivious. "Coop, let me handle this."

"But—"

He cuts me off with an I-will-strangle-you glare, then turns back to Helen, all smiles. "Well? How about it? Can you sing?"

Helen takes a step backward, a worried look in her eyes. "Uh, yeah . . . I guess . . . a little . . . why?"

"I knew it!" Dad throws his hands in the air in a hosanna way. "Ask and ye shall receive. Like manna from the gods."

Helen frowns, confused. "I'm sorry, I don't—"

"Our band here is suffering a lead vocal crisis." Dad laughs. "And we were *just* discussing the problem when you descended to us from the heavens."

Helen points up at the ceiling. "I just came down from upstairs."

"Listen to that voice." Dad gestures to us. "Can you hear it?" He waggles a finger at Helen. "I bet you sound like a cross between Stevie Nicks and Janis Joplin when you sing."

Helen's eyes dart around, looking like a trapped bird.

"Leave her alone, Dad," I say, a stabbing pain piercing my temples. "You're scaring her." Goddamn it. What the *hell* is he doing? If Helen joins the band, it will completely obliterate any and all rock-and-roll awesomeness that this whole thing was going to bestow upon me. I glance at Sean and Matt for support, but they don't seem nearly as supremely freaked out as me.

"I'm the manager of this dog and pony show, fella. So let me manage." Dad grins at Helen, placing a hand over his heart. "Would you do an old man a favor?" He stretches his arm out in our direction. "Would you join us for one song?"

"Oh, no." Helen takes another step backward. "I'd rather not."

"Please," Dad begs. "Just to satisfy my curiosity. A single song. What could it hurt?"

"I've never . . . sung in a band before. I probably don't know any of the songs you play."

"Of course you do." Dad gently guides Helen over to the microphone. "A Beatles song. Everyone knows the Beatles." He grabs a songbook and flips through it. "Here. We'll do 'Revolution.'" He folds the book back and places it on a music stand. "It's easy. You know the tune?"

Helen nods. "Yes, but—"

"Don't be shy." Dad makes a fist. "Just put some fight behind it. Think about something that really pisses you off. And sing from that place. Okay?" He pats her on the back.

Helen swallows hard and nods. "Sure. All right. But just one." She pulls the mic from the stand, and unwinds the cable.

Dad snaps his fingers. "Coop. Count us in. And guys? Balls to the wall."

Helen looks so fragile standing there, holding the microphone, staring down at the songbook and mouthing the words.

I grip my drumsticks tight in my hands, feeling like I just swallowed a fistful of broken glass. If she's any good, Dad will try to convince us to have her in the band. Which *cannot* happen. So why is there a whispering voice inside my head that wants her to do well?

Oh, man, this is totally screwed.

I take a deep breath, click my sticks together. "One, two, three, four."

I come down hard on my snare, launching Matt into the opening blast of guitar. We do three bars and then Helen leaps in with a perfectly-pitched knock-you-on-your-ass rock-and-roll scream.

It's so intense I nearly fall off my drum stool. Matt, Sean, and me look at each other like, "Where the hell did that come from?"

Then she starts singing the lyrics. And she's not only good, she's totally freakin' amazing. Her voice is beautiful and powerful and . . . Holy crap. I can't believe my ears.

Or my eyes. Because she's strutting around like she just got off tour with The Rolling Stones. Talk about attitude. Jesus Christ. This is not a woman you would want to cross. I don't even recognize her.

Helen saunters over to Matt, leaning in and singing to him that everything is going to be all right, all right, all right. And I get the strangest pang of jealousy in my chest. Wanting her desperately to come over and sing that to me.

Dad stands in the corner, his arms crossed. With the biggest shit-eating grin on his face I've ever seen. He's hearing exactly what I'm hearing. Our band suddenly sounds exponentially better. For no other reason than that Helen's voice is so damn good. It's like adding Wayne Gretzky to your beer league hockey team. Doesn't matter that the rest of you are tripping over your skates. Wayne's going backhand top shelf every time.

Helen spins the microphone around in fast circles on its cord, catching it in her hand just as the music ends.

I'm in a haze of confusion as the last crash of the cymbals dies out. If this were an alternate universe—one where Helen wasn't roundly despised by everyone at school—I'd be jumping for joy. She sounds great. She looks great. She's exactly what our "alternate-reality" band needs.

But since this is the *real* world we're talking about—where this band is supposed to *save* me from her corrosive reputation—I'm feeling like I want to scream.

Dad claps ecstatically as he walks over to us. "Now *that's* what I'm talking about. Finally we sound like we've got a pair."

Put a stop to this, dude. Before it's too late.

Helen laughs, out of breath. "That was fun," she says, her face glowing.

"Wow," Sean says. "You were totally stagg."

"Amazing," Matt adds. "You should go on *American Idol.*"

"It's been so long since I sang anything." Helen looks at me shyly. "I didn't know I could still do it."

"That was . . . insane," I say, a swirl of emotions filling my chest—awe and anger, annoyance and elation, attraction and repulsion—all at the same time. "You're incredible."

She smiles. "Thanks."

"I'd put it to a vote," Dad starts.

I open my mouth to protest but my throat is plugged with the thick stew of feelings roiling around inside me.

"But frankly, I don't give a tiger's tit what these chucklenuts think," he finishes. "You're hired."

"Dad!" I say. At least I think I say it. But no one is paying any attention to me.

"Oh, I don't know." Helen's beaming. "Are you sure? I mean it was really fun, but . . . Are you sure?"

"Surer than sure." Dad turns to us and glares. "And if anyone has a problem with it, they can take it up with my hairy ass."

Sean and Matt are all, "Yeah, of course," and "Absolutely. Are you kidding me?" while I sit on my drum stool, completely stunned.

How can they just stand there and agree to this? Can't they see what an absolute, complete nightmare this is going to be?

My heart beats hard in the center of my skull. A cold sweat blankets my entire body.

There will be no running of the bases, I can tell you that. This is not just a rain delay. It's a freakin' nuclear missile dropped right in the center of my baseball stadium.

CHAPTER THIRTY-SIX

UNWELL

I CAN'T BELIEVE OUR BAD LUCK," I say, jostling through the bodies in the crowded hallway. "Why did she have to be any good?"

"Tell me about it," Sean replies. "Now Helen's going to be the one who gets all the hottest babes."

I look at him sideways.

"And to top it all off," Sean continues, "I just found out Tianna's got a new boyfriend."

"Let it die, dude. We have *way* bigger problems on our hands here."

"But it means she lied to me when she said she wasn't ready to be in a relationship."

"Which is just another one of the *thousand* reasons you should be glad you're not together anymore."

"Yeah, I guess." He shrugs. "On the upside, Helen *is* an amazing singer. Which makes *us* look that much better.

Did you know she was in *Grease* in eighth grade? I looked it up in our junior high yearbook. I knew she had to have done *something* before."

"Yeah, well, I don't care if she was on Broadway," I say. "We have to find somebody else."

"Why? At least she gives us a chance to win. Which would mean that many more groupies."

"Don't you get it? We're not going to win. Because the boos are going to be so loud no one will hear us. Having her in the band defeats the whole point of being in the Battle of the Bands in the first place. We are *not* going to look cool with Helen Harriwick fronting us."

"What if we put together a persona for her?" Sean says. "Like a bank robber or something? She can wear a ski mask and nobody'll know it's her."

"Never mind," I say. "I'll figure something out." He doesn't get it. No one does. When I tried to explain to Dad how bad this was going to look for me, he just laughed and said there was no *I* in *band*.

The first bell rings, and Sean glances at his watch. "Dang. I've got to get to English. Ms. Murkin makes us read love poems in front of the entire class when we're late. I'll catch you in Health." He trots off down the hall and disappears around the corner.

"Woof, woof, woof, woof, woof!" a voice barks up behind me.

Before I can turn around to see who it is, my History textbook is batted out of my hand. It skitters across the floor, the papers I had tucked inside fluttering in the air like giant moths.

Dean Scragliano and Frank Hurkle tear past me, laughing like hyenas. They kick the book back and forth like they're playing in the FIFA World Cup.

"Goddamn it."

Sniggers and whispers fill the corridor as a prickling heat dances up my neck.

I pluck up the trail of papers that leads to my textbook, which is splayed open in a classroom doorway. It's in sad shape. Several of the pages are accordioned, and the cover is scratched to hell. Mr. Chumley's going to have a panda when he sees what I've done to his brand-new History book.

I rub the cover on my pant leg to clean off some of the dirt.

"What do we have here?" a girl's voice says as the loose papers are snatched from my hand.

I turn to see Bronte rifling through the pages and am momentarily spellbound by the tight white sweater she's wearing that hints at her lacy bra underneath. Then, like a fist to the face, it hits me that the Our Lady of Mercy form is somewhere within that stack.

"It's just garbage," I say, lunging for my papers.

Bronte dodges my hand and laughs. "Must be something pretty juicy if you want them back so badly. Love notes, perhaps?"

"Just give them to me. I'm late for class."

"Ah-ha!" Bronte shouts, waving the application and letting all the other papers drift to the floor. "I had a feeling there was something good in here. I'm psychic, you know." She winks at me, then looks over her shoulder and calls out, "Prudence! Come here. Look who's been holding out on us."

Prudence saunters over to us, looking fairly bored. "What's going on?"

Bronte triumphantly hands the application over to Prudence.

She flips through the form. "I thought you said you weren't done with this. This looks pretty complete to me."

"I just finished it over the weekend," I say, my palms starting to sweat. "But—"

"But what?" Prudence studies me.

"I still need to confirm a few things." Part of me feels like grabbing the papers and hightailing it down the hall but instead I just stand there. I don't want them to think I'm not still on board with the plan. Because I am. I'm just—well—I don't know *what* I am anymore. Life was so much simpler when I didn't have all these stupid "feelings" to contend with.

"Wow. You even got her mother's signature." Prudence grins like a cat with a cup of cream. "Pretty impressive, Coop." She chortles as she folds the papers up and places them in her purse. "Can you imagine the look on Helen's face when she gets her acceptance letter in the mail? Absolutely supreme."

"All she'll need is that one final"— Bronte makes a little shoving gesture—"*push* over the edge, and she'll be gone, baby, gone."

Bronte and Prudence bump fists, exploding their nugs on impact as they crack up.

I force a laugh, but inside I feel seasick. Like the whole world is canting.

Why, though? What's the problem here? If Helen transferred schools it would solve all of my problems. It's want I want. Isn't it?

Of course it is, you idiot. Do not let whatever evil seed Helen has planted in your brain cloud your logic. Maybe she's hot. And maybe she's funny. And maybe she's cooler than people think. But . . . that's the thing. None of it matters. Because perception is the key here. You can never forget that.

Oh, God, I'm losing my mind. Can you go insane at sixteen?

"That's the question, isn't it?" Prudence says.

"Huh?" I stare at her, wondering if she can hear my thoughts.

"What's the straw that'll break the Hot Dog's back?" Prudence peers at me. "You've spent quite a bit of time with her lately—"

"Not that much."

"More than the rest of us," Prudence says. "What have you learned about her? Something we can exploit. A weakness? Her biggest fear?"

My gut grips up. "I have no idea. I don't know her that well. All we've done is work on the project." I glance over my shoulder. "Look. I have to get going."

Bronte takes a step closer, boxing me in. "You seem nervous. Something wrong?"

"No. Nothing's wrong. I'm just . . . late for class."

"Oh, come on, Coopee." Prudence leans in and whispers in my ear. "Don't go yet. Just think for a sec. What would rock the Sausage Queen to her core?"

Her warm breath spreads out over my cheek, nearly making me swoon. "I- I don't know. I mean, people have been tormenting her forever and she still hasn't switched schools."

Prudence nods. "You're right. It has to be something big. So big she can't ignore it as just another prank."

"It should be public," Bronte adds. "To make it that much more humiliating."

Suddenly Prudence squeals with excitement. "Oh, my God. I've got it! I am *so* good."

"What?" Bronte smiles.

"Yeah, what?" I ask, my throat dry.

"Well . . ." Prudence stops herself. She looks at me sideways. "Actually. Now that I think about it. I'm not sure Coopee should know about it." She turns to Bronte. "He might try to put a stop to it."

"What?" I say, feeling like I've just been smacked. "That's ridic. Why would I do that?"

Bronte studies me. "Yeah, he'd probably leap in and try to save her at the last minute."

"What the hell are you talking about? I would not."

"Oh, be honest," Prudence teases. "You've developed a soft spot for the Hot Dog, haven't you?

Bronte laughs. "It's only natural. With you spending so much time with her and all. It's like Stockholm syndrome or something."

"I *haven't* spent that much time with her. And I haven't developed anything."

Prudence and Bronte crack up at this.

"Relax, Coopee." Prudence smiles and grabs my arm. "We're going to take care of this one on our own. It'll be painful for her. Like ripping a few hundred Band-Aids off her hairy arm. But it's the right thing to do. In the end, everyone will be happier for it."

The girls turn and head off down the hall, laughing and whispering to each other as they go. I stand there and watch them turn the corner, annoyed that they wouldn't tell me what they have planned for Helen.

But also glad that they didn't. Because there's a part of me that's worried for her. Even though I know leaving the school would probably be the best thing that ever happened to her. Not to mention how much it will help me and my sitch.

Still. I hope it's not something too, too awful.

CHAPTER THIRTY-SEVEN

(I CAN'T GET NO) SATISFACTION

ARE YOU OKAY, COOP?" Helen asks. "You look exhausted."

I pull my hands down my face, feeling totally drained. "Chorus people are brutal."

She clicks a link on the library computer. "I didn't know you were in chorus."

"I'm not. Forget it. It doesn't matter." I gesture at the screen. "Let's just get the stupid contraceptive statistics and get out of here."

Who knew it was possible to ask sixty different people the same question and get the exact same response every time? It's taken me two weeks to get through everyone in the school chorus, but it wasn't until I crossed the last five people off my list today that I lost all hope of finding a new singer for our band.

"Okay, write this down," Helen says. *"Teenage girls who are sexually active and avoid using any type of contraception have a ninety percent chance of becoming pregnant within a year."*

I scribble down this statistic in my notebook, though I'm not sure I get everything exactly right as my mind is spinning like a pinwheel in a hurricane.

My only chance now is that Helen gets her acceptance letter quickly and decides to transfer to Our Lady of Mercy before the end of the semester. Then Sean can go back to being our singer and we can still attain—if not full-on rock-god fame—then at least demigod status.

Helen reads, *"Forty-eight percent of all new STD cases each year will occur among people age fifteen- to twenty-four."*

And being a rock-and-roll demigod is certainly good enough to get a nice sampling of groupies who'd be willing to do some base running.

Helen scrolls down the screen. *"Nearly fifty percent of all Americans age fifteen to nineteen have had sex at least one time."*

I copy this down, wishing that I was one of the lucky forty-six percent. Thinking about how my plan of joining the more fortunate half of the population by year's end is in serious danger of being completely demolished. Wondering why Helen talking about contraception, pregnancy, and STDs is turning me on so much.

"Most teen pregnancies—over eighty percent—are unplanned," Helen continues.

I hate to admit it—and I never would to anyone—but the fact that Helen's such an incredible singer is just adding to my confused state of mind. It's like she's got this inner fire that comes blasting out when she sings that leaves me shifting on my drum stool with a colossal stalagmite in my shorts.

"Twenty-five percent of teen females and eighteen percent of teen males won't use any kind of protection the first time they have sex," Helen reads.

Though maybe it's not her singing at all. Because all she's doing now is talking and it's having the exact same effect on me.

"Cooper? Why aren't you writing this down?" Helen's deep hazel eyes are fixed on me.

I blink. Close my mouth which, apparently, has been hanging open. I look down at my pen hovering ineffectually over the nearly empty notebook page.

"I . . . um . . . got distracted. Sorry. I was thinking about something." *Come on, Coop. You can do better than that. Unless, of course, you want to tell her what's really on your mind.* "Your mother," I say, which wilts my wang like salt on a slug. "I was just . . . wondering how she was feeling. You know. If she was still stressed. And on stress leave. You know, Sean and her have already done several World of Warcraft quests together. He says she's pretty good."

Helen looks away. Her neck flushes. "Listen, I wasn't totally honest with you, Coop. About my mom. She's not on stress leave. She's on disability. She hasn't worked in over a year."

"Oh," I say, feeling like the biggest A-hole on the planet for bringing up her disabled mother in order to bail me out of an awkward situation.

"She has Lyme disease."

The question forms in my head, though I stop myself from actually asking it.

"It's a bacteria that affects your nervous system," Helen says, reading my mind. "It makes her dizzy and tired and shaky. A lot of the time she'll get bad headaches." Helen grabs the mouse and starts scrolling down the screen again. "It's not like she's going to die or anything. You just can't clean people's teeth very well when you feel like that."

"Huh," I say. "I'm sorry."

Way to go, Coop old buddy. You tricked a sickly woman into signing an application form for her tormented daughter. How do you feel about yourself now? What's next? Signing up to hunt baby seals?

Helen looks at me funny. "What?"

"What what?" I say, feeling like I might fall off my chair.

"All the color just drained from your face."

"Did it?" My voice squeaks. I clear my throat. "Did it?" I repeat in a lower register. "I guess . . . I haven't been sleeping very well lately." *Sure, go ahead. Shovel the lies on. Who cares that you've been sleeping like a near-dead dog on NyQuil? What's it matter now?* "I mean . . . It's everything, really. The band, and this project, and my dad being out of work. I guess it's all catching up with me." I rub my eyes. "Would you mind if I just copied down the URL and took these notes at home? I think I need to get some rest."

Of course, what I *really* need to do is to sort this whole mess out. And get my priorities straight. Oh, God, I sound like Mr. Tard every time I get sent down to his office.

But in this particular case it applies. I need to get clear. And stay focused on the goal: Hitting a home run with the babes this year. Preferably with Prudence. Or Gina. Or Kelly. Or Bronte. Or all four of them at once.

Everything else is just fogging the issue. I have to get back on course. Remove Helen from the situation. When that's done, everything else will fall into place.

I can't let anything distract me from that one simple fact.

CHAPTER THIRTY-EIGHT

I HEARD IT THROUGH THE GRAPEVINE

I LIE IN BED TRYING DESPERATELY not to think about Helen, but doing a piss-poor job of it.

My brain is no longer under my control. No matter how hard I attempt to imagine Prudence dancing around in see-through underwear, Gina and Kelly hot-oil wrestling, or stumbling upon Bronte's secret Internet porn site—all my mind wants to do is picture Helen.

And not even naked.

Just smiling. And laughing. And singing in our band.

What the hell's *that* about?

Whatever. It doesn't matter. Stay clear. Stay focused. Once she's accepted to Our Lady of Mercy and decides to go, she won't even be eligible to sing in the band. And that's the best of all possible scenarios.

Is that really true?

Yes, of course it's true. Jeez. Why wouldn't it be true?

But isn't there a flicker of—

No! There's no flicker of anything! Just shut the hell up!

I'm busy wrestling with my stupid brain, trying to smother my rogue thoughts with the pillow of logic, when my cell phone rings. I reach over and grab it from the nightstand. It's Sean.

"'Sup?" I say.

"Turn on your computer," Sean tells me, his tone urgent. "Go to the iTunes store. Right now."

"What? Why?"

"Just do it."

I groan as I swing my feet off the bed and slog over to my desk. Wake my laptop from its slumber and wait for the wireless to connect.

"You want to give me a clue here, dude?" I ask.

"Are you on iTunes yet?" he says.

"Working on it. Hold on." I click on the iTunes icon and watch it bounce. "This better not be you wanting me to hear the latest Michael Bublé 'masterpiece' again."

"Look at the banner. What do you see?"

"Lady Gaga's got a new album out. I'm absolutely stoked."

"Wait for it to change."

I wait. The banner shifts. And I can't say I'm not surprised.

"50 Cent's doing a Christmas album? That's a little bizarre, dude, but is it worth making a phone call for?"

Sean sighs loudly. "It's coming up next."

"Why don't you just tell—"

The banner turns again, and what I see makes me jerk back.

"Uh-oh," I say. "It can't be." I laugh nervously. "Do you think it could be the same—"

"Yes," Sean answers. "It's Understain. The Canadian band no one's ever heard of before. Go ahead. Listen to their first single. 'Grind the Rump Roast.'"

"Wow. That's crazy." My pulse quickens. My temples throb. "I must have listened to a thousand different bands. What are the odds?"

"You said they were unsigned."

"They *were*. Two months ago. At least according to their MySpace page. Maybe they don't update it. How the hell should I know?"

"What are we supposed to do now? I heard Mr. Tard suspended those three seniors—the ones who handed in that fake demo—for a month." Sean's tone is getting more and more panicky. "Someone in the music department's going to figure out we jacked our songs. We have to confess. Maybe they'll let us off easier if we do."

"No way," I say. "You never confess. To anything. Ever. Look, there are hundreds of thousands of bands on iTunes. And millions of songs. What are the chances they'll see this particular one?"

"It's called 'Grind the Rump Roast' for Christ's sake. Someone's bound to spot it."

"All right. Take a pill. Let me think." I stand and start to pace. Breathe deep. Run my hand through my hair. "Okay. Okay. I've got it. Here's what we're going to do."

CHAPTER THIRTY-NINE

I WANT YOU BACK

LEAVE THE TALKING TO ME," I say, as Matt, Sean, and me head toward Mr. Grossman's office before the first bell. "But while we're in there, you guys scout out his shelves. See if you can spot the demo. Just in case he decides to be difficult and we have to sneak in later and steal it."

We enter the chorus room and head toward the music offices.

Mr. Grossman is sitting at his desk reading the newspaper and drinking tea.

"Knock, knock," I say, sticking my head inside.

He looks up from his paper and sighs. "You're interrupting my 'me' time. This better be important."

The three of us step inside his mess of an office. Books, magazines, and a trillion CDs stacked up everywhere. Spilling out of every shelf of the floor-to-ceiling bookcases. I thought *I* was into music. We better hope to hell he hands over the demo because there's no way we're going to find it in here ourselves. I can tell by the look in Matt's and Sean's eyes that they're thinking the exact same thing.

"We need our Battle of the Bands demo back," I say.

"Is that so?" Mr. Grossman asks. "And why is that, pray tell?"

"My computer's hard drive died. So now you've got the only copy. There are a few places around town who are interested in us playing some gigs. But they wanted to hear something first."

"Yeah," Sean adds, for no reason.

"I'm afraid we don't return demos," Mr. Grossman says. "It states that specifically in the entry form you filled out and signed. Sorry." He lifts his newspaper as if that's the end of the discussion.

"We know about that," I say. "We were just hoping you might make an exception in this case."

Mr. Grossman lowers his newspaper again. "And why would I do that?"

"Because of what I told you. My hard drive—"

"Yes, yes. You said that already. But I don't understand. Why not just make another demo? Your band is rehearsing, is it not?" He glares at Matt and Sean accusingly. "Just record one of your rehearsals."

"Yeah, we could, I guess," I say. "But the demo *you* have was recorded in a studio. That we rented. And we don't have the money to do that again."

Sean and Matt nod their heads in agreement.

Mr. Grossman folds up his paper and places it to one side. "Do you have any idea *why* we hold on to the demos?" He addresses his question to Sean, who just shakes his head. "Well," he tents his fingers, "in the past, we've had some *issues*."

I can feel Matt's and Sean's rising panic. "Issues?" I say.

"Perhaps you're aware that we've already suspended a group of students for submitting a demo that was not, shall we say, thoroughly authentic. It might surprise you to learn that this is not the first time something like this has occurred."

"Seriously?" I lace my voice with what I hope is genuine indignation.

"And because of this," Mr. Grossman goes on, "prior to the competition, the judges listen to the CDs for a second time. Then, if there are any glaring discrepancies between the band's performance and what has been presented to us on the demos, we can take appropriate action."

Sean gulps but I pretend he didn't. Have to keep a calm front.

"That's chill," I say. "So, we'll just borrow the demo, make a copy, then return it to you first thing tomorrow."

Mr. Grossman exhales heavily and waves his hands around. "Never mind." He pulls out one of his desk drawers, rummages around, and removes our demo. "Here. Take it."

I look over at Matt and Sean, then reach out and slide the CD from Mr. Grossman's fingers. Talk about easy. "Thanks."

"Think nothing of it," he says.

I hold the CD up. "We'll get this back to you then. In a couple of days?"

"Don't trouble yourself." Mr. Grossman sips his tea. "Mrs. Ward, Mr. Blonsky, and Ms. Hosie all have duplicates. I'll just send one of theirs down to AV."

CHAPTER FORTY

STRAWBERRY FIELDS FOREVER

STICK A MEAT THERMOMETER up our butts," Sean says, all twitchy. " 'Cause we're done."

"First of all, dude, don't ever say that again." Christ. He hasn't shut up about the demo all morning. "Second of all, I'll figure it out."

I open the door to SaveMore Drugs and usher my buds inside. I've convinced the guys to come to the drugstore with me during lunch so we can pick up a few things I think will help pimp our rock-and-roll image: teeth whitener, tanning spray, hair color, hair gel, aftershave. I had to sell one of my iPods and a whole whack of old comics to raise the cash for all this stuff, but it's important we look our very best for performance night.

And while we're at it, I fig I can grab some of the contraceptives I promised to get for the Health project.

Sean's jaw pulses as we cruise the aisles. "I seriously think Mr. Grossman knows."

"He doesn't know," I say. "If he knew he would have called us out right there."

"Here's the teeth whitener," Matt says, pointing to a shelf.

"Later." I stride right by the oral hygiene racks and turn down the next aisle to find the Family Planning section. I stop and stand before a giant wall of colorful condom boxes, tubes of lubricants, and pregnancy tests.

"What are you doing?" Sean asks. "I thought you said we came for grooming products?"

"I need to get a few things for my Health project first."

"You didn't say anything about that." His eyes dart around like mad. "Someone's going to see us. What if my grandma comes in? Or Father Hurley?"

"No one's going to see us."

"But what if they do?"

"They'll think you're a responsible dude. I'll only be a second." To be honest, I figured I'd have the same anxious reaction as Sean when we got here. But now that he's acting all Chicken Little, it kind of makes me want to torture him a bit by dragging this out.

"What exactly do you need?" Matt says, more nonchalantly than I'd expect. Maybe he really has run the bases with Val.

"Let's do condoms first."

"Here." Sean quickly grabs a box of condoms off the

shelf. "What about these? Made from . . ." he reads the box, "real lambskin." He cringes. "Ew. Sick. That's like one step away from having sex with a lamb."

"You'd know better than me." I snatch the box from him and toss it into my shopping basket. "Isn't that why you were banned from the petting zoo?"

"That's not even funny." Sean screws up his face. "People actually do that kind of thing and—"

"You have all their Web sites bookmarked? Boo ya!" I give Matt a fist bump.

"Noooo. And even if I did . . . it's only because . . . your mother . . . e-mailed me the links." Sean blinks hard. "Because she's . . . into that sort of thing. With animals . . . and people . . . together. Doing stuff."

"Good one, Sean," I say as I reach over to the shelf, grab a Family Pack of Leviathans, and throw them in the basket. Odd that they call it a Family Pack when that's exactly what they're meant to prevent.

Matt stares down at the carton. "Those are for 'the extra-large man.' "

"Right," I say, dropping my voice an octave. "Might as well get some that I can use for when we win the Battle of the Bands, because the groupies are going to be swarming the stage."

"You probably want the fun size then." Matt grabs a random multi-colored box of condoms off the shelf and waves it in my face. "For your pygmy schwang."

"What's that, Matt Gratton?" I announce loudly. "You have a pygmy schwang? That's very brave of you to admit. Most guys would keep that to themselves."

Matt flings the box of condoms at me. It hits my chest and drops into the basket.

"Nice shot," I say.

Once we've grabbed a few other products—a bottle of lube, a Today sponge, a tube of spermicide, contraceptive foam, more condoms—we head over to the grooming supplies to finish up our shopping, then up toward the cashier.

"Are you going to be able to afford all of this?" Matt asks.

"Yeah. Of course. I've got a hundred and twenty bucks."

I look down at the mound of contraceptives in my basket. I'm trying to act all caszh but the closer we get to the cash registers the sweatier I start to feel. "We have to split this stuff up," I say, stopping at the end of the aisle. "It'll look too weird if I'm buying it all by myself."

Sean backs away. "I don't *think* so. This was your idea."

"I'll give you the money," I say.

"That's not what I'm talking about," Sean says. "I'm not about to go up there and have somebody see me buy all this . . . crap. They'll think I'm some kind of perv."

"I'm not asking you to buy a giant purple dildo, Sean. Grow up. People use this stuff to have safe sex."

"*Sex.* Exactly. And that's what the cashier will be picturing me doing as she rings it up."

"Well, then, go to a guy cashier. He'll think you're a player."

"Right. Unless he knows my sister," Sean says. "And then he'll tell her, and the whole world will find out. No. I'm not doing it. I'll buy the grooming stuff if you want. But none of the other things."

"You're a real pal." I turn to Matt. "What about you?"

Matt shrugs. "Sure. Fine." He shifts his weight. "But give me a mix of things. And we should probably grab some . . ."—Matt scans the endcap filled with school supplies—"notebooks. And pens. And highlighters." He pulls them from the shelves and chucks them into the basket. "So it's a jumble of stuff, instead of a never-ending line of sex products."

I nab two more baskets from the front of the store and return to Matt and Sean to separate the items. Sean gets most of the grooming products. Except for a bottle of lube, which I hide amidst the tanning sprays and teeth whitener, just because I can't resist. Then I split up the money—forty dollars each—and we hit three separate cash registers.

I head over to an ancient liver-spotted dude with an eye patch and glasses, in hopes that he won't be able to make out the things I'm buying. Matt goes the young-guy-maybe-he'll-think-I'm-a-stud route.

And Sean casually strolls over to the till being manned by somebody's grandmother because he has nothing to worry about. Or so he thinks.

I've got an anxious thrumming in my gut as I begin to place the items on the counter. Praying no one steps up behind me in line. I was busting on Sean for being such a pussy, but I have to say, I've never been so uncomfortable in my entire life.

My strategy is simple. Hair color first, followed by a couple of condom three-packs hidden under a package of pens, then a tube of spermicide and a can of contraceptive foam camouflaged nicely by a notebook and some aftershave.

"Nice weather we're having, huh?" the old guy says as he starts ringing up my stuff.

"Yeah, it's great," I answer. Oh, God, I hope I didn't land the chatty cashier. I need this to go fast and smooth.

I avert my eyes, employing the if-I-can't-see-him-he-can't-see-me technique. I pretend to be captivated by the check-out stand magazines. Well, well, look who has cellulite. Mm, wow, celebrities without makeup. They look so different. "Marry Me!" says Britney.

"So, big plans for this weekend?" the guy asks, scanning and bagging my items.

My eyes flick over to him, then dart back to the magazines. "What?"

"I was inquiring about your weekend plans. Doing anything exciting?"

I glance at the pack of multicolored condoms he's holding and feel my chest tighten. "Um. No."

He scans the item and places it in the bag with the rest of the stuff. "Weatherman says Indian summer. Which means the wife'll want me to do some serious humping on Saturday."

I blink. Not sure I've heard him correctly. "I'm sorry. What?" Christ. Why is he telling me this? Just because I'm buying condoms doesn't mean I need to hear about his exploits.

"It's not like I mind it." He scans the contraceptive foam. The notebook. The aftershave. "It's just, there are other things I'd rather be doing on a sunny day, right? Instead of having to lug all the garbage down to the junkyard."

"Oh. Right," I say. *That* kind of humping. It takes me a moment to supplant the image of this old dude going primal on his wife with the one of him lugging trash, but thankfully, my twisted mind obliges me.

"Hey, Ernie!" It's the old lady who's ringing up Sean. She's looking over at us and waving the red bottle of lube I snuck into Sean's basket. "Do you know how much the SlideRight Sensuous-Strawberry Personal Stimu-Lube is?"

Sean's face goes pale. His eyes wide with horror. He's shaking his head no and moving his lips, but no words are coming out.

"What?" Ernie says, cupping his ear with his hand.

"SlideRight Sensuous-Strawberry Personal Stimu-Lube!" the grandmotherly woman shouts. "Do you know the price?"

Ernie scrunches up his nose. "What is it?"

"It's sexual lubricant. Flavored. This kid wants to buy it. And it's not giving me a price."

Ernie throws his hands in the air. "I have no idea. Call Martin." He punches in some numbers on the register and squints at the screen with his one eye. "Thirty-eight seventy-three."

I look over at Matt, who is standing by the front door holding a plastic bag, shaking with suppressed laughter.

I hand two twenties to Ernie and watch as Sean tries to reach over the counter and grab the bottle of lube from the old lady. But she's turned away and already has the intercom phone to her ear.

There's a *beep-beep* over the store speaker, followed by the old lady's nasal voice calling out, "Martin. Can you get me a price on SlideRight Sensuous-Strawberry Personal Stimu-Lube? The four-ounce bottle?"

"No, no, no," Sean says.

I get my change, grab my purchases, and head over to Matt so we can watch the show together.

"I thought you only gave him grooming products," Matt says, laughing.

"I slipped him one thing," I say. "I thought for sure he'd spot it before it got rung up."

There's another *beep-beep* over the intercom. "Say

again?" a man's voice calls over the loudspeaker.

Sean's waving his hands frantically. "It's okay. It's fine. Never mind. I don't want it. I don't want it."

"Don't worry, honey," the old lady says. "It'll just be a second. We've got to get it into the computer anyway. I'll be right back." She steps from behind the counter and walks off toward customer service.

"All right," I say. "I guess we better go save him."

Me and Matt hurry over to Sean, who looks like he might blow a gasket.

"I'm going to kill you," Sean says to me through clenched teeth.

"Oh, come on." I laugh. "You have to admit. That was pretty funny. Just leave the cash and lets get out of here." I snatch the two twenties from his hand and toss it on the counter.

Matt grabs the bag of goods, I grab Sean's arm, and the three of us hightail it out of there.

Me and Matt hold ourselves together heroically as we hit the streets.

Until we both glance at Sean's scowling, something-stinks expression.

And then we're cracking up all over again.

CHAPTER FORTY-ONE

CHANCES

NO OFFENSE, DUDE," Matt says, his hair matted with sweat. "But don't you think your dad's maybe taking this band thing a little too seriously?"

"That was sick how many times he made us play 'Paint It Black.'" Sean flexes his fingers.

We're hanging in my room following our four-hour after-dinner rehearsal. The guys agreed to stay over again to get in some extra band practice. I tried to come up with a caszh way of inviting Helen to stay over, you know, just because. I had the whole scenario worked out in my head. Her lack of pajamas. Her need to borrow one of my T-shirts. Me explaining how there was plenty of room for both of us in my bed.

But the thought of someone from school seeing her leaving my house in the wee hours of the morning was all it took to kill that fantasy.

And honestly, she's not the one who needs to put in the extra work.

"We only have a few more weeks and he wants us to be good," I say, but even I can't believe how crazed Dad's getting. I tried talking to Mom about it but she says that he's just going through a phase. That it's the happiest she's seen him in a long time and she's willing to put up with the facial hair and silly clothes until Dad gets back on his feet with work. "Anyway," I continue, "we have something much more important to deal with right now."

"Sleep?" Matt says, collapsing on his sleeping bag.

"No." I move to my closet and take out the loot from the drugstore. "We're going to test out our rock-and-roll images. This way, if anything doesn't work, we'll have time to tweak our looks before the performance."

"Cool." Sean grabs the bag from my hand and looks inside. "I was wondering when we were going to get to use this stuff."

"Aw, man." Matt drops his head on his pillow. "Can't we do it some other time? I'm wiped."

"Don't be a tool bag." I grab his arm and pull him up. "You'll thank me when you see how kick-ass you look."

"You keep saying how I'm always going to thank you, but I never do."

"I know. You ungrateful bastard."

Matt laughs. "That's not really what I meant."

"What should we start with first?" Sean says, separating the grooming products from the contraceptives and tossing them on my bed. "Hair dye? Teeth whitening? Spray tan?"

"We're not doing it here." I collect up the various boxes, bottles, and tubes and chuck them all back into the bag. "We need access to water and towels."

The three of us retreat to the bathroom. I lock the door behind us so we won't be interrupted.

"Dude," Matt says. "Isn't it going to seem weird, all of us in the bathroom at the same time?"

"Relax, dawg." I clap him on the shoulder. "If anyone comes to the door, I'll just tell them we're giving you a bikini wax."

Sean cracks up. Matt just glowers.

"Everyone's asleep," I assure him. "No one'll even know we were in here. I promise." I take the hair dyes out and line them up on the counter. "Each of us has to choose a color. Since this is my brill idea, I get to pick first. And I want . . . green." I snatch up the green hair dye. "Because it's Pimp Daddylicious."

"What color do you want?" Sean asks Matt.

"I don't care." Matt shrugs. "Purple, I guess."

"Muy bueno." Sean grins. "*Rojo es el color del fuego!* And *El Mariachi* has a fiery passion like no other." He does his bullfighter prance, complete with concluding foot stomp.

Matt stares at him. "Please tell me you're not going to do that on stage."

"Si!" Sean waggles his eyebrow. "If dee mood strikes *El Mariachi.*" He laughs. "I knew my sixth-grade Spanish class would come in handy."

We shuck down to our boxers and wash our hair before attacking the packages of hair dye.

"Shouldn't we read the instructions first?" Sean asks, examining the miniature manual.

"Instructions are for pussies." I snatch the little booklet from his hand and toss it in the trash. "Obviously, we just slather all this crap on our heads and let it sit overnight. What could be simpler?"

I dive in first, squeezing the tubes of goop into my palm and scrubbing it all onto my scalp. Once Matt and Sean see how easy it is, they follow suit. We wrap the white bathroom towels around our heads and move on to the tanning products.

"I wasn't sure which brand to buy so I got three different kinds," I say.

"Which do you think will look most natural?" Matt finally seems to be getting into the spirit of things. He reads the label on each bottle. "BronzedGod? Tan-tastic? Or Natural spRays?"

Sean studies the containers. "I'm doing all of them. Us Latin lovers need to be tall, dark, and handsome."

"We got the dark part covered." I rustle through the

bag. "But I don't think we purchased any handsome lotion or Miracle-Gro."

"I don't need any lotions or potions." Sean places his hand on his chest. "I happen to have been told, on more than one occasion, that I am unconventionally good-looking."

"By who, dude?" I laugh. "Your mom? That just means you're butt ugly."

"And," he adds, "as far as my height goes, I'm sure you didn't notice, but I had a growth spurt this summer."

"Eww," Matt says. "I hope you cleaned it up."

"Screw you, yankcheese." Sean grabs one of bottles. "All right. Who's gonna spray me down?"

"That's what she said," I cough through my fist.

Matt laughs and takes the spray bottle from Sean. "I'll do it. Close your eyes."

We take turns basting each other with the various tanning sprays. Spinning around to make sure we get an even coat. By the time we're finished with all three products, a thick brown fog clouds the bathroom.

We cap off the evening by doing rock-paper-scissors for the three different teeth whiteners. I get the brush-on, Matt gets the strips, and Sean gets the mouth trays. We decide to leave these on overnight as well. Because, why not? You're teeth can't ever be too white.

It's three thirty in the morning by the time we stumble into my room in boxers and turbans.

Matt's passed out and snoring before I even get the light off.

"Dis bedda wak," Sean lisps through his mouth trays. "I feewl awl sdiggy."

"Don't worry," I say, settling into bed. "Tomorrow, you won't even recognize yourself."

CHAPTER FORTY-TWO

FLUORESCENT ADOLESCENT

ALL NIGHT LONG I HAVE DREAMS of being asked to model for the cover of *GQ* and *Esquire*. My agent can't handle the mounting requests and has to hire another assistant just to screen the calls.

As I walk down the street, swimsuit models attempt to tear the fur coat from my bronzed bod. Several babes in wet T-shirts yank at my purple Stetson to try and run their fingers through my emerald locks.

They're all shouting, "Cooper!" "Cooper Redmond!" "Cooper James Redmond!"

The yelling is so loud it actually jolts me from sleep.

"Cooperrrr! Bathroom! *Now!*" That's not the voice of any swimsuit model. It's Mom. And she sounds pissed.

I turn my head on the pillow. Squint at the digital clock on the bedside table, trying to focus my groggy eyes. 10:35. Jesus. What's going on? It's the weekend.

At least . . . I think it is.

Ew, my mouth tastes funny. What the hell are all these white marks on my pillowcase? I must have drooled like a basset hound last night.

"Don't make me have to come into your room!" Mom hollers.

Ugh.

I drag myself out of bed, still half-zonked and punch-drunk. Step over a couple of lumps on the floor and stumble out into the hallway wearing my sagging boxer briefs. Something slides off my head. A towel? Did I take a shower last night? Hard to think. I'm running on reserve power right now. All the switches have yet to be flicked on in my brain.

I wipe the sleep-crud from the corners of my eyes as I trudge into the bathroom. "What?" I groan.

"That's what *I'd* like to know," Mom says, gesturing angrily at our fluorescent-lit surroundings. "*What* are these brown streaks all over the walls? And the floor? And on the counter? And my brand new white towels?"

Whoa. She's right. There are rust-colored smears all over the place. "How should I know?" I say. "Maybe Angela had the goose-gravy splatters last night."

"Angela stayed over at her frien—Oh. My. God." Mom's staring at me with these big wide holy-crap eyes. "What have you done to yourself?"

"Nothing." I scratch my head to try and wake up a bit more. My hair feels weird. Thick. And gluey.

"Your skin. Cooper, it's orange!" she says. "And your hair. Is green! And your teeth! Good Lord!"

It hits me like a rogue wave.

My rock-and-roll image.

I turn to look at myself in the mirror. For a split second I'm confused. Who the hell is that?

"Oh, crap," I say, lurching back.

"What's going on?" Sean grumbles as he staggers into the bathroom, his eyes half-shut, plaid boxers pulled up near to his belly button. Sean's hair and forehead are fluorescent pink and his body is a bright pumpkin color.

Matt steps up behind Sean with a Day-Glo purple mop, a carroty complexion, and a blinding white grill. "We heard someone yelling," he rasps.

Mom has been stunned into silence.

Sean's eyes shoot open when he catches sight of me. He starts laughing. "Whoa, dude."

Matt starts cracking up, too. "The Oompa-Loompa look does not work for you."

"Go ahead. Yuk it up, Troll dolls," I say, pointing at the mirror.

Sean and Matt both glance at themselves and instantly reel backward.

"Jesus!" Sean shouts. "That's not fiery red."

Matt slowly approaches the mirror, staring at his alien reflection. "You have *got* to be kidding me."

"Walter!" Mom yells.

I hear Dad trot up the steps. "What is it?" he says, appearing in the bathroom door. He looks almost as ridiculous as us. A half-unbuttoned black satin shirt, a full goatee, angular sideburns, too-tight jeans, his red do-rag, and a forearm full of bangles. His "rock-and-roll" transformation complete.

"Say hello to your son and his friends." Mom gestures at us.

Dad flinches. "Yikes." He starts to laugh. "That's . . . an interesting look, fellas."

"It was an accident," I say, attempting to psychically will the images in the mirror to change. "We were trying to represent."

"Represent what?" Dad asks. "The Muppets?"

"This is what you've wrought, Walter," Mom says, her face going crimson. "Encouraging them to be rebellious. To rock and roll. Look at yourself. What kind of example are you setting?"

My stomach seizes. I pray this isn't going to degenerate into a fight. Not with Sean and Matt here.

"Hey, yo." Dad holds up both his hands, the bangles on his wrist clinking. "Don't trip out on me now."

"These walls are permanently stained." Mom wipes at the streaks on the wallpaper. "My towels. My counters. They're ruined." She rubs her thumb on a patch of green on the countertop, then studies me. "And our beautiful boy looks like some kind of freak!"

"We'll clean it all up," I say, trying to cut her off before she works up a full head of steam. Mom rarely gets mad, but when she does it's colossal.

"I've put up with this long enough, Walter. I've had it. This tomfoolery has to stop. I can't be the only adult in the house. You need to contribute. Start looking for another job. . . ."

Dad knits his brow. "But the band—"

"Hogwash. You're just using that as an excuse not to grow up. The boys can do the band on their own."

"Whoa, whoa, whoa." Dad shakes his head. "Let's not go crazy, now."

"It's over, Walter!" Mom glowers at him. "Understand?" With that, she marches out of the bathroom.

Sean and Matt look as embarrassed as I feel.

"Don't worry about her," Dad says. "I'll smooth things out. It's cool. Meanwhile, you guys make this"—he sweeps his hand at the bathroom and at us—"better. Somehow."

Dad turns and leaves. As he heads down the stairs I hear him sputter, " 'Trying to represent.' Jesus Christ." He wheezes with laughter. "Bunch of chuckleheads."

CHAPTER FORTY-THREE

WEREWOLVES OF LONDON

WE TAKE TURNS SHOWERING. And then we take turns showering again. Each time using more soap and hotter water. But still we look like the sort of freakish characters you'd see on a Saturday morning children's program. "Welcome to Creepy Street" or something.

"Hey, Coop," Matt says, rolling up his sleeping bag. "I forgot to thank you."

"For what?" I stare at my orange hand. Flipping it over and over in disbelief.

"You know. For how kick ass we look."

Matt and Sean break up in hysterics. Their glowing white teeth beam from between their stained lips. I'm glad they can see the humor in the situation. Though I can see their laughter turning to tears on a dime.

"It's too bad Halloween's over," Sean says, sifting through the remains of last night's junk food. "We could totally go as survivors of a nuclear meltdown."

"Yeah, yeah, yeah." I sit on my bed. The mattress springs squeak under my weight. "Have your laughs now. But you'll see. This is all going to tone down by Monday and then we'll see who's thanking who."

Matt and Sean share a look, then crack up laughing.

"Are you kidding?" Matt says. "Pale orange is still orange."

Sean points to his cotton-candy lid. "And what the hell is this going to lighten to? Certainly not red. I might have to do a buzz cut before I go back to school. And buzz cuts are definitely *not* mariachi-like."

I sweep this out of the air with my Martian hand. "That's why we did this early. So we can tweak things. Your hair color's the easiest thing of all. We'll just buy a darker shade."

"And maybe this time we'll read the instructions." Sean grabs a candy bar and waves it in the air. "Anyone want a Butterfinger?"

"That's what she said," I call out before I can stop myself.

Matt and Sean look at me, deadpan.

"What? It was too good to pass up. You have to admit."

Matt stuffs his sleeping bag inside his duffel and stands. "All right. I'm out of here."

"What are you talking about?" I hop off the bed. "We have a rehearsal. Helen's coming over this afternoon. We need to practice."

"Sorry." Matt shoulders his duffel bag. "I need a break. I'm going to soak in a bath for the next twelve hours before Val sees me looking all jack-o'-lanterny. I'll loofah myself until I bleed if I have to. And brush my teeth with coffee grinds."

"Yeah, I'm out too." Sean unwraps the candy bar. "I need to give my hands a rest from last night."

"That's what she said," Matt calls over his shoulder as he heads out the door.

"You guys are so last month with that." Sean pockets a few extra snacks before grabbing his backpack and taking off. "See you later."

I lie back on my bed and contemplate calling Helen to tell her practice is canceled. But to tell the truth, I'm actually looking forward to seeing her. In fact, I've been looking forward to it ever since she left my house after dinner last night.

I figure we can use the time to do some work on our Health project. I know I should be worried about what she's going to say when she sees me looking so ridic, but I have a feeling she'll find it funny. And who knows? Maybe I'll be able to play on her sympathy and parlay it into an all-afternoon chimney sweep.

Yeah, okay. And what happened to staying clear? Staying focused?

Oh, shut up. It's just a daydream. Dreams are harmless.

★ ★ ★

For the next hour, I imagine all the different ways the two of us could end up naked together.

And then the doorbell rings.

Suddenly all my confidence melts away.

I leap from the bed and race around my room trying to find something to disguise myself with. Hoodie. Ski jacket. Baseball cap. Nothing I find covers me up enough.

The doorbell rings again and I go into panic mode. Why the hell didn't I call her and cancel? When did I become so stupid?

"Would you get that, Coop?" Dad hollers from the bathroom. "I'm dropping bear bait in here."

The only thing I can find is my old rubber wolfman mask and paws at the back of my closet. It's pathetic but they'll have to do. At the last minute, I throw on my faux fur coat and play the story over in my head as I make my way to the front door: "This is part of my persona. The werewolf pimp. I'm going to see how it goes while we play."

As I grab the knob and open the door, I remember something. We aren't rehearsing today. Which blows that tale right out of the water.

Helen smiles and raises her eyebrows when she sees me. "My, what big hands you have, Grandma," she says.

"Hi." I wave my wolf paw, getting a nose full of that familiar rubber-petroleum smell from the mask.

She laughs. "Should I have brought my little red riding hood outfit?"

Oh, Lord. Don't go there, brain.

Too late. There she is. Red cape and hood. And nothing else.

I wonder if this will ever stop. If I will someday regain control of my thoughts when it comes to babes. And Helen in particular. Does Dad's brain go reeling off like this every time he sees a cute girl? Does Mr. Spassnick's?

Ew, God. I don't want to think about it.

"Come on in," I say, stepping aside.

She brushes by me, and it's like the slightest touch from her causes me to lose my breath.

"So, what's the deal?" Helen asks. "Are you having Halloween withdrawal?"

I shut the door as a new lie forms in my mind. Something about losing a bet to Matt and Sean. Having to wear this costume all day long. But just as I'm about to speak, the story barbs in my throat.

My shoulders deflate like a punctured bike tire, all my resolve escaping. "You promise not to laugh too hard at me?"

"Sure," she says, suppressing a laugh. "Why? Is there something funnier than this?"

I slowly pull off the wolf hands and remove my mask.

Helen claps her hand over her mouth. "Oh, no." I have

to give her credit. She's trying desperately not to crack up, but her body is shaking from the effort. "What—what happened?"

I shake my head. "We wanted to spruce up our image a little. It was only a test run but . . . things went sort of . . . wrong."

"*We?* No way. Do Matt and Sean look like this too?"

"Not exactly. Same skin. Same teeth." I flash my gleaming white Chiclets at her.

She shades her eyes. "Holy cow."

"Just different color hair," I say.

"You're very silly, you know that?"

I nod.

"To tell you the truth." Helen takes a step back, regarding me. "You're kind of cute like this."

Hello! I was thinking maybe she'd feel sorry for me, but if she actually *goes* for this kind of thing, who am I to question the strange ways of the female?

"You think?" I ask, standing a little taller.

"Absolutely." She laughs. "I bet we could rent you out for kiddie parties and make a fortune."

Oh. I see. *That* kind of cute.

"Thanks for the confidence boost," I say.

"Aw, don't be sad." Helen moves toward me and slings her arm over my shoulder.

Even through my fur coat she feels amazing. If I had any stones at all I'd lean in and kiss her right now. But I can't. Not looking like this.

"Besides," she continues, "this isn't a tragedy. I happen to have had some experience with this kind of thing."

"Really? You've looked like this before?"

"No," Helen says. "But my mother has. Sort of. She did something similar when she wanted to start dating after my dad left. It took us a week to finally find the right formula. Count yourself lucky. You get the benefit of our experimentation."

"Oh, my God. If you could fix this I would love you forever." The phrase leaps from my lips before I can snatch it back.

Helen's neck instantly flushes.

My cheeks and ears get hot.

We both laugh, nervously. Pretending I didn't just say those words. That everything is normal here. That the air isn't suddenly charged with something . . . different.

CHAPTER FORTY-FOUR

I WANT TO HOLD YOUR HAND

WOULD YOU RATHER BE BLIND or deaf?" Helen asks.

The two of us are sitting on my bedroom floor, playing "Would you rather?" as we search my iTunes library for a few more songs to add to the band's set list in case we're asked to do an encore.

After my baking-soda bath, which Helen steadfastly refused to join me for—even though I told her I wouldn't be able to scrub my back—I did several dish-detergent shampoos, followed by a series of mouthwashes involving grapefruit juice and black tea.

All in all, I look a thousand times better. My hair is still greenish, but in a pretty dope kind of way. And my teeth and skin have been toned down to acceptable shades of white and pale yam.

Helen wanted me to hold off telling Sean and Matt her cleaning secrets until tomorrow, just so that she could see what they looked like, but I couldn't risk having them still be pissed at me and bail on any more rehearsals.

"Blind," I say. "Definitely."

She stares at me in disbelief. "So you'd never get to see another sunset. Or watch another movie. Or see the faces of your wife and kids."

"Better than never hearing music or people's voices. I get freaked out when things are too quiet. What about you?"

"I'd rather be deaf. Because then you can still read books and get around places and see when someone's sad. Your turn."

"All right." I run through some options in my head. Sex in an airplane or submarine? On the beach or in the forest? Three guys or three girls?

"Well?" Helen says, breaking the spell.

"Um . . . okay." I blink hard to clear the slate and think about something completely unrelated to sex. "All right. How would you rather die? Falling off the tallest building in the world or being tied up and torn apart by feral squirrels?"

Helen laughs. "Building. No question."

"Seriously? But all that time you're falling you'd be thinking about what it's going to feel like when you hit the ground."

"And what would I be thinking about as the squirrels were gnawing off my eyelids?"

"Good point," I say. "Still, not a big fan of heights. I'd

choose squirrels and hope someone found me before they ate too much of my bod."

"No fair." Helen swats my shoulder. "You didn't say there was a chance somebody might find you before you died."

"Would that change your answer?"

Helen squints one eye, thinking. "No. Squirrels are cute but they have really sharp claws. And pincer teeth. It'd be too painful. Even if someone did finally rescue me."

We've been going back and forth like this for the last hour. Helen started the whole thing by asking me if I'd rather eat a soft-boiled duck fetus or a still-beating cobra heart. I chose the fetus because at least it was cooked but I told her I'd probably hurl either way. From there we moved on to monkey brains or maggot cheese. Then it was on to the old standards. Lose an arm or a leg. Have webbed feet or wings. Be a giant or a midget.

I'm glad Helen wanted to hang out even though we weren't having rehearsal. Sitting here right now, I wish the weekend could last forever. That Monday would never come and we wouldn't have to go back to school—and I wouldn't have to do acrobatics trying to avoid her all the time.

"All right," Helen says, twirling a strand of hair around one of her fingers. "Enough 'would you rathers.' Let's do some 'if you coulds.' I'll go first. If you could change one thing about your life, what would it be?"

"You mean, at this very moment? Or my life in general?"

"Your life in general."

"That's too intense. I don't know." Of course, a bunch of things cross my mind but nothing I can tell Helen without her slapping me across the face. "A million dollars without having to eat one of your disgusting foods, I guess. So I could buy some new drums to replace my taped-up ones. And my dad wouldn't have to worry about his job and the bills all the time. And my sister wouldn't have to fill out all these loan forms so she can go to college next year. And my mom could go to Greece like she's always wanted to."

Helen smiles. "That's nice."

"Mostly to get the drums, though. I just added all that other stuff so I wouldn't look like a dingus."

Helen laughs. "Yeah, yeah. I'm so sure."

"What about you?" Like I even have to ask. "What would you change?"

"My mom," she says without a beat. "I'd have her get better."

Oh. Right. I was way off on that one.

"You thought I was going to say all the stupid school stuff. But that'd be wasting a good wish on something that'll be over when I graduate."

"Does my face give me away *that* easy? Because I'm a damn good poker player and I'd swear I don't have any tells."

"Oh, really? Let me know when you're ready to lose your shorts and I'll take you on."

"Do you play for shorts?" I laugh. "Because I usually bet cash. But if you want to play for clothes, count me in."

"You don't want to play me for money *or* shorts."

"What is it? Do my eyes shift? Does my mouth twitch?"

Helen shakes her head. "If I told you, I wouldn't be able to read you anymore. What fun would that be?" She points at my laptop screen. "Ah-ha! I knew we'd find some good music on here eventually."

I look to see what she's referring to. It's my meager collection of U2 songs. "Really? I actually haven't listened to them much. I don't even remember where I got those."

"Yeah, well, you're missing out." She clicks on a song, "With or Without You," and taps up the volume. "I've seen them in concert three times. They're amazing. I love this song."

"I don't know, I—"

Helen grabs my arm. "Shh. Listen."

She closes her eyes as she breathes in the music.

I hear the song. It's slow and lush and sweeping. But really, all I can concentrate on is her warm hand on my skin.

And her beautiful face.

Christ, she's gorgeous. Why the hell doesn't anyone else see this?

It's hard to catch my breath. My heart's like a crazed windup toy in my chest. I want to kiss her so bad. I try to lean in, but it's like I've got a bungee cord attached to the back of my head that keeps me restrained.

Suddenly, Helen's eyes open. She knows what I'm thinking. She has to. I'm sure of it.

"What?" she asks.

"I want . . ." I say, trying again to lean forward. "I want . . ."

"You want what?" Her eyes give me nothing by way of a clue.

"I want"— I blink hard—"to dance with you."

The hell? Are you kidding? Dance? Here? In my bedroom? I don't even know how to dance! That's not what I want at all.

"Seriously?" Helen looks at me suspiciously. But also with a slight smile.

No, no, no! Kiss you! Kiss you! Goddamn it. Why don't my thoughts and mouth sync up anymore?

"Um . . . yeah," I say, encouraged by the glint of hopefulness on her face. "You seem to like to dance. At least, when you're singing." I swallow, my mouth drying up. "And . . . you like this song. So . . ."

Helen's smile grows.

And then, everything shifts. And dancing is exactly what I want to do right now.

I get to my feet and hold out my hand before I lose my nerve.

She laughs, but reaches up and takes my hand. "Sure. Okay."

My palms start to sweat. I wipe them on my jeans before putting my arms around her waist. She places her hands on my shoulders. And we sway gently in time to the music.

At first, it feels awkward. I can barely hear the music over the pounding in my ears. But Helen moves in closer and puts her head on my shoulder. She's humming the words softly against my cheek. My face right by her neck. She smells nice. Like sweet tea.

And that's when the world fades away into the background and everything feels perfect. There's only me, and Helen, and the music cocooning us in my room.

Her body feels good close to mine. The warmth of her through her shirt. If someone told me at the beginning of the school year that I'd be dancing like this with Helen Harriwick, I would have said they were out of their nut.

But I wouldn't want to be anywhere else in the world right now.

I hope the song never ends. The way I feel right now. My head buzzing. My skin tingling. It's like playing the perfect fill on the drums and scoring the winning street hockey goal in overtime and catching your chair right before you tip it back too far, all wrapped up in one and multiplied by ten.

Helen lifts her head from my shoulder and looks at me.

Right into my eyes.

I don't wait. I lean in slowly. Move my hands to her face. And kiss her.

She kisses me back.

Her lips taste like sun-warmed strawberries.

Holy crap. I'm kissing a girl.

And it's better than I ever imagined.

CHAPTER FORTY-FIVE

PLEASE MISTER POSTMAN

DESPITE ALL MY HOPES and prayers, Monday arrives on schedule. I've got that roller-coaster-just-cresting-a-twelve-story-drop feeling in my gut as I lie in bed, angsting over Helen and how I'm supposed to avoid her all day at school—and the rest of the year, for that matter—without hurting her feelings. Of course, it's not like we said we were going out or anything. All we did was dance a little. And kiss. But still.

Oh, who am I kidding? It's going to be a mess. And to top it all off, the guilt over the Our Lady of Mercy situation is eating me up inside. I kept waking up all night—my body drenched in sweat—nightmares of Helen slowly opening the acceptance letter. The look of confusion, anger, and horror on her face as she reads it. The slow dawning as to who was responsible.

Damn it. If only I could fig a way to get the application canceled. Of course, that would mean she wouldn't be leaving the school. And I'd have to come up with another way to get her out of the band. Or maybe convince her to wear a Kabuki mask or something onstage so nobody recognizes her.

But I just can't have that application on my conscience.

My brain clicks into problem-solver mode. Working out all the options. The various possibilities.

And then an idea.

One that might just work.

I spiral the plan out in my head. I'll have to stay home from school today. I need quiet. And privacy. And access to the Internet.

I pull the I've-got-a-killer-headache routine. Blow-dryer to the forehead for the back-of-the-hand fever test. Thermometer placed on a lightbulb while Mom ducks out of the room. Sure, I overdo it a little, let my mind wander and leave it on the bulb a bit too long. Scald my tongue when I stick it back in my mouth. But it's worth it. And Mom—who's already late for work—barely bats an eye when she sees my hundred-and-ten degree temperature. She just glances at it and shakes it down.

"Drink lots of fluids," she says as she leaves my room. "And no TV."

Once Mom heads out to her babysitting gig and Dad leaves for his morning shift at the machine shop, I've got free reign over the house.

First things first. I grab a Drumstick ice cream cone out of the freezer. I don't know why ice cream tastes so much better in the morning, but it does. When I leave home and have my own place, it's going to be Drumsticks for breakfast all the time.

Next, I google the Our Lady of Mercy Catholic School in Lower Rockville. Find their contact number, dial it on my cell, and drape a washcloth over the mouthpiece to help disguise my voice.

"Our Lady of Mercy," a cheery female secretary answers.

"Yes. Good morning," I say, in a low, gravelly tone. "This is Mr. Harriwick. Helen Harriwick's father."

"Is she a student here?"

"No. Not yet. But we've recently applied."

"Oh, well, all applications are currently being reviewed, sir. The responses will be sent in the mail over the next few weeks."

"Yes. I understand that. But the thing is, I wanted to *withdraw* our application."

"I'm afraid I can't do that, sir. I don't have access to the forms."

Damn it. All right. I need another approach. "Well, then. Can you give a note to the person who *does* have access? Telling them to throw away the form?"

"Your daughter is under no obligation to come to the school, sir," the secretary says. "If you receive an acceptance letter, you can simply discard it."

"Yes, but I don't *want* to receive a letter from your school. Of any kind."

"I'm afraid I don't understand."

"There's nothing to understand. Just don't send us a letter. Accepting or rejecting us. We don't like to waste paper, you see. My wife cries every time we receive any kind of junk mail. We're trying to decrease our ecological footprints . . . feetprint . . . I mean . . . Look, we don't want you killing any trees for us."

"Uh . . . okay. Let me see what I can do. What was the last name again?" the secretary asks.

"Harriwick."

"Can you spell that?"

"Of course I can spell it. It's my last name. What kind of question is that?"

"Right. Well. *Would* you spell it for me, then? So I can look it up."

"Oh. Yes. Fine. It's H-A-R . . ." Crap. You'd think I'd know this. But actually, I've only seen it the one time on the application. And I didn't even write that. I sound it out in my head. *Har-ah-wick. Har-oh-wick. Har-eh-wick.* If I get it wrong, they'll know I'm not her dad for sure. And that'll raise suspicion. Which could—

"Sir?" the secretary says.

"Yes?"

"The name? H-A-R . . ."

"Actually," I say. "Now that I think about it. Let's just leave it alone. Better to keep all our options open, right?

I'll deal with the wife's tears. But, um . . . you said that the letters will be sent out in the next few weeks?"

"Over these next few weeks. Yes. Although, to be honest, I believe some have already been mailed. If you'd like—"

"Shit."

"Excuse me?"

Uh-oh. Did I say that out loud? "Um. Nothing. I just . . . stepped on the cat. Thanks for your help. Good-bye."

I click off my cell phone and start pacing around the room. Okay, think. Her application was sent in close to the deadline. So, it won't be one of the first they look at. Still, who knows how many people apply in the middle of the school year. Probably not a lot. Therefore, it's possible the letter—rejection or acceptance—is already on its way. Which means I've only got one choice.

I kill a couple of hours on Xbox, wandering around Renaissance Italy searching for religious treasures and assassinating conspirators who try to get in my way. Just to give whoever delivers Helen's mail time to start their rounds. If I'm lucky—not something I can exactly count on these days—the letter will be waiting in Helen's mailbox ready for me to pluck out and tear up. If it doesn't arrive today, I'll just have to check back every day until it does.

As I coast up to Helen's house on my bike, I survey the neighborhood. Nobody's around, so I wheel my bike up the drive. Lay it down quietly on the ground. Then I walk super-quiet up onto the porch, holding my breath, praying Mrs. Harriwick is sequestered in the back of the house.

The black metal mailbox is secured to the right of the front door, above the doorbell. A little gold eagle sits on top of the latch. I reach over and raise the cover. It squeaks a little as I lift it.

It's stuffed with mail. I have to wiggle the mass of papers out of the cramped box, careful not to let the mailbox cover slam back down. There are several Christmas catalogs here, a few letters from the bank, a bunch from the medical center, a Visa bill, a couple of Christmas cards, something from the phone company, but absolutely nothing from Our Lady of Mercy.

Suddenly, I hear footsteps inside the house, coming toward the front door.

Damn it, damn it, damn it.

I try to slip the mail discretely back into the box, but there's way too much. It won't all fit in. The dead bolt snicks, sending my pulse soaring. I jam the letters and catalogs in, folding and crumpling them up, getting everything in just as the doorknob starts to turn.

I leap back and lift my hand like I was about to knock as the front door swings open.

"Oh. Hello, Cooper," Mrs. Harriwick says from behind the screen. "What are *you* doing here?"

Think. Fast. "Hi there . . . um . . . Is Helen home?" My voice cracks a bit.

"No. She's at school. Isn't that where you should be?"

"School?" I force a laugh. "Why's she at school?"

Mrs. Harriwick raises her eyebrows. "Because it's Monday?"

"What?" I say, feigning panic. "No. Are you sure?"

"Yes. Positive." She cracks open the screen door and checks the crammed mailbox.

"Oh, my God. I thought it was Sunday." I slap my forehead. "Okay, please do not tell Helen I was here. This is seriously embarrassing."

"Sure. No problem. You were never here." Mrs. Harriwick reaches into the mailbox and tries to tug the mangled letters out, but they are really stuck in there. "My goodness. We must have a new"— she pulls and pulls, rattling the metal box—"mailperson." Finally, it all comes free in a crumpled-up wad of paper. "Now, that's just wrong."

"Yeah, our mail guy does that to us all the time. Okay, so." I start backing down the steps. "I better get moving. I am going to be in *so* much trouble at school. See ya!"

I grab my bike, leap on it, and pedal away like crazy.

CHAPTER FORTY-SIX

WHAT'S GOING ON

FOCUS ON THE BREATH as you bring air deep into your lungs." A twelfth-grade girl who calls herself Willow and smells like a garlic factory walks around the classroom while four whackadoodles and me—all of us having given up our lunch to join Meditation Club—sit cross-legged on the gritty linoleum floor. "Quiet the mind. If a thought drifts in, let it just as easily drift out."

It's been a challenging few weeks to say the least.

No matter how stealth I've tried to be, Prudence won't give up any information about her big plans for Helen. Every time I attempt to extract even the tiniest hint from her, she laughs and says, "You're just going to have to be patient, Coopee. But don't worry, it's going to be supreme."

Which has only made me more worried.

On top of that, my efforts to intercept the Our Lady of Mercy letter have turned up nothing. I've ditched Study Hall every day to check on Helen's mail but the only thing I've discovered is that someone in the Harriwick house is seriously into catalog shopping. They get at least three or four a day from places hawking everything from tulip bulbs to pain-relieving copper bracelets.

At least I've got it worked out now how to avoid Helen at school and still keep everything chill with her in the afternoons. Health is the only subject we have together, and since Mrs. Turris isn't having us work on our projects during class anymore, that hasn't been an ish. I just come to class smack on time and leave right when the bell rings because—as I've explained to Helen—"I've got Bio right after and I'm on Mr. Forebutt's shit list for being late so often."

The hallways posed some difficulty at first, but I've memorized Helen's schedule and make sure I'm nowhere near her classes or locker in between periods.

The biggest challenge has been lunch. Now that she's in the band and we're "sort of" going out, Helen wants to eat with us all the time. Which would be great if she wasn't Helen. But she is. And so, other plans have had to be made.

Honestly, for the first few days I thought I was totally screwed. I had to come up with all sorts of excuses to get out of lunch. I was "nauseous." I had "lunch detention." I needed to "retake an English exam."

Finally, I came up with the solution. Matt and Val went to Chess Club three times a week. Why not join some clubs myself? To broaden my horizons. Or better yet, "because I'm being forced to by Mr. Tard for disciplinary reasons." Clubs no one else in their right mind—including Helen—would ever want to join.

And so, Monday and Wednesday is Meditation Club, Tuesday it's Astronomy Club, and Friday is Youth Alive! Club, which, to be honest, is still a mystery to me, as the nine geeks and myself just sort of sit around and talk about the news, or what's bothering us, or what we're "excited" about.

"Cooper, did you hear that?" Willow calls out.

"Hear what?" I say.

"Mr. Grossman wants to see you. Immediately."

"Oh." I shake my head. "Wow. I guess I was really deep into the meditation."

It's the "immediately" part that sends a chill down my spine. "Immediately" rarely means something good.

As I trek through the empty halls toward the music wing, I convince myself that this is not a big deal; that Mr. Grossman is the type of guy who likes to do everything "immediately."

It's not until I see Matt and Sean approaching the chorus room from the other direction that I realize they have been summoned "immediately" as well. Which can only mean we are royally screwed.

"What do you think he wants?" Sean asks as we enter

the darkened chorus room and head toward the offices in back.

"I'm sure it's nothing," I lie. "Maybe he's changed his mind. Maybe he couldn't make a copy. Maybe he wants the demo back."

"Or maybe he's heard about Understain," Matt adds.

We approach the office door, which looms like a giant oak tombstone.

"Admit to nothing." I grab the doorknob, push it open, and we step into Mr. Grossman's office.

"Mr. Redmond," he says, sitting at the desk with his fingers interlaced. "Mr. Gratton. Mr. Hance. Welcome."

Matt and Sean flank me as we stand there waiting for the accusation.

"Is there something you'd like to tell me?"

"About what?" I say, jumping in before Matt and Sean crumble and confess.

Mr. Grossman peers over his glasses. "About your demo tape. About a band called"— he looks down at his notes—"Understain. And how the two might possibly be related."

"Are you a fan of theirs, Mr. Grossman?" I ask.

Matt and Sean turn their heads to look at me. I give each of them a little let-me-handle-this kick to the feet, which I hope they interpret correctly.

"Not my particular cup of Earl Grey, no." Mr. Grossman stretches his lips thin. "Let's dispense with the subterfuge, shall we?"

"Okay. Sure. Whatever that means."

Mr. Grossman unlaces his index fingers and starts tapping them together. "Do either of you two ever speak? Or is Mr. Redmond here your official representative?"

"Sometimes," Sean says.

"But . . . yes," Matt adds.

"All right, then." Mr. Grossman picks up a remote control off his desk. He points the remote at a CD player on his shelf like he's planned this whole confrontation out, including his timing. "Let's take a listen, yes?"

"Grind the Rump Roast" starts playing over the speakers, and I'm still impressed with how I got it to sound like it was recorded live at some crappy studio.

"Grind it, grind it, grind it. Grab the handle and you wind it," the singer screams. *"When your meat is fully ground. Still you hear that mooing sound."*

"Mm-hmm," Mr. Grossman says, like he's made his point. He lets it play for a few seconds more, then shuts it off. Then he hits another button, and Understain's much clearer, brand-new version of the song begins to play. "And so we discover, this is *not* your original song."

"No," I say. "It's an Understain song."

"I'm aware of that."

"Okay." I look at Matt and Sean like, "Are you getting this guy?"

Mr. Grossman clears his throat. "Then why did you try to pass it off as an original?"

"Who tried to pass it off as an original?"

"*You* did."

"No," I say. "We *covered* that song. 'Burnin' For You,' 'Revolution,' and 'Grind the Rump Roast.'"

He tilts his head, his eyes full of disbelief. "Then where, pray tell, is your original song?"

"After that. At the end. 'I'm Sorry You're An Idiot.'"

"Excuse me?" Mr. Grossman's eyes burn into me.

I swear I hear Matt and Sean gasp. But I just couldn't help myself. It was too sweet of an opportunity.

I gesture at the CD player. "'I'm Sorry You're An Idiot.' That's our original song. It's on there. Right after the three cover songs."

Mr. Grossman raises the remote and clicks the skip button. Again and again and again. But nothing plays.

"What? Are you twisting me? Where is it?" I move to the CD player and hit the fast forward button. I look back at Sean and Matt. "Oh, man. The studio dude must have screwed us."

"Are you serious?" Matt says with the appropriate amount of irritation.

Sean huffs. "That jerk!"

"I'm sorry, Mr. Grossman," I say. "We should have listened to the CD before we handed it in to you."

"Indeed." He grabs a paper from his desk. "The submission form specifically states that 'each band shall submit a demonstration CD with *two* cover songs and one original.' Why then would you submit *three* covers?"

"Two covers? No." I reach over and snatch the paper from Mr. Grossman's hand. "Oh, man. You're right."

"Of course I'm right. I wrote the rules."

"This is totally my fault. I misread it. I thought it said three covers." I give him back the page. "I'm very sorry, Mr. Grossman. Is there anyway you'd let us hand in our original song tomorrow?"

"Well," he grumbles, shuffling papers on his desk. "This is . . . something that needs . . . I'm going to have to consult with the other judges. We admitted you on the basis that this last song was an original."

"We completely understand," I say. "Don't we?"

"Of course . . . Absolutely . . . For sure," Matt and Sean mumble.

I tap Mr. Grossman's desk. "You should definitely have a listen to our *actual* original song before you green-light us. It's the only fair thing to do. But I'm sure after you do you'll have no question you made the right call."

Mr. Grossman's eyes drift across the three of us. He *so* doesn't want to believe this, but what's he going to do? "Fine, then. *First* thing tomorrow. Or I'll have no choice but to disqualify you."

CHAPTER FORTY-SEVEN

CRAZY TRAIN

ALL RIGHT, ALL RIGHT, STOP, STOP." Dad whirls his arms in the air like he's being attacked by killer wasps. He's grown a full flipped-out-Jim-Morrison beard, and his rock-and-roll clothes haven't been washed since he's taken up permanent residence in the basement. "How is it that missy here keeps sounding better and better, while the rest of you clotloafs just get worse and worse? I don't understand. Explain this to me."

Rehearsal is not going well.

In fact, it's been a hellacious last few weeks.

I'd thought things were really looking up when we played our new demo for Mr. Grossman. Sure, I had to do a little tap dancing to convince him that Sean was going through a late puberty, and that his voice had started to change, which was why we had to recruit a new female vocalist, but once he heard "I'm Sorry You're An Idiot"—one of Dad's old tunes that we altered the lyrics to—we were in with a grin.

Now, though, we're just seven days away from the Battle of the Bands and everything seems like it's going to hell in a hammock.

Dad's rubbing his temples. "I had such hope. I can't believe this." He's pacing around and mumbling to himself. "I wonder. Could I play backstage? So no one sees me. Would we be able to get away with that?"

Sean, Matt, Helen, and Valerie are looking everywhere else but at Dad. I'm aware that they're embarrassed for me, but it's beyond that now as far as I'm concerned. I don't even know *what* to think anymore. Sure, I'm sorry he's out of work and all, but I'm pretty sure the band isn't such a good distraction for him anymore.

"Dad, listen," I say. "Let's just—"

He stops. Holds up his index finger. "Coop. No. I've sacrificed too much for this. I'm going to make this work. Just let me think." He drums his fingers on his forehead.

"Mr. Redmond," Valerie says from her perch on the couch. "Maybe they just need to take a br—" But Dad cuts her off with his traffic-cop hand.

We stew in awkward silence for a solid minute.

"Okay." Dad breathes deep. "I've got it. I don't know why I didn't think of this earlier. We have pyrotechnics. So we distract the audience and judges with our mighty blasts of sparks and plumes of flames. They won't even care how horrible we sound. They'll be so blown away by the visuals." Dad claps his hands together. "It's time for a test run."

Dad moves over to his "workshop" in the corner of the basement and grabs a plank of wood with five tin cans nailed to it. He's punched holes in the cans and rigged them with empty screw-in lightbulb fixtures.

"What are those?" Helen asks.

"Just hold your clown, Vocals." Dad places the board on the rug in front of my bass drum and snakes the wire and light switch off to the side. "I was going to surprise you wanks with this stuff the night of, but we need to make sure everything works prior to, since we're now relying on it to save your sorry asses." Dad plugs in the electrical cord and mans the light switch. "All right. Let's do something big. Rock my socks off with 'London Calling.' And try to match your chickee's passion this time, fellas."

I take off my fur coat—it's making me sweat like a pig—then count us into the song.

Helen, of course, looks and sounds brill.

Matt, Sean, and me? Not so much. It's like we've lost all our confidence or something. And our rock personas are doing nothing to help us. The music sounds thin and insubstantial.

I watch Dad out of the corner of my eye. He's got this wild-man look on his face as he crouches down with his finger twitching over the light switch.

My foot works the bass drum and I pound away on my toms, but no matter how much I try to put behind my playing, the whole thing feels sluggish.

And then, without warning, Dad leaps in the air and flicks the light switch, causing—

Nothing.

No pop. No flash. No sparks. No plumes of flames.

We continue playing as Dad toggles the trigger switch back and forth in rapid succession.

"What the . . ." He grumbles. "Come on! Goddamn it!"

Helen's eyes catch mine. I shrug and continue to keep the beat.

"Stop!" Dad hollers. "Cut! Enough! Something's wrong."

The music comes to a messy halt as each of us stops playing at different times.

Dad flips the switch a few more times. "I don't understand this. I got the build off the Internet."

"Off the Internet?" Valerie says. "Oh, well then it *has* to work."

"Hey, Groupie," Dad says. "Zip it. Guitars. How 'bout making yourself useful? Check to see if all the cans on that board are still connected."

Matt gives Dad a dubious stare. "I don't *think* so. What if they go off while I'm looking at them?"

"I'm going to unplug it, boobus." Dad reaches down, yanks the cord from the wall, and waves the plug in the air. "There. Happy?"

"No," Matt says. "It could be smoldering in there. Ready to blow at any second."

Dad rolls his eyes. "Jesus Christ. You're such a girl. Keyboards, take a look, would you?"

"Uh-uh," Sean says. "I like my face too much."

"Okay, fine." Dad slams the trigger box down on the coffee table and makes his way over to the flash pots. "I have to do everything for this band."

Dad shoves past Helen and nearly reaches the board of cans when—

WHOOSH!

A blinding flare fills the basement, like a thousand camera flashes going off all at once.

CHAPTER FORTY-EIGHT

SMOKE ON THE WATER

HOLY CRAP!" Matt shouts.

"Get down!" Sean screams.

I dive off my drum stool and hit the deck, covering my head.

But it's all unnecessary, because there's only the one explosion.

The dark smell of burnt firecrackers permeates the air. My eyes are in shock from the flash, but it doesn't take twenty-twenty to see that the basement is chock with black smoke.

I can't make out anyone, but I can hear people hacking up their lungs.

"Now, how the hell did that happen?" Dad grouses.

"Is everyone okay?" I call out.

There's a chorus of rasping "Yeahs" and "Fines" punctuated by coughing and wheezing. I tag the voices in my head. Dad, Helen, Matt, Valerie, Sean.

A second later, the smoke alarm starts to scream. A never-ending, eardrum-piercing shriek.

"Where are the windows?" Valerie calls out. "We have to open them up and get this smoke out."

There's the sound of scuffling as we all start running around. I hear someone trip over one of my cymbals, sending it crashing to the ground.

"Shit!" Matt shouts.

There's a loud "Oof!" as someone else runs into God knows what.

I reach out in front of me, trying to navigate through the dark fog. I'm doing well avoiding running into anything when my hands grab something soft and spongy.

"Hey!" Helen shrieks. "Watch the hands."

"Oops. Sorry," I say, though not as sorry as I probably should be. I'm pretty positive that was second base right there. Though I don't know if it actually counts when it's an accident.

"Are you *sure* you can't see?" Helen laughs.

"I'm trying to find the window. I swear. Why? Where did I grab you?"

"Never mind," she says.

I don't see why I should waste such a golden opportunity. So, I lower my hands in hopes that I might make it to third while I still have the excuse of sightlessness. My fingers blindly grope around at waist-level in the direction of Helen's voice. I'm getting nothing but air and so I shift to the right a little.

Bingo. My hand brushes something that's most definitely a jeans fly, and then I give a nice gentle squeeze.

"Whoa!" Sean hollers. "Who's palming my junk?"

I yank my hand away and wipe the hell out of it on my pant leg. I'm tempted to cry out but I manage to keep my trap shut. Crap. My first time to third base and it's Sean's meats? That is *so* not cool.

"Hello?" Sean says. "Please tell me that was a girl."

I quickly turn and stumble my way over to the windows. It'll be a cold day at the earth's core before I fess up to chalicing Sean's baggage.

Even with six of us it takes a while to get all the windows open, but we finally do. The alarm still blares, but hopefully the room will clear soon.

"Shut the door, quick," Dad says as we all tromp up the basement stairs. "I don't want it smelling up here."

I sniff the air as he closes the door. "It's a little late for that, don't you think?"

Dad pulls off his do-rag and blows his nose in it. "All right." Sweat beads on his forehead. "Let's open all the windows in the house. We'll spray some air freshener when it's all aired out. I don't want to have to explain this to your mother."

I move over to Helen. "You okay?"

"Yeah. I think so." She rubs her eyes. Even with dark smears on her cheeks, she still looks cute. I try hard not to, honestly, but I glance down at her chest anyway. Remembering the feel of her in my hands. Wondering if

I'll ever get a chance to do that again, without the cover of smoke.

"Chop, chop." Dad claps his hands. "Stop standing around. Let's get to work. We've got to get some cross-ventilation going. Keyboards and Vocals, you take the upstairs bedrooms. Coop, Guitars, and Groupie. Get everything open down here. I'll see if I can find some fans."

Sean takes off his sombrero and poncho and throws them on the couch. Matt removes his doctor's coat and chucks it on the coffee table.

We race around the house flinging open all of the windows. I throw open the front and back doors for good measure.

"Dude," Matt says, running up to me in the family room. "There's a hell of a lot of smoke billowing out of the basement windows. I think something might have caught on fire."

I poke my head out of one of the windows and see the streams of smoke spiraling into the air. My chest tightens.

"Dad!" I shout. "We've got a problem!"

CHAPTER FORTY-NINE

BURNING DOWN THE HOUSE

ME, MATT, AND DAD RACE down the stairs.

The heat belts me in the face instantly. The black haze from the flash pots has nearly cleared, but now gray smoke drifts from the flames that lick at my drum kit.

"My drums!" I run over to them, trying to stomp out the fire that's threatening to consume my rock-and-roll dreams.

Someone grabs my arm and yanks me back. "Don't be a moron," Dad yells. "You get burned alive and your mom'll divorce me for sure. Go outside and snake the garden hose down here. Hurry!"

"Shouldn't we call the fire department?" Matt asks, all shaky.

"No," Dad blurts. "It's not that big a deal. You guys get upstairs and start filling pots with water. We can contain this."

I tear up the steps, out the front door, and around the house.

The hose is coiled in a messy pile by the spigot. The spray nozzle still attached. I twist the valve and the hose comes to life. A small stream of water shoots out of where the nozzle connects to the hose.

The opened basement window is only a few feet away. I scoop up the whole whack of hose, chuck it inside, then charge back into the house.

Where I slam right into Sean, who's standing in the entryway like a statue.

"The hell?" I say.

"We can't find the pots." Sean looks panicked. Like he might start crying any second.

"In the kitchen!" I bark. "In the corner cabinet! Go! Move!"

I can hear everyone rummaging around in the kitchen cupboards, but I head straight down to the basement. Dad's got a hold of my fur coat and is beating my flaming drums with the pelt. He looks like a wild man who's just killed a small bear and wants to make sure it's good and dead.

"I've almost got the drums out." Dad coughs. "We're good."

I look over in the corner, where the couch is being consumed by fire. The flames climbing the drapes like fiery snakes. "Dad! It's spreading!"

I yank the neck of my T-shirt over my nose and mouth,

squinting to see through the gray smoke. My eyes sting as I follow the hissing sound of the hose, and I shuffle my feet on the floor so I don't trip over anything.

I reach down and grab the nozzle, spin around, and stride toward the other side of the basement, spraying the hell out of everything as I go.

"Watch it with that!" Dad hollers. "*I'm* not on fire. Hit the drapes."

The stream of water is forceful at first, able to knock the soda cans right off the bar, but it quickly slows to a trickle as I make my way across the room.

Until I'm standing right in front of the burning couch and drapes and there's no water coming out of the hose at all.

"It stopped!" I shout.

"What the hell are you talking about?" Dad continues to whip my drum kit with the smoldering fur.

"There's no water. We must have run out!" I shake the nozzle hard.

"The hose doesn't run out of water, you idiot. It's probably kinked. Untangle it. Before the whole house goes up."

I whip around and shake the garden hose. It feels heavy and snagged-up behind me. Even though I've still got my shirt over my mouth and nose, my throat is raw from the smoke.

An ear-piercing *POP!* comes from the drum kit. I drop to the ground like there's gunfire.

"Goddamn it!" Dad hollers, smacking at the drums even harder.

The basement door opens. I can see the shadowy figures of Matt and Sean trudging down the steps, hear the water sloshing in giant pots.

Sean coughs. "Holy crap, it's like an oven down here!"

"Get those pots over to the couch, stat!" Dad calls out.

Matt hurls his water on the flames with a splash and sizzle. Sean swings his pot but the momentum pulls him off course and the water comes crashing down all over Dad.

"Christ on the crapper, Keyboards!" Dad shouts.

Sean cringes. "Sorry."

Matt and Sean bolt back upstairs to get refills.

I trace the hose back several paces. It's all knotted up in a big rubbery ball. No time to get the whole thing untied. Just need to get the water flowing again.

Another thunderous *SNAP!* and flash.

"Jesus!" Dad ducks down. "What are these cheap-ass drums made out of?"

I hurriedly snake the nozzle through some loops, give the hose a few more shakes, and the water hisses inside, surging back up to the nozzle.

I whip around, get down on one knee, and shoot the stream at the couch and drapes. Steaming gray smoke billows up from the inferno.

The door to the basement opens again. It's Valerie and Helen hefting the pots this time.

"Give me some of that water over here." Dad gestures to them.

Helen goes right for the drums and hurls the water directly onto the smoldering kit.

"Now *that's* what I'm talking about," Dad says.

I keep my spray focused on the drapes and couch but the fire is spreading too fast. We're fighting a losing battle. My house is going to burn down, for sure.

And just as I'm wishing I'd defied Dad and called 911, I hear sirens in the distance. They get louder and louder as they approach.

Dad's head snaps up, listening. "No. No, no, no! Who called the goddamn fire department?"

CHAPTER FIFTY

SLEDGEHAMMER

THE SIX OF US SIT ON THE CURB outside the house as the firemen finish putting out our basement.

Dad glances over at the line of onlookers from our neighborhood. "I bet it was that busybody Mrs. Croucher," he grumbles. "She can't keep her nose out of anything. Ten more minutes and we would have had the thing out ourselves."

"What are we going to tell Mom?" I ask, my eyes still stinging.

"Well, obviously we're going to have to say it was your fault," Dad replies.

"What? Why?"

My friends all look over at Dad like he's truly lost his mind.

"I'm already in the doghouse," he says. "She finds out I nearly burned down the house, I'm done. You're gonna have to take the bullet on this one. I'm sorry." He clears his throat. "And I won't be able to take it easy on you, either. Otherwise she might get suspicious. So, don't be surprised if I have to ground you for a while. A month or two, maybe. This is a pretty major infraction."

"But—"

"Oh, Christ, there's her car." Dad hides his face behind his hand.

Mom's Volvo pulls over to the curb across the street because her regular parking spot is being taken up by a fire truck. She and Angela dash out of the car and over to us.

"What's going on?" Mom says frantically.

Dad leaps to his feet. I follow, a little slower.

"Oh. *Hey,*" Dad says. "There you guys are." He tucks his hands in his pockets, rocks back on his heels. "How was the mall?"

Mom stares at Dad. "Walter, what's with the fire trucks?"

Dad looks over his shoulder. "Oh, them?" He waves this off. "Nothing. Everything's fine. Just a tiny little itsy-bitsy fire. It's all under control. But it's a good thing we caught it right away and called the fire department. Otherwise it might have spread."

"What happened?" Angela asks. "Did anything in my room get damaged?"

"No, no. It was all contained in the basement. Your room is fine. The house is fine. Everything's fine."

"Goodness." Mom wrings her hands. "Well, I'm glad you're all safe." She grabs Dad and me in a hug. "Did they say what caused it?"

"They did not," Dad says. "But we know. Don't we, Coop?"

Oh, crap. Here it comes. I should just narc him out. It'd serve him right. For being such a nutcase. For burning my drums. For embarrassing the hell out of me.

I look over at him. I can't do it. I don't want Mom to kick him out. I just wish he'd go back to being my mildly-freaky dad rather than this bizarro whackadoodle.

"Did you start smoking again?" Mom asks Dad, her lips tight. "Is that it? Because if you did—"

"It wasn't that, Mom," I say. I look over at Sean, Matt, Helen, and Val. Standing off to the side. Each of them looking concerned for what I'm about to do. "It was—"

"My flash pots," Dad interrupts. He gives me a weary little thank-you smile. "Sorry, son. I can't let you do it. This is my mess. I've got to face the music." He looks back at Mom. "I was showing the kids what I'd been working on for their rock show. You know, sparks shooting in the air and such. It didn't go exactly how I'd planned."

"In the house, you did this?" Mom's jaw is twitching. "In *our* house? The one we scrimped and saved for."

"I know, I know." Dad looks like he's eighty years old. "It was colossally stupid."

"You *think*?" Mom says.

"Look, I'm an idiot," Dad goes on. "I've *been* an idiot. You were right. This whole band thing . . . I got carried away. I just . . . I don't . . . It made me feel alive again. Like I was part of something exciting. I thought maybe we could spin it into something bigger. And that people wouldn't look at me like I was, you know, a loser."

Mom's face softens. "You're not a loser, Walter."

"Yeah, well, the jury's still out on that one," Dad says. "Anyway, I'm sorry." He looks at me and my friends. "To all of you guys. Christ, I don't know how you put up with me. You deserve a medal, that's for sure."

"Are you kidding, Mr. Redmond?" Matt says. "We wouldn't sound half as good as we do without your help."

"Yeah, we were totally sucko before you came on board," Sean adds. "Now we might not totally embarrass ourselves at the Battle of the Bands."

Dad smiles sheepishly. "That's nice of you to say, boys." He drapes an arm around my mom's shoulders. "But I think my days of band managing are over."

Once all the firemen and fire trucks have left, my family and friends take a tour of the damage.

And it's bad. *Real* bad.

"Ooooh myyy God." Sean is absolutely goggle-eyed.

"Eh. It's not so terrible," Dad announces. Like if he says it out loud it'll be true.

But the wreckage is way worse than I had even

imagined. It's like an ash-filled swamp down here. There are giant blooming black stains on the ceiling. Brown scorch marks all over the walls. The couch and coffee table and bar are demolished.

And forget about my drums. *All* of our instruments are waterlogged and trashed.

Mom's mouth makes a perfect stunned O as she sloshes across the carpet.

"I'm gonna take care of everything." Dad gestures at the mess. "Don't you worry. By the time I'm through you won't even recognize this place."

"I don't recognize it now," Mom says.

Dad laughs nervously. "That's funny. Seriously, though. It looks worse than it is. And band? We're going to salvage as much of this as we can. Whatever we can't, I'm going to find a way to replace. Don't sweat it."

But I know, standing there in the middle of all that destruction, there will be no Battle of the Bands for us.

CHAPTER FIFTY-ONE

WHERE HAVE ALL THE GOOD TIMES GONE!

I'M VERY SORRY TO HEAR THAT," Mr. Grossman says after I tell him why Arnold Murphy's Bologna Dare is going to have to bow out of the Battle of the Bands. I didn't go into too much detail. I just said we had a fire and that our equipment was destroyed. "Is there no other option? Perhaps you could rent some instruments."

"Yeah, I don't think we can swing that," I say. "Financially and all."

"But surely your parents' insurance will cover things."

"They didn't have any," I lie. Dad says there's no way we can make a claim. Not with him being directly responsible for the fire. "Not only will they not pay," Dad insisted, "our rates'll be jacked sky-high if they find out who caused it."

I trudge from Mr. Grossman's office feeling totally bummed, but also—if I'm being completely honest—a little bit relieved. At least now I won't have to deal with the repercussions of taking the stage with Helen fronting the band. Especially since it doesn't appear she'll be leaving the school anytime soon, seeing as how she hasn't received an acceptance letter from Our Lady of Mercy.

At least, as far as I know.

I've had to cease my secret visits to her mailbox because Mrs. Harriwick caught me on their porch again. I'm pretty sure she bought my excuse that I wanted to ask her about Christmas present ideas for Helen, but I also think if she catches me a third time—especially in tandem with her jammed-up mailbox—it might raise some suspicion.

But Helen hasn't mentioned getting any letters. Even with my subtle and leading inquiries: "My parents are thinking they might want me to transfer schools next year. . . .", "I got this weird notice in the mail the other day that said I was accepted into the book of the month club. And I didn't even apply. . . .", "Someone told me that Mr. Tard is gunning for the principal position at Our Lady of Mercy. . . ." And so on.

Now that the Battle of the Bands thing has resolved itself, I'm really glad Helen's letter hasn't come. Sure, she's going to be the target of Prudence's teasing till we graduate, but at least she'll never put two and two together and find out that I played a major part in filling out her application.

"What did Mr. Grossman say?" Matt asks as I step up between him and Sean at our lockers.

I grab my lock and spin the combo. "He said he was sorry."

"Not half as sorry as I am," Sean grouses. "Do you have any idea how expensive a Mesa/Boogie amplifier is? My Uncle Doug will be garnishing my allowance for the next ten years to replace it." He sighs. "Even so, it'd be totally worth it if we were still going to play. Then Tianna would be all jealous watching me onstage, getting swarmed by a mob of screaming girls."

"Yup." I grab my Health text and notebook. "It's too bad."

Out of the corner of my eye I see Prudence strutting down the hall. It dawned on me last night that her big plan to humiliate Helen will most likely involve the Health presentation that we're giving in a few days. It's why she didn't want to tell me about it. I don't know how I missed that.

I wonder if there's any way I could get Prudence to abort her mission without her getting suspicious. Because, yeah, it'll be bad for Helen. But if Prudence does whatever she's planning on doing while I'm standing in front of the class next to Helen, it'll be humiliation by association.

"I'll catch up with you guys after detention." I snick my lock shut and head off to catch up with Prudence.

"Hey, can I talk to you?" I say, matching Prudence's step.

She smiles "What's up, Coopee?"

"I think you need to postpone whatever it is you have planned for Helen."

Prudence's eyes narrow. "And why do you think that?"

"She hasn't gotten her acceptance letter yet."

"You know this, how?"

She heads down the stairs. I move with her.

"Let's just say I've been doing some covert ops. Just to make sure everything was going smoothly. I'm ninety-nine percent sure it hasn't come. And personally, I think the whole thing works best if she's already got her escape hatch when the embarrassment happens. Otherwise, her anger might fade."

"That's a very good point, Coopee," Prudence says, heading toward the front doors. She stops before leaving the school and turns back to me. "But I don't care. It's happening." She smiles. "And you know what else? She's never going to forget it."

With that, she pushes open the door and disappears outside.

Leaving me standing in the hallway, feeling like I've just been hurled off the Brooklyn Bridge with cement blocks tied to my feet.

CHAPTER FIFTY-TWO

STAND BY ME

TODAY HELEN AND I ARE GIVING our Health presentation. Several pairs have already gone this week. Most of them were pretty lame and boring. Andy Bennett and Nicky Hickey just sat on stools at the front of the room and read alcohol facts off sheets of paper. Prudence and Sam were not much better. Sam did most of the talking while Prudence just pointed to things on a poster like the world's hottest game-show hostess.

At least Matt's and Sean's project provided plenty of gross-out moments with giant pictures of herpes sores and parasitic crabs projected on a screen at the front of the room.

Helen and I have a pretty kick-ass presentation, but I'm glad we didn't have to go first. And even though I'm happy we're finally getting it over with, I feel like I've got a noose cinched tight around my neck and the milk crate

I'm standing on is wobbling beneath my feet. Especially since—if I'm right about Prudence's plans—things could get seriously ugly today.

Hopefully, Mrs. Turris will be able to keep a tight rein on the class. Though somehow I doubt it.

Anyway, once it's done, I can put this whole stupid semester behind me.

Helen and I get to class early so that we can set up. She connects her computer to the projector for the PowerPoint presentation while I put together our contraceptive diorama.

I've got a whole whack of fruits and vegetables—ends cut and glued down—standing triumphantly on a poster board: a zucchini, a carrot, a banana, a parsnip. I roll a different type of condom on each one. Ribbed, glow-in-the-dark, lambskin, Leviathan. I unfurl the female condom and insert it into an "everything" bagel. Take out the pack of birth control pills I "borrowed" from my sister's nightstand. Place the bottle of spermicidal lube next to a gargantuan cucumber for a hands-on demonstration.

Then I carefully display the extremely graphic eleven-by-fourteen-inch posters I printed out in the computer lab. There's one of a woman inserting a diaphragm, another of an X-ray showing an implanted IUD, and, for good measure, a giant wrinkly scrote with its vas hanging out, ready to be snipped.

"Good morning," Mrs. Turris says, bustling into the classroom. "You guys look like you're all—" She does a double take as she passes my grand display of grotesquerie. "Well. That's . . . very . . . visual."

I smile. "Yeah. We want to make sure people remember what we have to say. All the things we learned doing this report, Mrs. Turris—how to protect yourself from disease and unwanted pregnancy. This stuff is super-important. I, for one, am very grateful we were assigned this topic."

"Yes," she says, giving a little head shake as she averts her eyes from the vasectomy poster. "I'm glad." She moves to her desk and takes out a coffee thermos. "Don't forget to leave some time for questions. That's ten percent of the grade."

When the class arrives and is settled, we dim the lights. Helen stays standing, and I take a seat on one of the stools.

"Good morning, ladies and gentleman," Mrs. Turris says. "Today's lesson on contraception will be taught by Helen Harriwick and Cooper Redmond. Please give them your undivided attention."

I was feeling nervous before, but now it's like someone's got their hand clenched around my nads. Finding it hard to breathe. To think. To speak. I try to remember what I'm supposed to say first, but all I get is this whooshing sound in my head.

Helen clicks the remote in her hand, and the first PowerPoint slide is projected onto the screen at the front of the room. A picture of a pregnant teenage girl. "Over thirty percent of women will get pregnant before the age of twenty."

"That's my baby!" Andy calls out.

Mrs. Turris slaps the legal pad she's taking notes on. "Another word out of you, Mr. Bennett, and I'm taking points off your project. Something you can scarcely afford."

I use this diversion to flip through my notes. But somehow they're all mixed up. And the light's too dim. My first page is missing. Damn it. I try to shuffle the papers quietly, but I can't find my opening line.

Helen goes on. "Eighty percent of these pregnancies are unplanned."

"Was *yours*?" some dude coughs from the back of the room, which sends a wave of laughter throughout the class.

"Who said that?" Mrs. Turris cranes her neck. Does she really think anyone's going to confess?

It suddenly feels like my shirt collar is too tight. I should probably say something. Tell everyone to shut the hell up. But I'm too preoccupied with trying to remember my part of the presentation.

At least, that's what I tell myself.

Helen seems unfazed. She doesn't miss a beat. Just keeps rolling forward. "Nearly all of these pregnancies could have been avoided if some form of contraception had been used."

"Spay that bitch!" a girl bellows.

Mrs. Turris leaps to her feet. "Excuse me! I will not put up with these shenanigans. I expect you to give Helen and Cooper the same attention you'd like for yourselves."

Helen clears her throat and continues. "Teen mothers are at a much greater risk for dropping out of high school, and less than two percent of them will end up getting a college degree before they're thirty. Eight out of ten teen moms will have to turn to welfare to support their families." She clicks the remote, and the slide switches to a dude with thick syphilis sores glazing his back.

"Ewww. *Nasty!*" I hear someone shout, followed by more mutters and mumbles.

This slide is my cue. I sit up on the stool. Take a deep breath. And magically, the words appear in my brain. "Every year, twenty-five percent of teenagers who are sexually active will be infected with a sexually transmitted disease. And while all of the contraceptive methods we will be discussing today can help prevent pregnancies, only latex condoms can help protect against STDs."

Just then, something greasy, gray, and limp hits Helen's forearm and clings there. Muffled laughter flutters from somewhere in the center of the room.

Mrs. Turris is too busy scribbling notes on her legal pad to notice.

Helen looks down at the thing on her arm, lying there like a deflated jellyfish. She pinches the edge and peels it off, leaving an oily stain on her skin.

The laughter spreads as the entire class turns to see

Helen holding up a very large unfurled condom. Her face contorts into a look of horror as she flings the condom onto the floor and angrily wipes the goo off her arm.

The slurs come fast and furious: "Doggie bag!", "Wiener wrap!", "Pigs in a blanket!"

I glance over at my diorama and see that one of the condoms is missing from the display.

Mrs. Turris finally looks up from her desk. "All right! One more outburst and I'm handing out detentions."

A hot anger roils inside me. The movie plays in my head where I flick on the lights and save Helen from this torment.

But I can't move. I just keep spewing more statistics, my voice thin and reedy. "Fifty to sixty percent of sexually active teenagers use condoms. Twenty to thirty percent use the pill. And upwards of ten percent will not use any method at all."

Someone's cell phone starts playing "Who Let the Dogs Out?"

And then . . .

Several people at the back of the room launch raw hot dogs in the air.

And they rain down all over Helen.

The color drains from her already pale face.

Dive in front of her, goddamn it! Smack them away with your papers! Do something *for Christ's sake!*

But it's too late.

Helen's papers fall from her hand. I think she might be crying but I can't tell because she runs from the room.

Mrs. Turris bolts up from her chair. "How dare you!" she shrieks. "Principal Tard will hear about this!"

And I just sit there on the stool. My pulse thrumming in my temples. My jaw clenching so tight my teeth ache. Feeling like a complete and utter tool.

CHAPTER FIFTY-THREE

SCAR TISSUE

I RACE UP HELEN'S DRIVEWAY, drop my bike, and bound up the steps to her front door. I left school so fast after the final bell that I forgot my coat and now I'm freezing. My nose and cheeks are stinging from the cold.

My mouth is all chalky as I reach for the doorbell. I have no idea what I'm going to say. Or if it'll seem weird that I'm coming over like this. Maybe she wants to be left alone.

I glance over at my bike. Think about leaving.

But then I remember how I stood there and did nothing while Prudence and her goons threw hot dogs at Helen, and instead I press the doorbell, which makes its familiar tinny *BING-BONG.*

I tuck my hands in my pants pockets to keep warm. It's a while before I hear any movement inside the house.

The door opens and there's Helen, her eyes red-rimmed and puffy, a tissue in her hand.

"Hi." I feel my body tense, trying not to shiver. From the cold or from nervousness, I'm not sure. "Are you . . . okay?"

She shrugs.

"Mrs. Turris went ballistic after you left. I thought her head was going to explode. She marched the entire class down to Mr. Tard's office. It was nuts. But nobody was narcing anyone out."

"Typical," Helen says.

"Anyway, she said we could finish our presentation for her after school. Any time we want before winter break."

"Fine. Okay."

I shift my weight. Feel my throat get thick. "Can I . . . come in?"

She looks over her shoulder. "My mom's sleeping," she says, her voice hoarse.

"Look. Helen. I just . . ." Just what? Feel like an ass because I didn't stand up for her? How could I have? I'd never live it down. And things are bad enough as it is without me compounding the problem. Still, I can't pretend it didn't happen. "I just . . . wanted to make sure you were all right."

She smiles. Her face softening. She glances over her shoulder again. Then looks back at me. "Come on in. But be quiet until we get upstairs."

I step inside her house. We walk past the living room. I peek in to see Mrs. Harriwick asleep on the couch and hear her heavy sleep breath rising and falling.

"What's she think about all of this?" I whisper as we head up the stairs.

"She doesn't know."

"Seriously?"

Helen leads the way into her bedroom and closes the door halfway. "I just told her I had a really bad stomachache."

We sit on the plush light-blue carpet. The whole room's all pale yellow and powder blue. Neat and clean like the rest of the house. My mom would faint if my room were ever this tidy.

"So . . . I don't get it," I say. "Why didn't you tell your mom what happened?"

"She doesn't know about any of it." Helen bites the corner of her lower lip. "She's got enough to deal with. She hasn't been able to work for more than a year. I don't need to bother her with my stupid stuff."

"Don't you think she'd want to know?"

"I tried telling her once. When it all first started. But it was the worst time for her." Helen's gaze drops to her leg, where she picks at a thread on her jeans. "Her boyfriend had just broken up with her, and then she started having these dizzy spells. It was like she just couldn't hear what I was saying. I haven't brought it up since." Helen clears her throat. "I don't know. It's weird. Sometimes I feel like she's making the whole thing up. Because she feels bad for herself. I know she isn't. I've been with her at the doctor's. It's just . . . a big coincidence, right? The timing of it all. And you want to know something even worse? I get mad at her. How mean is that? She can't help that she's sick. But I get angry sometimes when she goes on about it. And then I hate myself for getting so upset. Horrible, right?"

"I don't know," I say. "Makes sense to me. It's like, everything's out of control so you get mad because it all sucks. Doesn't mean you're a bad person."

"Feels that way sometimes."

"Yeah, well, you're one of the nicest people I've ever met, so . . ."

She glances up. "Thanks. And thanks for coming by. It was sweet of you." She lowers her gaze.

"So what are you going to do now?" I ask.

She shrugs. "What's there to do? I'll get over it. Or not. I mean, look, there's only four hundred and fifty-seven actual school days left until I graduate, right?"

"You're *counting* the days?"

"Not really. Not anymore. I was last year, for sure. I downloaded a counter onto my computer. I guess I never took it off."

"What about going to a different school?" The question isn't one millisecond out of my mouth when I feel my stomach clench, remembering the Our Lady of Mercy application. But then I relax, recalling that she never heard from them.

"Sure, I've thought about it. A lot. But then the bad guys win, right?" Helen looks at me, her head tilted and her eyes a bit narrowed. My gut grips up again. "It's funny you'd ask that, though." She stands and moves over to her desk. Flips through a small stack of mail and finds an envelope. Oh, shit, she got the letter. How could I have missed it? Okay, just stay chill. "I received this last week. It's totally bizarre." She pulls a page from the envelope. Oh, God. I think I'm going to puke. "It's an acceptance letter from Our Lady of Mercy."

My lungs constrict. It's hard to get a full breath. Is she remembering all those questions I asked her? My unexpected chattiness? Still, would she be able to put it together so fast? She didn't see the application. She doesn't know the questions on it. But what if she takes the time to follow the bread crumbs all the way to my doorstep?

I get a sudden urge to confess everything. About Prudence and Bronte and Gina and Kelly. About the pranks. About the application form. Laying it all out for her.

Yeah, right. Just going over it in my head, it sounds so awful. It's too much. She'd never forgive me. Ever.

No. I just have to remain calm. I know nothing about

this. She'll never make the leap. Unless I give a hand by acting all suspish.

"Huh," I say, feeling majorly carsick. "What's bizarre about that?"

She stares at me. "I didn't apply."

"Well . . . maybe they made a mistake. Or, you know, maybe they have scouts. Like in sports. Maybe they saw your grades and said, hey, we'd like her at our school." Maybe I should just shut up now before I dig my own grave.

Helen's expression grows cold as she studies the letter. "No. It says they've reviewed my application form." She tosses the papers back on her desk. "Somebody must have filled one out with my name on it and sent it in."

You better tell her now, dude. Before she figures it all out on her own.

Why? What does it matter? Either way she's going to hate my guts. Why throw myself into the fire before I have to?

Because it'll be better coming from you. She'll respect your honesty.

Ha! What a crock! That's what parents say to their kids so they won't try to get away with stuff. No. I can't risk Helen never wanting to speak to me again. I like her too much.

The other voice in my head is stunned into silence.

Neither of us can believe I admitted it. But it's the truth. I don't want to lose her. Besides, *how* would she find out? Sure, the dots are all there, but it'd take a hell of a lot of connecting to see the whole picture. It'd be stupid to implicate myself. Never confess to anything, remember?

I take a breath. Keep my composure and say, "Why would anybody do that?"

"To get me to leave the school." Helen plops down next to me. "Don't you get it, Coop? People like Prudence and her friends think they can just maneuver people like pawns. If you give into it then it never stops. I've been able to deal with it. Not always as gracefully as I'd have liked but . . . I don't know. What about the next girl they target? What if she's not as strong as I am? I don't even want to think about it." She shakes her head. "What I'd like to know is where they got all the information to actually fill out an application."

I turn away. Remembering how she was able to read my thoughts when we were playing "If you could."

I need to change the subject. Find something else for us to talk about before she sees the guilt on my face. My gaze drifts around her room. Helen's got several U2 posters framed and hung on her walls: I could get her talking about her favorite band. A chair in the corner with an old teddy bear sitting square in the middle: Or ask who gave her the stuffed animal. Some running trophies on her desk: Maybe guide the conversation around to cross-country.

It all seems too jarring. Like I'm not listening to her.

And then I get an idea.

"Can I ask you something?" I say.

"Sure."

"How did this all start?"

Helen rubs her hand along the plush of the carpet.

"I mean, you don't have to tell me if you don't want to."

"No," she says. "It's fine. It's just . . . the whole thing's so dumb." She takes a deep breath. "It was in eighth grade. You probably didn't see it, but I was in the school musical. *Grease.*"

"Sean told me he saw you in the junior-high yearbook."

"Yeah, well, back then, Prudence and I were best friends. And this guy she was dating, Drew Avery, had already been cast as Danny. So we decided to audition because we did everything together. She'd go for Sandy so that no other girl would get to kiss Drew in the show. I just went along to support her. I thought I'd try out for one of the Pink Ladies. 'Cause it'd be fun for us to hang out and do a musical together."

"Uh-huh."

"So, I do my audition, and Mr. Krantz, the director, stops everything and says that he doesn't need to audition anybody else. That I was going to play Sandy. Prudence didn't even get a part. I told her I wasn't going to do the show but she said I had to. She'd rather have someone she could trust playing Drew's girlfriend than some skank she didn't know." Helen shakes her head like she's still trying to figure it out. "Anyway, everything seemed fine until a few weeks later, when Drew started acting all weird around me. Saying how talented I was. How exciting it was to work with me. The next thing I know he dumps Prudence and asks me out."

"Oh, crap."

"Yeah. 'Oh, crap' is right. I mean, what am I supposed to do? Even if I did like him—which I didn't—I was never going to date him. Prudence was my best friend. And so, Drew is furious with me when I turn him down and then he goes crawling back to Prudence, saying I was the one who came on to him. That I convinced him to break up with her by saying all this nasty stuff about her."

"The hell? And she believed him?"

"I tried to tell her the truth but she wouldn't even listen. And that was it. She stopped talking to me. Except to tell me that she'd make sure I never stole anyone's boyfriend ever again. It only took her a few days to get all our friends to ignore me. And shortly after that, the whole Hot Dog Helen rumors started spreading."

"Jesus," I say, feeling this rage rise up inside. At Prudence. At her friends. And at myself for being sucked into it all.

"For the longest time I tried to figure out what I could have done differently. I kept questioning everything. Was it my fault? Did I lead him on? It got to a point where

I almost felt like I deserved it or something. It's totally warped."

"And she's still pissed about it, two years later?"

Helen laughs. "You obviously don't know girls very well. We're like elephants. We have long memories. Even if those memories aren't true. Besides, it was right around then that she became so popular. I think it gave her this weird sense of power. Like she could crush anyone she wanted. I don't know. I stopped trying to figure it out."

"Did you ever think about trying to get revenge?"

"No. Not really. I guess I was hoping it would blow over eventually and I'd get my old life back. Pretty pathetic, huh?"

"We should do something. For payback. What do you say?"

Helen looks at me with her gorgeous hazel eyes. She smiles. Then leans over and kisses me.

Deeply.

Intensely.

Until I think I might lose my mind.

We part and I swallow hard. "Is that a yes?"

Helen laughs. "No. I just thought it was sweet of you. I couldn't help myself."

Sweet of me? Oh, God, if she only knew . . .

I can't believe what a supreme mess I've made of everything. All I can do now is pray that she never finds out the truth.

CHAPTER FIFTY-FOUR

BRAND NEW DAY

WHERE THE HELL HAVE YOU BEEN?" Dad says the second I walk through the door. He's vibrating with excited energy, his fingers wiggling, like he's been standing there waiting all day.

I drop my backpack on the floor of the vestibule. "I had to stay after school with Helen to do our Health presentation for Mrs. Turris."

"Oh." He looks a little embarrassed. "Well. How did that go?"

"Fine," I say. "She gave us an A." I don't mention the fact that it was probably because she felt sorry for us. But I'll take it anyway I can get it.

"An A? Wow. That's great." He claps his hands and rubs them together. "So. You ready for a surprise?"

"Sure."

He grins and waggles his eyebrows. "Okay, then. Follow me."

I trail Dad to the basement door. He covers my eyes with his hand and carefully leads me down the stairway.

"What's going on?" I ask. "Why all the secrecy?"

"Just shut your pie hole and wait."

For the last week he's only come up from the basement for meals and to shower. We've heard a lot of hammering, sawing, carpet tearing, and drilling down here, but nobody's been allowed to see what he's been up to.

"We're almost there." Dad's got a hold of my right arm as I feel for the next step with my outstretched foot.

Finally we reach the bottom of the stairs, and Dad guides me across the basement floor. The air smells of sawdust and lacquer and fresh paint.

"Okay. Are you all set?" he asks, his calloused palm a scratchy blindfold on my face.

"Yup."

He repositions me and then pulls his hand away from my eyes in a ta-da gesture.

Holy crap. For a second I feel like we've entered someone else's house. The basement has been completely renovated. Hardwood floors, a brand-new bar, beautiful carpet laid out across half the space, and a fresh coat of buttercream paint on the walls. It looks like it belongs in a magazine.

"Wow," I say. "It's amazing, Dad."

"It's almost all recycled stuff I got from the junkyard." He smiles proudly, standing up tall. "You think your Mom'll like it?"

"Uh, *yeah*. Maybe too much. She'll probably make you get to work on the rest of the house now."

Dad laughs. "Good point. Maybe we don't show it to her until I'm back at work full-time. Which shouldn't be too long hopefully, since I started sending out resumes again." He grabs my shoulders. "Okay. You ready to see the best part?"

He spins me around, and what I see makes my mouth fall open in shock. In the far corner of the basement is an entire band setup.

A really bizarre looking setup. But a full one, nonetheless.

There's a Pearl drum kit with orange flames painted on the shells and a demon airbrushed on the bass head, stacks of beat-up Marshall amps covered in old bumper stickers, four dented microphones in listing mic stands, a neon-green electric guitar with a spread-eagle naked woman painted on it, and two gigantic keyboards with chipped, yellowing keys.

I look at him, confused. "Where'd you get all this stuff?"

"Made a few calls." He's acting all caszh but I can tell he's pretty pleased with himself. "Got in touch with my old band members. When I told them our situation, they offered to loan us their instruments for the performance."

I walk over to the gear, take a seat behind the drums, grab the drumsticks, and twirl one around my fingers. "I already told Mr. Grossman we weren't going to be able to play."

"Well, tell him you can now."

I give the floor tom a little tap. The head is loose and muddy sounding.

I think about what this means. That I'll now have to perform in front of the entire school with Helen. That my chances of tagging all the bases—*any* of the bases—will be officially shot. But the thought of being up onstage with Helen no longer fills me with dread. Not after everything we've been through, and everything I've learned about Prudence.

I look at my dad, who's still struggling not to bust into a huge grin. He did all this for me. For us.

"Dad?" I say. "You think we have a shot? You know. To win?"

He smiles. Considering the question. I expect to hear the "as long as you're in it, you've got a shot to win it," speech, even though I wouldn't quite believe him.

But what he says to me is, "Who knows?" He shrugs. "But, really, who cares? At the end of the day, it matters shit one what anyone else thinks about you. Just have a good time. That's what rock and roll is all about anyway."

CHAPTER FIFTY-FIVE

YOU SHOOK ME ALL NIGHT LONG

No FREAKIN' WAY," Matt says, staring at the sprawling-naked-woman guitar.

Tomorrow night's the Battle of the Bands, and I've called an emergency rehearsal so that we can shake off the rust and get used to our new instruments. Of course, we can't get started until I convince Matt to play the pornographic six-string.

"Oh, my God," Helen squeals. "It's obscene."

Valerie laughs. "Well, at least they'll have something else to focus on besides your music."

"Jesus." Sean shields his eyes like the image is blinding him. "You can practically see her pancreas."

"It's not so bad." I tilt my head to get a different perspective. "It's like . . . a work of art."

"They should hang it in a museum, then." Matt crosses his arms. "Because I'm not playing that thing."

"You *have* to," I say. "It's the only guitar we have. People will love it. It's rock and roll."

"That's easy for you to say," Matt huffs. "You have a demon on your drums."

"Yeah, but he's also naked."

Matt glares at me. "He's *red*. And he's got no . . . bits. So it doesn't really count, does it?"

"All right, just a minute." Valerie looks around the basement. "What if we cover her up with something?" She marches over to Dad's toolbox and grabs a roll of duct tape. "With this. We can fashion a little tape bikini. *Problème résolu*."

"That's genius," I say, taking the duct tape from Val.

Ten minutes later, I've cut out a tiny silver bathing suit and magically we've gone from an X-rated guitar to one you could safely play in front of a group of kindergartners.

"Better?" I hand the instrument off to Matt.

"Much," he says, lifting the strap over his head.

Sean plunks away at his ancient synthesizers. "Hey. Some of these keys are dead, you know?"

"How many?" I ask.

Sean counts them out. "Six that I've found so far."

"Can you work around them?"

He shrugs. "I'll guess we'll find out.

I move behind my drums and grab my sticks. "Okay, then. Let's run the set."

I count us in, and we proceed to trip and stumble through our eight songs.

Then we trip and stumble through them again. And again. And again. Helen sounds absolutely stagg, it's just us "musicians" who are having all the difficulty.

Matt looks pale. "Are we sure we want to go through with this?"

"I don't know," I say, feeling like an empty wind sock. "We sound pretty sloppy."

Sean plunks at one of the yellowed keys. "Maybe we should re-quit."

"No," Valerie protests. "Don't say that. You can't give up. You're just getting used to the new instruments. That's all."

"Val's right." Helen puts her mic back into the stand. "We need to do this." She fixes us with her gaze. "You guys have put too much work into this band to give up now. We all have." Helen takes a deep breath. "Look. You think I'm not terrified? Getting up in front of the entire school when I know what they all think of me? But here's the thing. Every time the fear starts to set in, I tell myself, 'Helen, you're not in this alone. Your friends are behind you. And you *love* singing. Don't let that get stolen from you.'"

Her words nearly knock me off my stool. I've been so focused on myself—on how embarrassing it would be for *me* to be seen with *her*—that I never actually thought about how incredibly ballsy it is for Helen to be doing this in the first place.

She grabs the mic from the stand and unfurls the

cable. “We’ve been given a second shot here. Let’s take advantage of it and prove to everyone we have no fear.”

Matt straightens up, smoothes his hand down the lapel of his lab coat. “You’re right. We’re in this thing together. It’s way less terrifying than when you’re on your own.”

“Yeah,” Sean says, adjusting his sombrero. “They can take our manager. They can burn our instruments. But they can *not* take our friendship. *Vamanos mis amigos!*”

Everyone looks at me, waiting for my verdict. This means way more to Helen than I realized. I can’t bail on her now. Not after all the crappy things I’ve already done to her.

“Okay.” I nod, feeling slightly queasy. “Let’s do this thing!”

A collective cheer goes up as I count us in once again and we tear into our first song.

CHAPTER FIFTY-SIX

TONIGHT'S THE NIGHT

THE BIG NIGHT HAS FINALLY ARRIVED, and I have to say, I'm feeling pretty chill. It took a while yesterday, but by the time our rehearsal was over, we were sounding almost half-decent. Helen was right. Once we shook off the jitters, we were able to make the songs come alive. I know Dad doesn't think we have much of a chance of winning, but with Helen's killer voice, and the added adrenaline rush we should get from playing live, I think we might just surprise everyone tonight.

"Come on, hurry it up," Dad calls out as we bring all the equipment up from the basement. He looks up at the cold gray sky. "We want to get on the road before Frosty starts dumping on us."

Matt, Sean, Val, and Helen have all come by to help get ready. We pack three cars—our station wagon, Matt's mom's Buick, and Sean's parents' Volvo—with the drums, amps, guitars, keyboards, stands, microphones, cables, and PA system. And even though Dad tries to hurry us along, by the time everything's loaded, the flurries are coming down with a vengeance.

"Are you sure they're still going to have this thing?" Matt's mom says as we head out my front door, everyone bundled up in their winter coats. "It seems dangerous to be on the road."

"It'll be fine," Dad assures her. "Just follow me. I'll make sure I hit all the cars and pedestrians to get them out of your way."

Matt and Val go in his mom's car with his grandpa Arlo and Mrs. Hoogenboom, Sean rides shotgun with his father, and Helen joins me in the backseat of our car. Mom starts in with Christmas carols as soon as we're out of the driveway.

"God rest ye merry gentlemen, let nothing you dismay," she sings.

"No, Mom," I say. "It's *Undress these married gentlemen, their long things on display."*

She turns and looks at me over her shoulder. "Now I know you're pulling my leg."

"I think he's right, honey," Dad says. *"Renouncing nice behavior, their dingle-dangles sway."*

I laugh as Mom gives Dad a stern look.

"To save us all from Satan's power when we were gone astray," Helen sings, picking up the song.

"That's right." Mom croons, *"O tidings of comfort and joy. Comfort and joy. O tidings of comfort and joy."*

Helen looks over at me and smiles. She takes my hand and gives it a squeeze.

"How are you doing?" she asks.

"Good," I say. "You?"

"Nervous." She takes a deep breath. "But no fear, right?"

"You're going to be great."

We get to school and Dad pulls up to the gym doors, the car skidding a few feet on the slushy pavement before it comes to a full stop.

Dad's out of the wagon first, playing traffic cop and waving the other two cars into position next to ours.

It's a short walk to the gym doors, but the ground is slick and we have to be extra careful as we lug all of the equipment inside. Thankfully, it takes less time to get all the stuff out of the cars than it did to pack everything in them.

The gym is crazed with activity. Teachers and students setting up refreshment tables, stringing crepe paper streamers, hanging posters, filling balloons. The other bands are unpacking their instruments. Someone has a stereo blasting Radiohead over the loudspeaker.

Standing there, taking this in, I'm suddenly feeling all shaky inside.

"You need help setting up?" Dad asks as he carries the last few things into the gym.

"No," I say, acting way more caszh than I feel. I glance back over my shoulder at the pile of equipment sitting on the gym floor. "We got it. Thanks." I look up at the caged-in clock on the wall and see it's just after six. "The show doesn't start for another couple of hours. You guys should go to the diner and grab a dessert or something."

"All right, then. We'll leave you to it." Dad claps me on the shoulder. "Don't forget. Bring the attitude. And have fun."

"We will," I say.

He gives me a thumbs-up and then proceeds to do his "big junk walk" across the gym and out the door. At any other time, I'd be hiding my face with embarrassment. But right now, it just makes me smile.

Each of the four bands have been designated a wall in the gym. The band names written on butcher paper and taped to the floor of our respective "stages." Cheeba Pet is by the bank of windows. Mjöllnir is opposite them in front of the foldaway bleachers. The Wicked is setting up at the far end of the gym under one of the basketball hoops. Which leaves the area under the opposing hoop for us.

"How should we do this?" Sean asks, standing amidst the heap of equipment with this bewildered where-do-we-even-start look.

"We'll set up the drums at the back," I say, gesturing at the spot directly under the basketball hoop. "Then we'll do your keyboards on my left. Helen's mic in front, of course. And the PA and guitar on my right."

★ ★ ★

It takes around an hour to get everything up and running. The drums put together, the keyboard stands fully assembled, the PA wired up, all four of the microphones connected, the cables taped down to the floor.

"May I have your attention?" Mr. Grossman says, standing in front of the judges' table. "Would all band members please join me over here."

The bands all leave their respective stages and congregate around Mr. Grossman. When Matt, Sean, Helen, and me approach, it's the first time any of the other group members seem to notice that Helen is part of our band.

Prudence, Bronte, Gina, and Kelly are the ones most visibly distressed. Glaring at us, then turning to each other and whispering. Justin Sneep and his baked boys don't even bat a puffy red eye. And Andy Bennett appears to find the whole thing hilarious.

"Well, well, well," Andy says. "Look who's been adopted from the kennel."

This gets a big laugh from his band members.

I feel my face flush. A rising sense of uneasiness. Like maybe it was a bad idea to go through with this after all. But I force the feeling down and look over at Helen. Standing there. Being strong. And I want to be strong for her.

"Does she howl?" Andy says. "I mean . . . sing?"

More laughter. Prudence and her pals joining in.

I ignore them, like Helen's doing. Keep myself calm. And wait for Mr. Grossman to tell us why he called us over.

Finally, he clears his throat. "I've written the numerals one through four on sheets of paper and placed them in this receptacle." Mr. Grossman indicates a small red cereal bowl on the table. "The number you pick will determine the order in which your band will do their sound check, as well as the order in which you will perform. Please choose a representative to pick a number for your party. We'll do it alphabetically by group name. That means Arnold Murphy's Bologna Dare will draw first."

I tap Matt's elbow. "Go pick number four," I say.

Matt rolls his eyes. "I'll see what I can do."

He approaches Mr. Grossman, reaches his hand into the bowl, grabs a small square of paper, and unfolds it.

Matt shrugs. "Got it."

I give him the thumbs-up.

"Why'd you want us to play last?" Sean asks me.

"Last band is always the headliner. And the one everyone remembers."

Once all the numbers are chosen, the performance order is set: Cheeba Pet, Mjöllnir, The Wicked, Arnold Murphy's Bologna Dare.

We listen to Cheeba Pet as they run through their ten-minute sound check. Playing a few bars of a tune by The Doors, the opening of a Bob Marley song, and then a couple of minutes of some kind of thrash-metal jam. It's a bizarre mix of stuff, but they sound amazing. So much for all the other bands being tragic.

Mjöllnir does their sound check next, performing

something completely unrecognizable as music. It's a whole lot of hiss and distortion with Ernie Plingus screaming over it. If that's the best they've got, then at least I know we won't come in last.

Matt picks up his bikini-girl guitar and starts tuning it up. "Jesus, I'm getting nervous. Is anyone else getting nervous? All of a sudden, I can't remember the chords to any of our songs."

"It's okay," Helen says. "It's normal to be a little anxious before a performance."

"You don't understand." Matt looks down at his fret board. His hands are shaking. "I'm not just a *little* anxious. I'm terrified. My palms are sweating. I'm going to rust out my strings." He wipes his palms on his jeans.

I step up next to Matt. Put my arm around his shoulders. "You're going to be dazz, Matt. Trust me. You *know* the chords. We ran through these songs a million times yesterday." I look across the gym at Valerie, who's talking to Ms. Hosie. "Just chill. We're going to have Val stand right in front during our set. You focus on her. It's just going to be Val and The Doctor in this room. No one else."

Matt nods as The Wicked start in on their warm-up. They do part of a Beyoncé tune and part of a Pink song. I can't say I'm too impressed. Maybe they're just holding back.

"We're up," I say when The Wicked put down their instruments.

"Can I put on my outfit?" Matt looks all twitchy as he plugs in his guitar.

"No." I get myself settled on the stool behind my drums. "We're saving that for the show."

Sean hits the switch on his keyboards. "What do you want to play?"

"Let's do 'Go Your Own Way,'" Helen says. "Since we're not doing that in our set."

"Everyone ready?" I get nods from Matt, Sean, and Helen, then count us in.

We play through the first chorus. Sean hits a few sour notes and I speed up the beat a little too much, but Helen's voice is pitch-perfect.

I catch Prudence and her gang hanging by the doors, listening to us and looking totally green, which makes me smile.

"Matt," Sean says when we stop. "I can barely hear your guitar. You need to turn it up."

He winces at the suggestion. "Can't I just keep it in the background?"

I stand and look over my drums. "Dude. Come on. You've got this. It's go monster or go home time."

"I know. It's just . . . when I've got my doctor's coat on I can pretend I'm someone else. But like this"—Matt gestures at his street clothes—"I feel so . . . exposed."

"Just close your eyes then," I say. "And *pretend* you're wearing your coat."

Matt nods apprehensively. “Okay. I’ll try.” He turns up the volume on his amp and closes his eyes.

I start the drum intro to “Dani California” and we roll through the first two verses. We’re much tighter during this song, which makes me breathe a whole lot easier.

“Sounds good, guys,” Helen says, placing her mic back in the stand.

Valerie approaches and grabs Helen’s arm. “We better start getting your outfit ready.”

I laugh. “It’s *that* complicated?”

“Good things take time,” Valerie says. “Come on, we’ll use the second floor bathroom so we’re not disturbed.”

The girls exit and make their way down the hall. I catch sight of Prudence and Bronte heading in the same direction, and I get a bad feeling. I’m up off my drum stool, starting to go after them, when Sean grabs my arm.

“Coop, I’m getting some serious popping in my amp,” he says. “What do you think it could be?” He flips the switch on the amplifier to demonstrate. There’s a heavy buzzing sound punctuated by a series of loud snaps.

I glance toward the gym doors and tell myself that everything’s fine; that Valerie’s with Helen; that I’m just being oversensitive; and that we only have a few minutes to take care of this problem before the first band starts playing.

“Let’s take a look,” I say, moving to the back of Sean’s Marshall stack. “It’s probably just a loose cable or something.”

CHAPTER FIFTY-SEVEN

CRUMBLIN' DOWN

I'M CROUCHED BEHIND SEAN'S AMP, about to apply electrical tape to the suspect cable, when out of nowhere this miserable feeling crashes over me like a tidal wave. It's totally bizarre. I've never felt anything like it before in my life.

It's like this knowing drops down into me and I am aware now that something's wrong with Helen. I don't know what it is, or how I know it. I just do.

I move from behind the amplifier, stepping by Matt. "I'll be right back."

"Where are you going?" Matt asks.

"To check on the girls," I say.

Sean calls after me but whatever he says doesn't register.

I bust through the gym doors and start walking down the hallway toward the stairs. The endless succession of blue lockers lining the walls, the shiny beige floor, the fluorescent lights on the ceiling, seem to stretch out forever. I've got that panicky I'm-not-going-to-make-it-in-time feeling thrumming inside me.

In time for what? I have no idea.

I pick up the pace, walking faster. But still the staircase at the end of the hall feels like it's a mile away.

Prudence and Bronte come down the steps. They're both laughing like they've just heard the greatest joke ever. As they approach me, they attempt to compose themselves.

"Good luck tonight," Bronte sputters as they pass me. She waves Gina's Flip Video camera at me. "You're going to need it, traitor."

And then both of them are busting up again.

I break into a run, taking the stairs two by two. Bolting down the second floor hallway, I have to skid to a stop when I finally reach the girl's bathroom. I knock on the hollow metal door, trying to catch my breath. "Helen? Are you okay?"

There are voices coming from the other side but I can't make out what they're saying.

I pound the door with my fist. "Helen! Are you in there? Is everything all right?"

Several eternal seconds pass. I raise my fist to knock again, when Valerie cracks open the door. She has this I-hate-your-guts scowl on her face. I can hear Helen's heaving sobs coming from inside the bathroom, and it breaks my heart.

"You're such a bastard, Coop." Her tone is contained but you can tell she's pissed because her French accent is thicker than usual. "How could you?"

The terrible look in her eyes startles me more than her words. "How could I what? What happened? Let me see her." I try to look past Val but she doesn't budge.

"Didn't she have enough to deal with already?"

Helen's sobbing is suddenly louder, like she's just been hit with a wave of impossible grief. Valerie glances over her shoulder, then returns her accusing eyes to me. "Is it true? You helped Prudence and her friends pull all those pranks? Took a dead frog from biology so they could put it in her sandwich? Stole her locker combination so they could break in?" Valerie's voice is laced with anger and disbelief. "And then helped them fill out an application to Our Lady of Mercy?"

"Did they tell you that? They're full of crap." But my stomach heaves with guilt, because I *was* the one who stole her locker combo. And who filled out the application. But the rest was all Prudence. Prudence and her minions.

"That's what we thought, too." Valerie shakes her head. "Then they showed us the video of you guys planning it all. And the text message you sent Prudence, the one with Helen's locker combination."

"OK, Val, listen—"

"And then," she says, "they handed over a copy of the filled-out application form. In your handwriting. Helen told me about all the questions you asked her. To 'get to know her better.' You're despicable, Cooper."

"No, it wasn't . . ." I can't get the air deep enough in my lungs. "Look, let me—"

"I hope it was worth it," Valerie says. "You completely destroyed her."

"Let me talk to her, please!" I try to push past her.

Valerie doesn't move. "She has nothing to say to you. You're an asshole, Coop."

"Helen!" I call over Valerie's shoulder. "It's Coop. Listen to me. I'm sorry! Come out. I can explain. Please!"

Valerie glares at me. "Go away."

"But—"

She cuts me off with her dark stare. "Do the right thing for once in your life and leave her alone."

Valerie disappears into the bathroom, the door swinging slowly shut behind her.

My body sags, like my skeleton's turned to rubber. I lean back against the wall, trying to steady myself. Just as I turn to go, I see Matt and Sean approaching.

"Hey, Coop," Sean calls out.

"They're about to start," Matt says, jittery with nerves. "We should—" The look in his eyes suddenly shifts. Restlessness replaced by concern. "What's going on?"

"I fucked up," I say, feeling dead inside. "Completely and absolutely."

"What happened?" Sean asks.

"I'm a huge tool. What can I say?" I gesture with my head toward the bathroom door. "They'll tell you all about it. I have to get out of here."

I turn and start walking toward the stairs.

"Coop, what's going on?" Matt calls after me.

I don't answer. Just keep moving.

"What about the show?" Sean says.

I trudge down the steps and head out the side door, into the blizzard. My feet crunch the snow on the ground. It's dark. And freezing cold. But I don't care.

I just keep walking.

CHAPTER FIFTY-EIGHT

LANDSLIDE

BY THE TIME I LOOK UP from the snow-caked ground I realize I've walked at least a mile from the school. All the way up to the Rockville Avenue Pool.

Everything's so quiet. Like the world is holding its breath.

I step up to the fence and grip it. Press my forehead against the chain links. They've emptied the pool for the season. It's just a concrete hole now, filling up with snow. It's weird being here in the winter. I forget all about this place once they close it down at the end of August. I mean, I know it still exists. It's just that it's like a television that's been turned off. You pass by, you know it's still there, but you just sort of ignore it.

I scale the fence. Don't care if anyone sees me. It's like I've gone numb. Don't even feel the rawness in the air anymore, the sting on my skin.

It's a good thing they take the diving boards down in the winter or I might be tempted to see if I could survive a cannonball into the powder that's accumulated on the bottom of the pool. It's only a few inches deep, so probably not.

Instead, I climb the ladder down into the empty pool and walk through the snow blanket. Kicking up the perfectly smooth whiteness as I go.

I hate the fact that I can't run away from myself. No matter where I go, my stupid voice still rattles around in my head. Telling me that I shouldn't have done this or I should have done that. Like I don't know all this already? Like I need to keep hearing it again and again? It's not as though I sat down and planned to ruin everything.

It just . . . happened.

Keep telling yourself that, Coop. Maybe you'll start believing it.

I believe it because it's true.

Really? So how did you imagine things would turn out?

All right, shut the hell up, okay? Just, leave me alone.

But you are *alone.*

You see? This is what I'm dealing with. My own brain has turned on me. Trying to use logic and facts to confuse me.

I make my way past the lifeguard stands, to the deep end of the pool, and sit down with my back against the twelve-foot wall. I grab a handful of snow and press it into a sad looking snowball. Matt, Sean, and me could totally have a killer snowball fight down here. No place to run and hide. It'd be a free-for-all. Sean would end up huddled in the corner, pleading for us to stop barraging him.

It would be good times.

Although, after they hear what I did to Helen, I doubt they'll ever want to hang out again. I wouldn't blame them, either. *I* don't even want to hang out with me.

I hurl my malformed snowball into the air and it lands just a few yards away, rolling a wobbly path through the snow.

There's no fixing this. Valerie's right. I'm despicable.

And I've completely blown it. With Helen. With my friends. Everything.

Stupid.

How could I be so stupid?

I punch the ground.

Ow. Damn. That was stupid, too. I rub my throbbing knuckles.

At least I'm not frozen yet. I wonder if I'd freeze to death if I stayed here all night. Like Jack Nicholson at the end of *The Shining*. Would I really turn blue like that? Have icicles dripping off my face?

My nose starts to run but I don't bother wiping it away. Just sniff it back, which does nothing. I tilt my head up and watch the steam stream from my lips. Let the snowflakes land on my face.

The way the light's shining, and how the snow's falling, it looks like I'm traveling through hyperspace. The stars hurtling by me.

If I was the Silver Surfer and I had the Power Cosmic, I'd travel through time and go back to this summer. When everything was dope and all my plans worked like a charm. And Matt, Sean, and me stuck together no matter what. Back before the school year. Before being partnered with Helen. And all the crap with Prudence, and the hot dogs, and the Battle of the Bands.

Several ice crystals land in my eyes. Making them water. Snapping me from my daydream. Tears stream over my temples and onto my ears, almost like I'm crying. But I'm not crying. I'm not. It's just the snow.

I level my head and stare out at the empty pool.

The snowfall is slowing. Just flurries now, floating softly to the ground. Slowly drifting down. Reminding me of the drifty feeling of dancing with Helen in my room.

And then it comes to me. The realization.

I don't want to take it all back. Not the hours of playing "Would you rather?" with Helen. Or dancing to U2 in my room. Or our first kiss. Or hearing what an awesome singer she is. I wouldn't trade any of that stuff for a million nights with Prudence Nash. Because who wants Prudence when there's Helen?

Helen, who was ready to stand up there in front of the entire school and sing with our crappy band because she didn't want to let the bad guys win. Who has more courage in her pinky finger than I have in my whole body.

I mean, look at me! Sitting here feeling sorry for myself. Bailing on my friends. Leaving them high and dry to explain to everyone why we're not going to play. Just because I screwed up and don't want to deal with it.

Jesus Christ, what kind of friend is that?

I get to my feet. Brush the snow from the backs of my legs.

No. If they still want to play—if *Helen* still wants to play—I'm going to be there to play. I owe it to her. To give her what little I can. She deserves to be allowed to show off her talent. The school should know how incredible she is.

I turn my cell phone back on to check the time—8:52 p.m.—and notice that I have fifteen messages. Don't need to listen to them to know who they're from.

Mjöllnir's probably already three songs into their migraine-inducing set. If I hurry, I should be able to get back just as The Wicked hit the stage.

I climb out of the pool and over the fence.

And start running down Rockville Avenue.

CHAPTER FIFTY-NINE

I SHOT THE SHERIFF

WHERE THE HELL WERE YOU?" Sean says when he sees me coming down the hall.

"I had to clear my head." I rub my hands together, trying to get the blood flowing.

The Wicked have already started playing in the gym. Even muffled through the doors I can tell they're rocking it. They were holding back during the sound check, for sure.

"We called you a million times." Matt waves his cell phone. "Jesus, Coop. Is it true? What Valerie said you did to Helen?"

I nod, not able to meet his eyes.

"But . . . why?" Sean asks. If my heart wasn't already destroyed, Sean's totally baffled expression would break it.

I take a deep breath. "I could give you all my lame-ass excuses but they don't amount to a weasel's wang. All

I want to do right now is talk to Helen. Apologize. And hopefully, make it up to her."

"I don't know if that's possible, Coop." Matt looks at me. "Val says Helen's super upset. You really screwed up."

"Tell me about it. And you don't even know the worst part." I swallow. "I think . . . I'm in love with her."

Sean's eyes widen to the size of Ping-Pong balls. "Seriously?"

"Yeah. Seriously. Which is why I have to at least give it a shot." I glance over my shoulder at the stairs. "Are they still up in the bathroom?"

"Helen is," Matt says. "Valerie went to get her a drink from the soda machine."

"Good." I brush some of the melting snow off my shirt. "Look guys, I'm really sorry about all of this. And I don't deserve your forgiveness. Or to ask you for any favors. But when Val heads back, could you maybe try and stall her for me? I just . . . need a little time with Helen alone."

Matt and Sean share a look.

"Sure," Matt says. "We'll try."

"Thanks."

I turn and head off. As I climb the steps, my mind tries to spin the story every which way possible. The excuses, the justifications, the explanations. All the ways I could make myself come out looking not so heinous.

But as I walk down the second floor hallway, I know there's only one way through this mess.

The truth.

Which is something I've never been very good at.

"Helen?" I call out, pushing open the door to the girls' bathroom. "Are you in here?" My voice echoes off the sage-green tiles as I cautiously step inside.

When I turn the corner, I see that all of the stall doors are open except the one at the far end, which is just now shutting. I hear the latch sliding.

"Helen, it's Coop." I approach the closed door. "Is that you?"

"Go away," she rasps. "Leave me alone."

"I can't. I just want . . ." I take a shaky breath. "Could you please come out?"

Helen sniffles. "I don't want to see you."

There's a weight on my chest as I search for the right words; what I need to say to make this all better. "Listen. I know an apology isn't nearly enough but . . . I *am* sorry. I was a complete asshole."

"Worse."

"A *major* complete asshole. Look. I'll be totally honest with you, okay? I didn't do everything they said I did, like the frog and stuff like that. But I did give your locker combo to Prudence, and I did help them fill out the Our Lady of Mercy application. I told myself it was for the best, that you'd be better off at another school." I close my eyes. Feel the swell of self-loathing filling me up. Oh, God, this is even harder than I thought it would be. "But the truth is . . . I was worried about us being partners . . . and how it would affect the way people saw me. And I was afraid. I was afraid it was going to ruin my reputation. So everything I did—joining the Battle of the Bands, filling out that application, trying to weasel my way out of spending time with you—they were all done to save myself. To impress Prudence and her gang. It was totally cruel and selfish and stupid." I sigh. "Seriously, if I had any brains at all I would have figured out those girls weren't worth impressing back in third grade, when Prudence and Bronte stole my Pokémon lunch box and threw it on the roof of the school." I shake my head. "But let's face it, I'm a slow learner."

I think I hear a little laugh from Helen but I'm not sure.

I place my hand flat against the door. Feel the cold painted metal on my palm. "And *all* of that was before I realized how amazing you are. Like, *really*. You're the coolest person I've ever met. And you're a million times more beautiful and smart and talented than those girls could ever hope to be."

Helen shifts behind the door. "I trusted you."

"I know, and—"

"I feel cheated, Coop." I can hear her starting to cry again. "It's dumb but I felt like . . . we had something special, you know? Something hopeful. And it was all a big lie."

My heart is breaking all over again. "Helen. Please—"

"I don't know what to believe anymore," she says. "Everything's turned upside down. I thought . . . I don't know. I thought you were different from everyone else."

"No. Listen. I *am* different. I mean . . . I wasn't . . . but I am now. And everything we had was real. I swear." I take another trembling breath. There's a boa constrictor around my rib cage. "I don't know how else to tell you. I am so, *so* sorry. If I could take it all back. All the bad stuff. I would. Every single bit of it. I just . . . I didn't know who you were. How brill you are. And I didn't know that"—I press my cheek up against the door—"that I was going to fall in love with you. By the time I finally figured it all out, it was too late. Everything was already set in motion. I didn't know how to get out of it. I thought, if I told you what they got me to do, I'd hurt you even more."

I shake my head. Feel the tears running down my face. "Please." The word hitches in my throat. "Don't tell me I've ruined us."

There is silence. I wish I could see her face. Gauge her reaction to all of my words. But the only things I have to go on are the sounds on the other side of the door. And now with her so quiet, I don't even have that.

Finally, Helen takes a long, deep breath. And lets it

out. "You haven't . . . ruined us," she says. "It's just . . . going to take a bit of time. That's all."

"Of course," I say, feeling the heaviness start to lift from my chest. "I completely understand. I'd feel exactly the same way." Finally I can get enough air into my lungs. "But . . . will you open the door at least?"

"I don't know. I'm in my band outfit." I can hear the hesitation in her voice. "I feel . . . kind of stupid."

"But don't you still want to play?"

"Oh, Coop. I don't think I can face everyone. Not now."

"Helen, no. Come on. Remember what you said. Don't let the bad guys win here. Don't let them steal this from you. Once you get up there and start singing, everyone's going to be totally blown away. And they'll all fall for you. Just like I did."

"You really think so?"

"How could they not? You're the best singer I've ever heard. And besides, we're in this together, remember?"

There's another long silence. I can sense her weighing my words.

And then . . .

"Okay," she says. "But I have to fix my makeup. How much time do we have?"

I check my cell phone. The Wicked should be wrapping up their set right about now. "I think we're on in the next few minutes. How much time do you need?"

"Five minutes, maybe. If Valerie can help me."

"All right. Do what you have to do." I pocket my cell. "If the time comes, we'll just start the intro to the first song and keep playing it until you can get to the stage."

"Okay," she says shakily.

I start to go, but at the door I turn back. "Helen?"

"Yeah?"

"I meant what I said, you know. About . . . I really do love you."

She's quiet for a while, and my heart starts beating faster. But then I hear her. "I know. I believe you. See you out there."

CHAPTER SIXTY

CARRY ON WAYWARD SON

THE WICKED ARE WRAPPING UP their final song as Matt, Sean, and I enter the gym. Each one of the girls is dressed in a painted-on, pastel-colored racing-style jumpsuit: Prudence in pink, Kelly in baby blue, Gina in green, and Bronte in yellow. And even though I'm beyond pissed at them, they still look unbelievably hot. Which is why they've always gotten away with everything they've gotten away with, I guess—until now.

The gym is chock with students, parents, and teachers, all dancing and swaying and clapping to the music. Kelly does a pick drag up her guitar and Gina does a drum fill and then hits her crash cymbals to end the tune. The audience breaks into wild whoops and catcalls and applause.

The three of us make our way through the crowd toward our equipment.

I clap Matt on the shoulder as we get to our stage. "You gonna be okay?"

"Me? Sure." He puts on his doctor's coat and stethoscope, lifts his guitar, and slips the strap over his head. "How about you?"

"I feel pretty damn good, actually." I slip into my smoke-drenched fur coat, dangle the chains around my neck, slide on my "ruby" ring, and don my purple Stetson. "The school is finally going to see how incredible Helen is. Let's make this great for her."

"Okay," Sean says, flipping his keyboard and amp switches. *"Levantemos la azotea!"* He grabs his poncho and sombrero and completes his *El Mariachi* transformation.

"Right." I point at Sean with a drumstick. "What he said."

"Our final band of the evening," Mr. Grossman announces over the gym's PA, "is Arnold Murphy's Bologna Dare. Please make your way to the north end of the gym."

The mass of people turn around and herd their way toward us. There are so many bodies out there, it's like the entire town showed up. Which is surprising, considering the weather outside.

Seeing everyone's faces in the gym makes every muscle in my body tighten, the saliva in my mouth drying up. I pray this goes well. That I didn't just convince Helen to come out here to be slaughtered. That people really do see how incredibly talented she is.

All of a sudden this means so much more than it did before.

I try to shake the tension out of my arms. Flex my fingers. I tilt my head to one side, then the other, stretching out the muscles in my shoulders.

I look over to the doors, hoping that Helen will step through them any second now.

As soon as everyone has gathered around, Mr. Grossman points to us from the judges' table, giving us the go ahead.

"Okay," I say, filling my lungs to capacity and slowly letting the air out. "Here we go, boys." I sit up tall on the drum stool and clack my sticks together, counting us in, "One, two, three, four . . ."

Sean starts in with the keyboard intro to Journey's "Separate Ways (Worlds Apart)." Obviously, another one of his keys has died on him, because there's a very noticeable silent pause each time he comes around to that note. He glances over at me, a look of distress in his eyes, but all I can do is shrug and start in with the drum beat.

Matt joins in on guitar, and the music fills out a bit, thank God.

Still, we sound horrible. I don't know if it's nerves or what, but we are serving up a giant bowl of weak sauce.

I look around desperately for Helen. It's been more than five minutes since I left her. She should be here by now. Her voice is the only thing that can right this thing.

Maybe she's having second thoughts about performing. Or maybe she really doesn't forgive me, and this is her revenge. To humiliate me in public.

I think about how I left her. How she didn't say "I love you" back. Maybe she was shaking with barely controlled rage the whole time I was pouring my heart out.

We play the intro several times over, but still there's no sign of her.

We're only thirty seconds into our set and already the crowd looks lifeless and bored. No dancing. No swaying. No head bobbing or hand clapping. Nothing.

"Hola!" Sean shouts into his mic in an attempt to liven things up. *"Buenas noches!"*

"Pendejo!" a girl calls out over the music.

Now I don't know a lot of Spanish. But I do know that's not the response Sean was looking for, God love him.

Matt—who obviously knows even less Spanish than I do—steps up to his microphone to join in with the enthusiastic stage banter. "How's everybody doing tonight?" he asks the audience, having difficulty playing and talking at the same time.

"Great!" I hear Dad shout from way in the back.

"I see this crowd could use some medicine," Matt says. "Well, The Doctor has made his diagnosis, people. Looks like I'm going to have prescribe a heavy duty injection . . . of *rock*!"

Matt shoots his right fist into the air triumphantly.

"You suck!" some dude shouts through cupped hands. Which gets a huge laugh from the crowd.

Matt's arm goes limp. His body deflating. He lowers his head and goes back to playing his guitar.

And that's when the boos start, loud and clear and forceful, nearly drowning out the music.

We're dying. If Helen doesn't get out here soon, there'll be no reviving this fading patient.

I can't believe she would do this. Leave me to hang out to dry in front of the entire school. I mean, if she didn't want to seek revenge against Prudence, why would she want to do it to me? Unless . . . I hurt her way more than Prudence ever did.

I clench my eyes shut and realize it's true. I deserve this. And probably a whole lot more.

Still. We're up here. And we're playing. So we better get this song moving.

Which means, we've only got one choice.

Sean's going to have to sing.

I open my eyes and lean in toward my mic. I take a deep breath and am about to tell Sean to take it away when . . .

The jeers suddenly subside. And everyone is quiet. Our terrible music—like a skipping CD—the only thing filling the gym once again.

I'm thinking maybe some of the parents and teachers stepped in. To hush everyone up. But then the crowd parts and I see that it's something else entirely.

It's Helen.

She's come into the gym and is walking over to us, looking so far beyond smokin' that it nearly makes me drop my drumsticks.

She's wearing a skintight red leather bodysuit unzipped to the belly button. It hugs every curve perfectly. Not a chance she's got anything on underneath. Her hair is styled and flowing around her face. Her full lips glistening with crimson gloss.

She makes Prudence and her gang look like a bunch of hairy wood trolls.

Jesus Christ. I think I might faint.

Sean and Matt glance back at me.Their mouths are hanging open but miraculously they're still keeping the beat.

There's some loud barking coming from several guys standing by Prudence, but Helen completely ignores them and saunters over to her microphone with all the attitude Dad was trying to get us to display. She lifts the mic from the stand, raises it to her beautiful lips, and starts belting out the lyrics.

I've never heard Helen sing with so much power, fire, and emotion. She's always been amazing. But this is beyond belief. And while I know that it's because I screwed up and pissed her off, I can't help feeling really proud of her.

Matt, Sean, and I somehow plug into her energy and raise the level of our play from plain miserable to passably unexceptional. Which is all Helen really needs to soar.

The crowd is completely hushed as she carries us through the rest of the song. Completely astounded by Helen's awesomeness.

We end the tune with a flourish, Helen spinning the microphone around and around, then throwing it high in the air, and catching it right on time with the last note.

There is a moment of stunned silence as the crash of my cymbals dies down.

Helen is actually smiling. Matt and Sean are standing up tall and proud. I sit up high on my drum stool.

And then . . .

Someone yells out, "You can't polish a dog turd!"

An explosion of laughter ensues. Followed closely by a tidal wave of boos and hisses and insults. Louder than ever. Someone hurls a cup of soda at Helen. It barely misses her and explodes on the gym floor.

There's panic in her eyes. Her neck and cheeks glowing red. The confidence and high spirits she had moments ago . . .

Gone.

Poof.

And just like that, all the dreams of rock-and-roll glory—for me and for Helen—die at our feet.

CHAPTER SIXTY-ONE

REDEMPTION SONG

THE EXPRESSION ON HELEN'S FACE. That look of total despair. And the fact that all these jerks are responsible.

It sends me over the edge.

The rage wells up from my gut. I hurl my drumsticks down. Leap off my stool. And yank my microphone from its stand.

"Shut the hell up!" I roar, shoving the mic right up to the PA speaker. A loud piercing squeal of feedback floods the gymnasium, causing everyone to cower and cover their ears.

I hold it there a few seconds more, just to ensure that I've made my point. And when I pull it away, the squealing stops, and every eye in the place is on me.

"What the *hell* is your problem?" I holler at the crowd.

"*You* are!" Dean Scragliano shouts back.

I stick the mic right up to the speaker again, sending another brain-blowing screech howling over the PA.

Once I've regained everyone's attention, I calmly raise the microphone back to my mouth. "Keep talking. I've got plenty more where that came from."

"The squealing's more enjoyable than your mus—"

SCREEEEEEECH!

I give them a little more feedback. People's faces scrunching up in pain. Someone punches Dean in the shoulder to keep him quiet.

"I'm going to say something here," I announce. "So just shut it!"

A stunned hush falls over the crowd.

I take a deep breath and feel everything go calm inside, like I'm finally doing the right thing for once in my life.

"I'm not going to let you do this. It's not fair. Helen Harriwick is an amazing person." I look over at her and meet her eyes. "She doesn't deserve this. She's a great friend. And she has more talent in her left toe than any of you combined."

"Then bring her to the dog show!" Andy hollers.

I dole out another serving of head-exploding feedback and watch as Andy cringes in pain.

"As I was saying," I continue. "I will not sit here and watch you disrespect the girl . . ." I look over and catch Helen's eyes again. "The girl that I love."

There is a collective gasp from a good portion of the audience, quickly followed by a great deal of laughter.

"That's right," I say, turning back to the audience. "Laugh all you want. I don't care anymore. But like it or not, we are going to finish our set uninterrupted. And even though you are not worthy of listening to her, Helen is going to sing. And you will give her the respect she deserves." I glare out at the audience. "Or so help me, I will crank up the volume on the PA and blow your goddamn eardrums out."

"Yeah!" Dad whistles and claps loudly at the back. "That's right!"

I don't know if my outburst has shocked everyone else into silence, or what, but there's not another word from the crowd.

I turn to head back to my drums. "Knock 'em dead," I say to Helen, who stands there with tears welling up in her eyes.

I wonder if what I said made no difference at all—if she's still humiliated to be standing up here in front of all these people. But before I can ask her if she's okay, she raises her mic to her lips and says, "Let's do it."

I return to my drum stool and find my sticks on the floor. "Haul out your big junk, dawgs. Don't hold back. We're gonna give these bastards a show they'll never forget."

Matt's and Sean's eyes light up. They stand tall,

smiling big, like they've just been waiting for permission to let it all hang out and go crazy.

"Arriba!" Sean trills.

"Arriba!" Valerie echoes, raising her fist in the air.

"Yeah, okay." Matt grins. "What the hell." He moves to his amp, spins up the volume, and then tears into the opening riff of "Revolution."

Helen hits the audience with her kick-ass rock-and-roll scream, then starts to sing so passionately it nearly brings tears to my eyes. She whips her microphone around on its cable throughout the rest of the set, dancing and leaping in the air, kicking her performance up to an absolutely supreme level.

And the guys . . . well, they are just going completely nuts, having more and more fun with each successive song.

Matt rips it up on guitar, doing windmills, air splits, playing behind his back, playing with his teeth, falling on the gym floor and having rock-and-roll convulsions.

All the while, Sean sweeps his elbows up and down the keyboard keys, gets his poncho spinning wildly around his neck like a hula-hoop, and even pulls off his shoes and socks and starts playing a solo with his toes.

And me? I wail on the skins like never before. Spinning my sticks around my fingers. Tossing them in the air. Doing insane drum fills I have no right even trying.

Honestly, we still don't sound very good. In fact, some of the crowd-pleasing stuff makes us sound downright awful. But the four of us are having such a blast, it really doesn't matter anymore. And I don't know if the people in the crowd just can't believe what they are seeing, or if our insane energy is contagious, but there is a definite shift, as more and more of the audience starts hooting and laughing and cheering.

And maybe it's seeing how much fun we're all having. Or the fact that Helen is really going for it. Not letting anyone take this moment from her.

But something tells me, this is a night people will be talking about a hundred years from now.

CHAPTER SIXTY-TWO

LET IT SNOW!

WE BUILD THE LAST FEW BARS of "Twist and Shout" to a grand crescendo, finishing on a wild rush of crashing cymbals and roaring guitar and pounding keyboards.

Right on cue, as the last note dies out, Matt saunters up to his microphone. "The Doctor has signed your release papers! You have been . . . *discharged*!" And with that, Matt rips the top off the tape bikini on his guitar, exposing the naked babe's bouncers.

"Now *that's* what I'm talking about!" Dean Scragliano calls out.

"Adios!" Sean shouts, Frisbeeing his sombrero into the crowd, which is caught by a pretty girl who whoops and places it on her head. *"Feliz Navidad!"*

We don't get the loudest applause of the night, for sure. But we've definitely gained some new fans with our enthusiastic display. And I don't hear a single "Hot

Dog Helen" or "Corn Dog Coop"—not even from Andy Bennett himself, who is busy taking pictures of Matt's guitar with his cell phone.

"Come on now!" Dean Scragliano encourages everyone, clapping his hands loudly over his head. "Give it up! These dudes have balls! Encore! Don't put away that guitar!"

"Thank you, Arnold Murphy's Bologna Dare," Mr. Grossman says over the gym PA. "That was extremely . . . interesting." He clears his throat. "Now, may I have all of the bands over to the judges' table for the announcement of the winner?"

"How cool was *that*?" Sean says, a huge grin on his face as he shuts down his keyboards.

"Totally *uncool*-cool!" Matt cracks up, lifting the guitar over his head, sweat dripping down his face.

"That was awesome." I give my buds a shoulder squeeze. "Talk about a 'big junk' performance!"

Matt and Sean laugh, pleased twinkles in their eyes.

I look over at Helen, who's coiling up the mic cable. I want to talk to her. Make sure everything's okay between us. But I'm suddenly feeling really shy. Unsure of myself.

I breathe deep and force my feet to move.

"Hi," I say, when I step up beside her.

"Hi."

"Can we . . . talk? In private?"

She nods. "Yeah. Okay."

"Everyone," Mr. Grossman calls out, still trying to wrangle the hordes. "Over here, please."

I turn to Matt and Sean. "We'll be right back to help with the breakdown."

"Wait," Sean says. "Don't you want to see who wins?"

"Doesn't matter." I clap him on the back. "We didn't let them get us down. We had a good time. And Helen kicked ass. That's all I care about. See you in a few."

I grab our coats, and Helen and I head outside. Just as we step out into the snow, I hear Mr. Grossman make an announcement but I can't make out what he says. There's a mix of cheers and groans which is cut off as soon as the heavy metal door snicks shut.

A lot of people are hanging around the parking lot—smoking and chatting and clearing the ice off their cars—so Helen and I make our way across the football field and up to the top of the bleachers.

I brush the snow off the benches and we take a seat. The cold soaking through my jeans.

"How's your mom doing?" I say as we stare out across the winter landscape. "I didn't see her in the audience"

"She couldn't make it. She wasn't feeling up to it."

"I'm sorry. She would have been mega-proud of you. I know I was. You were absolutely incredible, you know?"

"Thanks." A shy smile on her face. "You too."

"I don't know about that."

Helen looks at me. "No, Coop. You were. What you

did tonight. Saying those things. In front of the whole school. Standing up for me. It was really brave. It meant a lot."

"Yeah, well . . ." I feel my eyes starting to fill up. "I should have done it earlier, back in Health class. Except I wimped out. But there's no way I was going to make the same mistake twice."

Helen reaches over and wipes the tears from my cheeks with her thumb. Then she leans into me. Her body warm against mine. I put my arm around her. Nestle in close. Breathe her in.

I had all these things I thought I wanted to say. Questions I wanted to ask. Are we really okay? Can she actually forgive me for all the stupid, horrible things I've done? Does she even want to be with a loser like me now that everyone knows how amazing and totally hot she is? Sure, Andy Bennett and Prudence Nash might not let the name-calling drop, but I bet there are guys who would totally go for Helen after tonight's display.

But sitting here now on the bleachers, comfortable in the silence, curled up together and watching the snow come down . . .

I have all the answers I need.

We stay there for a while. Watching people come and go. Car lights switching on in the parking lot. Just being with each other.

And it's the only place in the entire world I'd want to be right now.

"There you guys are," a voice calls from down below.

It's Matt, standing at the bottom of the bleachers with Sean and Valerie. All of them in their winter coats.

"We're packed up and ready to go," Sean says.

"No thanks to you two slackers." Valerie laughs.

Helen and I stand up. Brush ourselves off. I take her hand, supporting her as we carefully make our way down the icy steps.

"Are you guys good?" Matt asks when we reach them.

Helen smiles. Looks at me. "Yeah. We're good."

"Cool," Matt says.

"Hey, so who won?" Helen asks.

"Cheeba Pet." Sean groans. "I mean, can you believe it? After that killer show we put on? They didn't even have the courtesy to announce a second or third place. Just one winner. That's all."

"Yeah, well," Matt says. "If it had to be anyone else but us, I'm glad it was them. Now, let's get the hell out of here."

The five of us head out across the snow-blanketed football field. Back toward the parking lot.

"Okay," I say. "So, this is probably as good a time as any to start discussing our next gig."

"*Next* gig?" Sean's eyes saucer. "Don't you think we should just go out in our blaze of glory?"

"Oh, come on." I put my arm around Sean. "Are you

really ready to say goodbye to *El Mariachi*?" I swing my other arm over Matt's shoulder. "To The Doctor?"

"I think I'd survive." Matt laughs.

"Okay, but hear me out," I say, letting go of my buds and making a "marquee" gesture. "Just picture it. Arnold Murphy's Bologna Dare at the spring talent show. It's much less pressure. We only have to do two or three songs. Which we can certainly polish up in the next few months. And best of all, they don't serve refreshments. So there's nothing for people to throw."

"You can't be serious," Val says.

"Helen, come on." I turn to her. "You're with me on this, right?"

"I don't know, Coop." Helen laughs. "I think Arnold Murphy's Bologna Dare should probably retire."

"Absolutely," I say. "You're right. We retire the name. It's too quirky. We need something slick. Something more in your face. Like Sock Monster. Or Bag of Pants."

Nobody says anything. They just keep walking.

I look left and right at my friends. "Don't tell me I'm the only one with faith here. So we didn't win the Battle of the Bands. Big deal. How epic will that look in our rockumentary? 'Nobody knew just how famous they would become.' It's just like The Beatles and the Decca audition."

Still, we walk in silence.

"Just say you'll think about it."

"No," everyone responds in unison.

"All right." I nod. "I'll take that as a yes."

Matt quickly scoops up a hunk of snow, compresses it, and chucks it at me. The snowball explodes on my chest.

I look down at the crystals clinging to my coat. "You didn't just do that."

"Oh yes, I did." Matt laughs and points at me. "And there's plenty more where that came from, if you don't zip it."

"Okay, then." I throw my hands up. "It's on." I reach down and grab some snow. Matt starts running. He's too far away by the time I've got my snowball formed.

So, I turn and hurl it at Sean, whaling him in the shoulder.

"Hey!" Sean shouts. "What the hell?"

"Oops," I say. "Friendly fire."

I tear off toward the goalpost—the only cover available—and the snowball fight begins.

It doesn't take long before a stray throw hits Valerie. And another clips Helen. Before you know it, everyone's involved. Racing around the football field, laughing, and dodging snowballs. The winter air filling our lungs. The lights from the parking lot casting a faint glow, catching the flurries that drift down around us.

And I have to say, it's the perfect cap to this insane semester, which was, as I predicted, epic.

ACKNOWLEDGMENTS

This book had to be steered through some rocky and treacherous waters along the way and could not have been guided home without the help of some wonderfully patient and dedicated people.

For that—and all the love and support I received for *Swim the Fly*—I would like to offer my heartfelt gratitude to:

Kaylan Adair, my amazing editor, who co-captained and righted this sometimes-canting ship with me, and whose ideas, suggestions, encouragement, cheerleading, and overall fabulousness were much appreciated.

Liz Bicknell, for offering the all-important "other perspective" on the book.

Jodi Reamer, my stalwart literary agent, for her conviction and support.

Caren Bohrman, my film agent, for her enthusiasm and constant good humor.

Karen Lotz, Tracy Miracle, Elise Supovitz, Jeanne Emanuel, Nicole Deming, Jennifer Roberts, Jenny Choy, Sharon Hancock, Andrea Tompa, Chris Paul, Hilary Van Dusen, Nicola Makoway, and everyone else at Candlewick Press and Random House Canada (I hope I'm not forgetting anyone but I'm sure I am and I'm sorry) who have helped get the word out and who have been so incredibly kind to me on this journey.

Caroline Lawrence, for her persistence and effort in creating an awesome cover, and James Weinberg and Sherry Fatla for their kick-ass work on the interiors.

Maggie Deslaurier and Sarah Chaffee Paris, for catching all my mistakes.

Ken Freeman and James Fant, for reading and re-reading and re-re-reading the many drafts of this novel.

Greg, Paul, Dean, and Rich, the original Spiroketes.

Chris "The Doctor" Conroy, for making me laugh and regaling me with his Battle of the Bands war stories.

Ron Harner, for his friendship and honesty.

Will, David, and Emily, for their continual inspiration.

My wife, for being my rock, my muse, and the greatest thing that ever happened to me.

And everyone who wrote to tell me (or told me in person) how much you enjoyed *Swim the Fly*. Your words kept me going through all the drafts of this book.

Three boys, one summertime goal: to see a real-live naked girl

SWIM THE FLY

★ DON CALAME ★

"Raunchy hilarity ensues." —*People* Magazine

"Serves up jokes and gross-outs in the style of film-makers like Judd Apatow. . . . Boys will probably love it. This one did." —*New York Times Book Review*

"Hilariously raucous scenes stuff its pages. *Swim the Fly* is a set apart from the run-of-the-mill."
—*Los Angeles Times*